ABOUT

ROXANNE

A PSYCHOLOGICAL THRILLER

NINA ATWOOD

About Roxanne: A Psychological Thriller

Copyright © 2021 by Nina Atwood Enterprises, LLC. All rights reserved, including the right to reproduce this book, or portions thereof, in any form. No part of this text may be reproduced, transmitted, downloaded, decompiled, reverse engineered, or stored in or introduced into any information storage and retrieval system, in any form or by any means, whether electronic or mechanical without the express written permission of the author. The scanning, uploading, and distribution of this book via the Internet or via any other means without the permission of the publisher is illegal and punishable by law. Please purchase only authorized electronic editions, and do not participate in or encourage electronic piracy of copyrighted materials.

This book is a work of fiction. Permission has been granted to the author for name use by those with specific references. All other names, characters, places, and incidents are either the product of the author's imagination or are used fictitiously. Any resemblance to actual persons, living or dead, or actual events, is entirely coincidental.

Published by Nina Atwood Enterprises, LLC
Dallas, Texas

[E-book] ISBN-13: 978-1-7363470-1-0

[Print] ISBN-13: 978-1-7363470-2-7

OTHER TITLES BY NINA ATWOOD

Unlikely Return: A Novel, is available on Amazon.

Free Fall: A Psychological Thriller, is available on Amazon.

Nina's next full-length novel, book one of the electrifying Jill Rhodes mystery/thriller series, is scheduled for release in 2022. (See excerpt at the end of this book.)

Get Nina's FREE Novellas when you join her VIP Reader Club. Go to:

> www.ninaatwoodauthor.com/freenovella

Reward Special note: If you introduce me to someone in the moviemaking industry [big screen, streaming content, etc.] that results in a signed contract and paid advance on <u>any of my books</u>, I will pay you a reward of $10,000!

– Nina Atwood

Contact: nina@ninaatwoodauthor.com

PROLOGUE

Exhausted after a long day at work, Erin reached over to her phone on the dash and pushed the button to ring her husband's cell. She quickly returned her eyes to the road, swerving slightly to get back in her lane.

"Hey," he answered.

"Hey. It's me."

"Hey, me. Are you on your way?"

"Yep. Just passing the freeway, so I'll be home in about five minutes. How did it go with your dad today?"

"Okay, I guess. I mean, he knew me when I got there, and we actually talked for a while. But then he forgot who I was. I tried to remind him that, 'Hey, I'm your son, remember?' But he got all upset, and I had to leave after that." He sighed over the phone.

"I'm sorry, honey."

"Yeah, I know. Hey, did you get the chow? The game is tonight, and I thought—"

She glanced in the backseat at the two large pizza boxes, the aroma of pepperoni permeating the air. She smiled. "Chow?" Just the right note of puzzlement in her voice.

NINA ATWOOD

"*Seriously?* Did you forget? I sent, like, five text messages today." He went silent.

After a meaningful pause, she giggled. "Did you honestly think I'd forget your favorite pizza? *After all this?*" It was one of their little jokes. Do you still love me *after all this?* Followed by, *still, after all this?* And then the affirmations, the kissing, the laughter.

The vehicle in front of her slammed on the brakes, so she slammed hers as well. She halted a few feet from the back of the SUV. She couldn't see any kind of traffic jam ahead.

Really? Some people just didn't know how to drive, always pumping the brakes for no reason. The SUV moved forward and increased speed, so she did as well.

"What was that?"

"Oh, nothing. Somebody slammed on the brakes. But traffic seems to be moving."

She glanced at the backseat again, and that's when she saw the pizza boxes. Still stacked, but both now teetering on the front edge of the seat, about to fall onto the floorboards. She glanced at the road. The SUV was far ahead.

She reached back, glancing back and forth between the road ahead and the pizza boxes in the back seat, straining to reach them. Her fingers outstretched, she pushed and, finally, made contact. She gave it one more push, lifting up a little in the driver's seat, and the boxes slid back.

When she looked up, bright headlights were headed directly for her. She slammed on the brakes as hard as she could, but it was no use. The next second, she heard and felt a sickening, grinding slam. Her vehicle swirled and rolled in impossible ways, and when it was over, she lay there, her body mangled.

She whispered her husband's name, and then, "I love you."

ABOUT ROXANNE

Then darkness.

Roxanne strained to make sense of the road ahead. It was just a bit out of focus. *Wait, was she in her lane or in the other lane?* She swerved to compensate but suddenly found herself on the side of the road, tall weeds slapping the underside of her car. She swerved back the other way.

She couldn't remember why she was driving. She always took an Uber or Lyft car after she'd been out. But tonight was different, for some odd reason. *Oh, right.* Her husband needed the car early tomorrow to take it in for servicing.

No problem. She'd only had a couple of drinks. She could drive safely.

She hummed to herself and reached over to turn up the music. When she looked up again at the road, two bright headlights were headed right for her.

She had no time to react before impact. She didn't feel anything. Didn't hear the terrible grinding of metal on metal as the darkness claimed her.

When EMTs arrived on the scene, they found two women in the mangled wreckage of the two vehicles. Both were rushed to the nearest hospital.

One was dead on arrival.

PART ONE

CHAPTER ONE

Roxanne opened the front door of her home. Henry and the girls' voices wafted in her direction, his murmurs, their laughter. She paused for a moment. *What an incredible day.*

First, the case, and something not sitting well with her partners. Then, the letter, the one that had set her off and led to...but nothing else came to mind. She shook her head in confusion, something she rarely felt.

In the kitchen, Henry stood cutting up vegetables while six-year-old Rose, sitting on the massive marble-topped island near her dad, talked animatedly. Rose's legs swung, and she painted pictures of her day in the air with her small hands, eyes wide, curls flying around her head.

What a relief. Henry making dinner, a glass of wine close by, within reach in seconds. One of the best decisions she'd ever made was encouraging him to work part-time, so he could take over most of the parenting duties.

"And then what happened to her?" Henry prompted.

"And Miss Taylor told her to sit down," said Rose. "She was in *trouble*." She exaggerated the word drawing out the last syllable. Rose was a bit of a rebel and could stir up trouble, usually at bedtime when she wasn't ready to curtail the evening's fun, which mainly consisted of following her sister around begging for a game or a story. But Rose was primarily a pleaser, so the thought of being in trouble was clearly disturbing.

"I don't think Katie did anything wrong," observed Annie, her older sister. She sat on a stool at the island with an open book. "She was just trying to pick up the papers from the floor. It was James's homework, and he was crying. That wasn't very nice of Miss Taylor, was it, Dad? I mean, what kind of teacher punishes a kid for that?"

"But if the teacher says—" began Rose.

"Just because the teacher says it doesn't mean it's right," interrupted Annie, glaring at her sister. Annie had a keen sense of justice and probably had a career ahead in law. *The apple didn't fall far.*

Rose's eyes began to well with tears. Henry put down the knife and swooped her up for a hug. She wrapped her arms around his neck and tightened them, hiccupping a bit.

Annie rolled her eyes and went back to reading, mumbling something about teachers who abused their power and students who put up with it, not to mention parents who condoned it.

She was definitely going to be a handful in a few short years.

Henry's long-sleeved tee with the sleeves pushed up exposed toned forearms. His shaved head and muscular frame might have given him a harsh appearance. But his innate kindness, and the way his eyes caught the light over his daughter's head as he held her close, made him almost too good to be true.

Roxanne's stomach relaxed for a moment. She couldn't remember the last time she'd really looked closely at her husband, noticed him, or registered the tender way he cared for their daughters.

For the first time in longer than she could remember, she reflected on the way he covered for her with the girls, making excuses for her absences, for her shortness, for all her many sins. Not to mention how he'd let her off the hook countless times.

ABOUT ROXANNE

Annie's birthday party, only recently. *When was that?* It was fuzzy, but it couldn't have been very long ago because one memory was still fresh in her mind. Noticing her cell phone lying on the bar, face down, too much noise to hear the buzzing and ringing.

She remembered picking it up and noting the voice messages and texts, followed by the familiar twist of shame and guilt. Henry had been calling her frantically to remind her to pick up the cake and refreshments, which she'd never had time to make, but could count on Central Market to provide. Later, the defenses constructed, the lies behind which she hid, as always. *You said you were going to pick up everything, remember? How am I supposed to get things like that done after a case that lasted until the courthouse shut down?*

How had she forgotten? She had no clue, but it didn't matter.

There had been no case that day. It was simply another evening of doing what she loved best, her daughter's special day forgotten. By the time she got home, they were already eating cake. She'd swooped in to kiss Annie and apologize for being late, but her daughter's accusing eyes pinned her. At least she'd managed to buy a few gifts weeks earlier. Pulling them out had distracted everyone.

Henry hadn't said anything accusatory. Instead, he'd reminded Annie that her mom worked hard and was doing the best she could.

But even as he'd excused her that day, Roxanne's teeth had ground.

Most women would be flooded with gratitude, would reward a husband like Henry with tenderness and appreciation. Most women would give a thought or two, once in a while, to his wants and needs.

Most women were not her.

After giving Rose a few gentle rubs on her back, Henry set her down, then resumed the vegetable chopping.

Roxanne stood, oddly frozen, watching her family.

Annie looked up again, starring hard at her dad. "So, Dad, what are we going to do about Mom?"

Henry's shoulders dropped a bit as he looked at his daughter. "There's nothing we need to do about your mom, Annie."

What? They were talking about her like she wasn't there.

"Mom's going to be fine," Henry said quietly.

"No, she's not," said Annie, dragging out the words slowly, as if she were the adult speaking to a child having difficulty tracking the conversation. "She *works* all the time, and we know what she does after work, and now she's—"

"Don't bring that up," said Henry sternly but gently, nodding his head toward Rose, who was listening intently.

"Dad, you can't ignore it forever. She's just going to get worse and worse. That's if she even makes it home." With that final statement, Annie's eyes took on a sad look.

Henry spoke gently to her. "That's not your concern, Annie. There are some things that the adults have to take care of, and this is one of them. You are only ten."

"So, because I'm ten, I'm not supposed to notice things that are right in front of me?" challenged Annie, roughly swiping away her tears, anger replacing the sadness. "I'm ten, not *stupid*." She glared at Henry.

"Mommy!" Rose began crying again. "I want Mommy," she wailed.

"I'm here, baby," said Roxanne. "I'm here. Shhh, everything's okay."

Rose continued to cry. Biscuit, their golden retriever, padded into the room, went to Rose, and nuzzled her. True to her breed, she couldn't tolerate anyone in the family in pain or upset of any kind.

"Now you've upset your sister," said Henry, looking at Annie and shaking his head.

"Rose, stop being a baby. We're just talking," said Annie, but she'd softened her tone. "Come here. Let's play a game." She got up, went into the living room, and came back with a tablet. She set it up on the countertop, and Rose climbed on the stool next to her sister, the beginnings of a smile playing across her lips.

ABOUT ROXANNE

Amazing. Annie always knew what to do to help her sister feel better. Roxanne was envious of their relationship, of having a sister to love and shelter, someone to sympathize with about their parents.

She'd wanted a sister so badly, and she'd found the next best thing. A face swam into view. The face expanded into a wispy form standing in the corner, staring at her. *What was she saying?* Whatever the words were, they placed a cold piercing in her gut.

A piece of paper, with spidery handwriting, floated to the floor. She reached to grab it but found only air.

"Thanks, Annie," said Henry, giving his daughter a grateful smile. He went back to chopping vegetables. "She's coming home," he added firmly.

"Henry, *I'm here*. Why are you talking about me that way? I'm already home," she said, glancing between her husband and her eldest. But neither acknowledged her. Something was terribly wrong, but understanding was elusive. And with the mystery of the moment, swam memories of a friend like a sister, who now danced nearer.

Hayley? Had she spoken out loud or merely thought the name of her long-lost friend?

Biscuit looked up sharply in Roxanne's direction. She whined and padded over to Roxanne, who reached out to pet the dog. Her hand touched Biscuit's head, but she felt nothing. Biscuit continued to whine, looking directly into her eyes. A cold shiver trailed down Roxanne's spine.

A disturbing sense of separation from everyone else gradually swept over her. She tried to feel her arms, crossing them, and hugging herself, but everything felt so far away. Her own body felt distant, disconnected. She looked down but couldn't really see her feet. "Henry?" she asked in a small voice.

But he ignored her as he transferred the chopped vegetables into a large skillet on the stovetop.

"Henry, I don't feel so good," she said, feeling a watery sensation flood her body and brain. *"Please,"* she said.

Biscuit barked once, and then again. Henry shushed her.

"Henry! No!" Roxanne cried as her family slipped away. Then there was nothing but the whisper of a friend.

CHAPTER TWO

"I can't believe this didn't happen sooner," said Jessica. "How long have we been saying that this day was bound to happen? Poor Henry."

"Poor Henry? I think he's doing great, don't you?" said Claire defensively. "He's amazing—a great dad, a totally nice guy. He's holding the family together while she—"

"Yeah, we know," said Jessica abruptly. "But who is he doing that for? I mean, if you were Henry, how would *you* feel? There he is, taking care of the kids, always supporting her, while she—"

"While she what?" said Claire. "What else is he supposed to do? He's a good guy. We all know he's going to do whatever it takes."

The women sat in Jessica's tastefully modern living room, the remains of an assortment of appetizers strewn on the table in front of them.

How nice to relax with her two closest friends, especially after whatever it was that had happened with Henry. He was probably tucking the girls in bed, and now, it was girl time.

There was Claire, her paralegal and friend. They'd gone to college together, but while Roxanne went on to law school, Claire had married the guy she'd dated all through college, and later divorced. She'd dated for a couple more years, then gotten pregnant with Maya, now nine. Maya's father wasn't interested in parenting, but at least he sent small but regular child support checks.

Claire was completely devoted to Maya, who was the happiest, most joyful child Roxanne had ever known. She seemed utterly secure, her focus entirely on school and creative pursuits. Roxanne had never heard Claire utter even one harsh word to Maya.

What would that be like? To never be impatient with her daughters, never yell at them, or order them to their rooms because she didn't have the time to figure out what they needed.

They'd lost touch over the years, but one day, Claire had interviewed at Roxanne's firm and won the position as her paralegal. They'd re-bonded over work, toddlers, and more. Roxanne felt her chest tighten as she thought of the loyalty Claire had shown her more than once over the years. "Hey, girls, you won't be*lieve* the day I had."

Claire stopped talking suddenly.

"What?" said Jessica, staring at Claire.

"Nothing," said Claire, but she sat still, listening.

"What do the partners think?" asked Jessica.

Claire clutched her wine glass in one hand and gestured with the other. "They don't think anything," she said defensively.

Roxanne stared at Jessica—the first friend she'd made after law school. They'd both dated the same guy, before she'd met Henry. Jessica had dated Kyle first, then they'd broken up.

Kyle and Roxanne had met later, started dating, and one night at a party, he'd introduced her to Jessica, his ex. It was an odd way to make a new friend, but the two women had immediately hit it off, and Kyle soon became history. It turned out he wasn't any better as a boyfriend to Roxanne than he'd been to Jessica. How much fun they'd had over the years telling people that *they'd once dated the same guy*. Pause. *Oh, not at the same time!*

ABOUT ROXANNE

Jessica was still single. She kept her dark hair cut blunt and short, and loved painting her full lips a deep red. Yes, she'd done some modeling in college, but now she had a successful career as a commercial realtor. She was so intelligent and complex that she drove guys away as quickly as she attracted them.

"Anyway, I find that hard to believe," said Jessica. "Maybe if you could stop defending her—"

"That's ridiculous," said Claire hotly. "She's a valued partner. She's won more cases than the rest of them put together! And she's brilliant. She's had a few problems focusing lately, that's all." But the argument lacked conviction and was laced with sadness.

"Maybe so, but there's only so many times you can show up at work and compensate when your boss is nursing a—" said Jessica, stopping abruptly. She sighed. "Come on, Claire, you know what's really going on. If we don't see the truth about Roxanne, how are we going to help?"

Roxanne's teeth clenched, but she remained uncharacteristically silent as the conversation wound around the room, she the unwilling topic, shame roiling her insides.

Claire took a sip of wine and mulled over Jessica's comments. "You're right. Things have gotten worse over the past year. She shows up late but not too late. Though she's always early for court dates," she conceded. "But, it's the afternoons. She takes off around 2:00 or 3:00. The partners think she's doing research or picking up her kids from school, but Henry does that. They think she's working remotely a lot of the time, but the truth is she's down the street at the bar... in that beautiful historic hotel, you know the one?"

"Leaving you to cover for her," Jessica finished for her.

"Exactly," Claire said, pointing her finger at her. "It's been hell," Claire said, her voice trailing off. She tugged forlornly at her wispy blond hair.

Roxanne stood in shock. *It's been hell? What were they talking about? And why weren't they looking at her?*

The women looked down, quiet. "So, what about Roxanne?" asked Claire to no one in particular.

"Hey guys, I'm here. I'm fine, I'm great. Yeah, really great," said Roxanne. But fear threaded her chest and her bowels felt odd. *Was she afraid of the power of their words? Or was it something else?*

Again, the familiar face swam into her mind, but this time, nothing. No whispers, just a sad stare. And in Roxanne's heart, the familiar guilt, the recriminations, the blame, and the self-loathing.

She yearned for the familiar relief, the elixir that spared her the aching that dogged her daily, always there, ignored, denied, and shoved away.

Claire looked up, her blue eyes glistening. Then she looked down sadly. "Oh, Roxanne," she whispered. "I hope you get better soon. We miss you."

They lifted their wine glasses and clinked them. "To Roxanne."

Roxanne looked down as the floor simply dropped away. A scream tried to work its way out of her throat, but there was only silence.

CHAPTER THREE

THREE DAYS EARLIER

Roxanne picked up the envelope with the spidery, cursive handwritten address on the front. Her office address, her name.

What an odd throwback, a handwritten note or letter.

No email. No phone call. No text.

She took in the return address and felt an immediate jolt, tugged to another part of her life that had been safely tucked away. Tearing open the envelope, she read the short note inside, and as soon as she finished reading, the letter fell out of her hand.

Why now, after more than two decades?

Everything she'd believed about what had happened long ago began spinning out again in her mind, and the familiar tightening in her belly propelled her. She stood, grabbed her briefcase, and stuffed in that day's files, turning to the door of her office, feet already in motion. But something tapped her shoulder blades, and she couldn't go. She stood frozen, indecisive, wavering between the long ago and the press of today.

This was ridiculous, really. She could send a quick note, or make a call, then push all of it back into the tiny envelope out of which it had escaped, and into the recesses of her own dark memories. She gripped the handle of her briefcase so tightly her nails dug into her palms, stimulating a different kind of pain. She gasped and looked down at the red scores in her palm, one of them welling with blood.

Quickly, before she could second-guess herself, she picked up the phone to place a call, heart reverberating.

But before she could finish, Claire beckoned frantically from the doorway. "It's Richard, and he doesn't look happy."

On the way down the hallway, her mind continued to spin, and memories swirled about the worst day of her life, over two decades ago. The day she'd walked down her best friend's street, oblivious to the devastation she was walking into. Then, she'd realized there was an ambulance parked in front of the Strickland's house. Also, a police car.

The front door opened, and two firemen came out with a stretcher. On top lay a small body, covered.

Roxanne walked faster. She dropped the grocery bag filled with goodies to make up for their recent rift. Then she ran, but sluggishly, her limbs heavy, her heart pounding, her breath more ragged with each agonizing step. As the firemen reached the ambulance, and as she reached them, she began to moan.

She tried to grab the covering on the stretcher, but Hayley's mom was there, tugging her away. "No, Roxanne, don't look!" she cried out, sobbing. But Roxanne fought her and yanked it back anyway. What she saw would be seared in her brain for a lifetime.

Her beautiful friend now lay waxy and still. But her neck—her neck was twisted and swollen and deeply bruised. Her face was grotesque, swollen so much the skin was stretched, her mouth partly open, and her tongue partly extended.

Roxanne screamed. "What happened to her? What happened?" She shook Hayley once, twice. "Get up! Get up, Hayley! Stop this!"

The two firemen gently pushed Roxanne aside and slid the stretcher into the ambulance as she continued emitting unearthly sounds of shock and pain. Then, Mrs. Strickland's arms were around her, and they collapsed together, both wailing. Mr. Strickland stood silently nearby, his face red, his eyes streaming, choking with barely suppressed sobs.

She stood outside Richard's door, memories tugging at her, thinking. She could leave for the day now. It would be for research, remote work on her cases. She had no court appearances for the rest of the day.

She could place that call, seek absolution, put something to rest that had eaten at her soul for too long. But first, she would need something to help her wind down and focus, to help set the memories aside for now.

She took a deep breath. With a plan in place, and the promise of a respite at her destination down the street, a sense of relief brought her heart rate down.

The door flew open, and all thoughts of winding down were displaced by the frown on the face of her colleague, Cory Holloman. "It's about time," he said, opening the door wider and inviting her in with an exaggerated hand wave.

"Roxanne. Please, sit," said Richard Driscoll quietly. As the Managing Partner of their small firm, Richard exuded his superpower—a calm presence. He maintained a quiet, yet strong, demeanor in court while presiding over raucous internal meetings at the office and with clients. Roxanne had never seen him rattled. He gently smoothed his graying hair and placed his hands on the conference room table, linked together. He looked worried, and that was new.

Cory, a Senior Associate, sat nearby, tapping his manicured nails on the table, vibrating visibly as if he were ready to explode. Cory was always primed to 'fire, 'then, 'ready,' followed by 'aim.' A few years younger than Roxanne and hard-wired for aggressive action, he was a good litigator.

But not so good as a colleague, except for those times when he could be the hero, be the star in court. She'd co-counseled with him a few times when she needed his specific expertise, but she hadn't enjoyed the experience. Too much testosterone and ego.

Cory was one of the many reasons Roxanne chose to dress demurely for work, following her grandmother's advice of many years ago. Slacks were preferred, although skirts could be worn if they landed just above the knee. Tailored jackets over cream or shiny gray blouses, buttoned well above cleavage. Pearls. Low-heeled pumps. Minimal makeup. Hair pulled back a bit severely, although she couldn't hold back all of the riotous curls.

Of course, at night at the bars, she let her hair down, literally. But years ago, she'd perfected the 'hands off, dude,' radar signal that allowed her to have lively conversations, over cocktails, in the male-dominated, evening legal universe she inhabited without having to constantly fend off unwanted advances.

Cory, though, was the kind of guy who ignored the radar, so she avoided being alone with him. Not that she was afraid of him. She figured she could hold her own with him, or any other guy, in any situation. She just didn't want the aggravation.

Now, Cory fired his first shot. "What the hell do you think you're doing?"

"Now, Cory—," began Richard.

"That case is a moneymaker for us, and she's blowing it! You can't give her a pass this time," shot back Cory, glaring at Richard.

ABOUT ROXANNE

The Patterson case... of course. This was a come-to-Jesus meeting. She'd seen it coming, but did it have to be today? Her head throbbed.

Richard held up a hand. "We're going to give her a chance to talk. Roxanne, please enlighten us." He slid a thick file toward her. "Motions not filed, depositions not done, at least one hearing postponed for reasons that your team wasn't told. What are you doing?" Richard asked firmly but compassionately. Richard always gave the benefit of the doubt, especially to her.

Roxanne gazed at Richard. She did her best to project her trademark intensity that always worked. But it wasn't her best day.

"Look at her, Richard," spat Cory. "She's hungover, as usual."

"Shut up, Cory," said Roxanne, waving him off. She thought about the case. The 40-something son of the owner of a large, privately held company with over 400 employees, based in a small town in southeast Texas. The company was one of the largest employers in the town of 30,000 or so people, and the owner and his family were high profile.

A female employee had stepped forward and claimed sexual harassment by the son, who was the acting CEO. The woman, a long-time employee, had crumbled due to emotional stress and was now unable to work.

Roxanne had begun to discover evidence that it wasn't the first time or the first employee. She also strongly suspected that the woman was raped but didn't want to deal with a criminal trial. She mainly wanted to be compensated for her inability to work and her medical bills.

"How do you explain your actions, Roxanne?" said Richard.

"That's just the tip of the iceberg!" declared Cory.

Roxanne fumed but didn't answer. *What could she say?* It was completely unlike her. Even when she felt a little... off at times, she showed up and did her job. And she did it extremely well. But not this one. And she had no good answers.

When she said nothing, Richard sighed. "You know I have to answer to the other partners for this one."

That spurred her. "No, you don't. You don't owe them anything, and especially not for me. I will speak with the partners. We can't represent this guy. He's poison."

"That's just great," scoffed Cory. "I'm sure when you're done talking to the other partners, we'll all be better off. *Poison*." He shook his head. "Thanks, but no, thanks."

Richard let out a breath. "What's done is done, and now, we have to put our heads together and figure out our strategy going forward."

"Strategy?" Roxanne looked incredulous. "It's a no-brainer, Richard. We give the retainer back to the scumbag client's company and we're on our way. We give them a referral to another firm."

"You know it's not that simple, Roxanne. This is a firm that we've done business with for well over a decade. We are talking about close to a million in fees on an annualized basis. And this guy is the owner's son."

"Right!" threw in Cory. "We're talking about the down payment for my lake house—gone, poof. Thanks to you!" He steamed visibly.

Roxanne spoke directly to Richard, pointedly ignoring Cory. "Richard, can you honestly tell me you believe this guy? He's a snake—a lying, womanizing, possibly a rapist, snake! How can we defend him? He deserves to go to prison, but he'll probably have Daddy pay his get-out-of-jail ticket in the form of some kind of payoff to the woman and continue doing what he does!"

"We don't know that will happen," Richard offered, but weakly. "And our job isn't to believe or disbelieve. It's to do our job, and you know what that is. Every person we see deserves to have a well-represented day in court, a fair defense, no matter who that person is, or even what they've done."

"That is bullshit. Tell me something, Richard. If this were any other client, someone who walked in the door randomly, no big corporate meal ticket, what would you do?"

Richard looked uncomfortable. He started to speak, but Roxanne interrupted. "Save it. I can tell already you're just going to spout some

ABOUT ROXANNE

kind of nonsense about our mandate as legal counsel, which you know I believe in just as much as you. But what you're not willing to say is that you don't believe this guy any more than I do, and you know this case is about helping him win while we watch that poor woman sitting through it, weeping every day. And we haven't even gotten to court. Can you imagine what that's going to be like for her?" She stared at him, and he had the grace to look contrite.

"While I can't say I disagree with you, still, this is a client, and he's a valuable one," he said. "The company stands to lose a significant amount of money, not to mention the negative publicity. We can't leave the owner in the lurch. We're counting on you—the client is counting on you. You are a partner in the firm. We can push him to settle, and that will spare her having to show up in court."

"I can't do it, Richard," she said, knowing she would lose that argument. She *could* do it, but she didn't want to do it—represent that snake.

Richard sighed again, then pushed a brochure toward Roxanne. "Look, I know you're dealing with personal issues—"

"I'm not. I don't have any personal issues," Roxanne spat. The handwritten letter came to mind, and she quickly reconsidered. "Actually, I do have something personal I need to deal with."

Richard waited, and Cory scoffed again.

"There's someone from my past who died... I don't want to get into the details, but it's a loose end, and I heard something about it today from someone who..." She stopped, unwilling to say more.

"This is unbelievable. A dead person from the past? *That's* why you can't do your job? Richard, you have to tell her." Cory's eyes pierced Roxanne.

"Roxanne." Richard cleared his throat. "Take this brochure. There's a number there for someone who can help you. I want you to talk to me again tomorrow. Let me know if you're going to work on the case, do your best for the client. If not, I'm afraid the next time we talk, it's about your status at the firm."

Cory smiled triumphantly at Roxanne.

"Fine." She looked hard at Cory. "You weasel. I should have known." She stood indignantly and turned to go.

"Take it," Richard said firmly, holding up the brochure. She snatched it out of his hand, tore it in two, and threw it down before stalking out, slamming the door as she went. She avoided the stares of everyone else as she left the office.

Later, sitting at the bar, Roxanne shook for—how long, she wasn't sure—until the first few pours of gin entered her system. To hell with Cory Holloman, and as for Richard, she could deal with him later. As for the ill-fated Patterson case, it paled in comparison with the looming specter of the past that had wound its way into her consciousness earlier that day, with the arrival of the oddly worded letter.

She'd place that call, go see Mrs. Strickland tomorrow. It had been a long time, and a visit was long overdue. It would be good to talk about the past, maybe put some things to rest. Maybe find a way to loosen the terrible tightness, the stretching of her skin all over, that the long-ago events had permanently planted.

Yes, it would be good to talk, to understand the letter, and the questions it raised, about Hayley's death and about the events that had led up to that devastating day. And, perhaps, she would gain a measure of comfort.

Who was she kidding? It would be excruciating.

She ordered another drink to help reduce the knot in her belly. It was a couple of drinks later before she felt normal again. And two more drinks after that before she stumbled out to her car.

CHAPTER FOUR

PRESENT DAY

Henry stroked Roxanne's hand. He adjusted her blanket. He picked up the warm washcloth and lightly bathed her face. He brushed her hair aside. He sighed deeply. "Roxanne, we miss you. You need to wake up. The girls and I are doing our best to keep up, but we need you."

The doctor had spent time with Henry that morning explaining long-term care for comatose patients. It sounded like a terrible warehouse for human shells to him. He couldn't imagine leaving Roxanne to waste away in a place like that. But she couldn't occupy a hospital bed forever, either.

He shuddered again. Time was running out. Three days had passed since the accident, and soon, his wife would be in the timeframe of long-term coma patients, past the early window of likely return to full functioning.

He dipped his finger in the water glass on Roxanne's bedside table and dripped it on her cracked lips. "Annie's a little behind in school. Not in English, of course, her favorite subject, and not even in math, her least favorite subject. But she never really liked science, to begin with, you know, and now, well, she had a project last week. She was supposed to build a solar oven—you know, a box that you set up and it cooks something without electricity. You can imagine what she had to say about that." He smiled, remembering his conversation with Annie, her logic threaded with pre-teen sarcasm.

What do I need a solar oven for, Dad? What is this, the Stone Age? Ours is gas, and gas never goes out even if electricity does. Plus, I can order something to eat in a couple of seconds with your phone since you won't let me have that kind of app yet. Although I don't know why. I'm certainly old enough and mature enough to do it. What if you're gone, and we run out of food? I think it's time for you to give me some responsibilities like that.

"But she wound up making a wand, of all things, a wand like Harry Potter's. She got points for creativity from her teacher, but I'm afraid that didn't get her a good grade since it wasn't really a science project. More of an art project. She already had a wand, the one I gave her for her birthday, but she said she needed one she made herself, with special powers."

He stopped. Roxanne still wasn't showing any signs of consciousness. He'd been sitting here for hours every day, talking away to a comatose woman. Something built up inside, something unlike him, but undeniable. "Roxanne!" he shouted. He stood, paced around the room, running his hand over his shaved head. "I'm sick of this! I can't keep doing this! The girls can't keep wondering why you don't come home, crying and...regressing! Rose is acting like she's three again. Annie thinks she's the boss of the house."

He stood over the bed. He couldn't stop his hands as they reached for her shoulders, gripped them, and shook them. "Wake up! WAKE UP!" he shouted.

The door to the room opened. In walked Dr. Stevens, who quickly surmised the situation. He walked to Henry and put out a steadying hand to his shoulder. "It's okay."

ABOUT ROXANNE

Henry released Roxanne, stepped back. A small, wild animal thrashed in his chest. "Oh, shit, oh shit, oh SHIT," he said as tears sprang into the corners of his eyes.

Grateful for the moment to collect himself, Henry watched as Dr. Stevens moved to Roxanne's side and began his routine. He opened one of Roxanne's eyes, shone a penlight into it, then did the same with the other. "Mrs. Fairchild? Can you hear me? Can you see me?" he called out. "Make a sound if you hear me."

Nothing happened. Dr. Stevens lifted one hand and squeezed each of her fingers firmly. He pressed her fingertips with a sharp metallic instrument. He used his fingertips and pressed just below her eyebrows. He pinched the muscle at the top of her shoulders closest to her neck.

He pulled the blanket off of her feet and touched, then tapped her soles with the metallic instrument. There was no response. Then, her foot twitched just a tiny bit. He did a couple of other tests.

Henry stood numbly nearby, barely registering what was happening.

"Well, there's a little improvement. Her eyes registered a reaction to light. She reacted to the foot stimulus test. There's room for some optimism, but it's still a long road, and there aren't any guarantees. I'm sorry it's not better news." He turned to go, then stopped. "Try to stay calm, Mr. Fairchild. Maybe take some breaks. You don't have to be here all the time."

Henry threw himself into the bedside chair. He stared at Roxanne with a glazed focus, his mind whirling. What was he going to do if she didn't wake up? How would he manage their two girls without a mom? Well, he could manage them. He could get their meals together, get them to school, buy clothes, run the household. He'd been doing that for a long time.

But how would he manage their loss? Their bereavement? What about the things only a mom could give to two little girls? Especially as they got older.

How would he manage his own loss? Did he even feel any loss? Guilt stirred in his gut. Even so, he picked up his phone. "Hey, it's Henry. I'm at the hospital. Can you meet me?" The familiar, warm voice, so ready to make time for him.

CHAPTER FIVE

A nurse entered the room and began checking the equipment. The woman on the bed stirred. It began with a few twitches. First her toes, then her fingers. Her eyes, under her lids, moved right and left rapidly. Her breathing hitched into a faster pace. Her mouth fell open, and small sounds emerged.

The nurse noticed the woman's slight movement and gently shook her head. "Poor you. Your husband has been sitting here night and day, waiting for you to wake up. I've never seen anyone more devoted. He looks completely lost, like he's missing his best friend. Which I'm sure he is.

"And the little girls—they are adorable." She tsked and chattered and set things right before pausing at the door. "What about you, Roxanne? What's your story? What was it before this, and what will it be after this? You have to wake up to find out, you know, to see how it turns out." She turned and left quietly.

The woman on the bed twitched, and her eyelids moved rapidly.

Roxanne meandered along the shoreline of the ocean. The sand was warm beneath her bare feet. She stared at her toes as she slowly walked. Sometimes, she dipped them in the water as gentle waves lapped at her feet.

The sun was low in the sky, the air warm, and the wind—but there was no wind, and she found that odd. There was no one else in sight. The shore stretched away in a long curve to the horizon, which was hidden from view by…she couldn't quite see the horizon, but it didn't seem to matter.

She reflected on the strange day she'd had. Henry and the girls, her two friends, and the sense of separation from everyone. And something about the long-ago past, things that had happened which she'd done her absolute best to forget.

Where was this place? Was she in heaven?

Or perhaps it was some kind of quiet hell—as defined by finding yourself separated from your life and the people you loved, wandering forever with no sense of purpose, nothing to do, and nowhere to go.

She shuddered at the thought. That would be hell for her.

Her head jerked up. Someone approached, walking purposefully, face unclear. Who was this? She felt oddly calm as she stood still, waiting.

Then, the shape of his head, the walk, the athletic gait. She knew this person; she was sure of it. Warmth slowly spread in her belly.

He came into view, and she registered the broad shoulders, the slender torso, and the muscular legs. He wore white shorts and a tee shirt. She ran to him, and he wrapped his arms around her. "Henry!" she breathed. "How did you find me?"

ABOUT ROXANNE

He pulled away and smiled at her. "I had to find you, silly. You've been gone so long, and it's time to go home." He took her hand, clasping it tightly, and pulled her away from the shore.

"Wait! Where are we going? I thought this was hell, you know, maybe a milder hell than the one Pastor Kenneth used to talk about, but, still, hell. And why are you here? Wait. What are you doing? Henry!" She tried to pull away, but he tugged harder, still smiling, though the warmth she'd felt drained away.

Suddenly, he stopped smiling and grabbed her shoulders. He shook her hard, and she felt terrible. It was like a giant shaking her, not her husband, not Henry, with his always gentle hands, his soft approach.

In the sterile hospital room, her eyes opened. She was terribly disoriented. *Where was she?*

This room smelled of antiseptic and crispness and machines, which she now heard. There were soft clicks and hums nearby. She tried to raise her hand, but it wouldn't cooperate. She strained mightily, and her fingers twitched. She tried to see her toes, but they were covered. Still, she could move them a bit.

It was too exhausting, and something else pulled at her, dragged her into an unrestful sleep.

CHAPTER SIX

ROXANNE, 1999

Mrs. Strickland asked again, "Are you sure you don't want to come over for dinner?"

"Thanks, Mrs. S., but my mom's waiting for me."

"Okay, but you're always welcome, you know that, right?" As always, she gave Roxanne a reassuring smile.

Mrs. S. was so nice to her. Hayley was so lucky. "For sure. Later, Hayley?"

"Yep. While we do homework, right?" It was their tradition. Call on the phone and talk while they did homework. Roxanne climbed out of the car and waved goodbye. She waited until they were out of sight before going in the door.

The house was quiet. Roxanne dropped her books on the table in the breakfast room then went in search of her mother. She found her in her bedroom, dozing. Books and magazines were strewn over the bed, which was unmade. One of the books lay across her mother's abdomen—something about how to befriend your daughter—some flavor of self-help, her mom's preferred reading. So ironic. Several coffee mugs crowded the surface of the bedside table. A bottle of prescription pills sat nearby. "Mother."

Ellen opened her eyes, saw her daughter, and smiled. She stretched and slowly sat up. "Hello, dear. How was school?"

Roxanne stared at her mother, whose face dropped. She turned and walked out of the bedroom, tense with irritation.

"Roxanne, dear. Sweetie?"

But the more her mother called out in that syrupy voice, the further away Roxanne wanted to be from her. She heard her mother get up from the bed, then a minute later, she padded down the hall and stuck her head in the door of Roxanne's bedroom. Why hadn't she shut the door? But still, she stood there, gazing at her daughter, apparently at a loss for words.

"What?"

"Nothing, dear. I just...I, well, I wanted to see how you were doing. Are you okay?"

She stared at her mother, who said nothing further.

"I have homework."

"Of course, you do, darling." And she stood there looking lost for another agonizing minute. Roxanne felt her mother's neediness in the air. It caused every bit of compassion to squeeze tight until it disappeared. She felt nothing but cold inside.

And her mother turned and padded away, back to her own room, like a child who'd been banished. Roxanne knew she was on her

ABOUT ROXANNE

own for dinner. Her mother was back in her own world again, sleeping, reading, or watching television in her room. It was a relief, and it was agonizing. She flopped back on her pillow, longing for something to ease the inexplicable ache in her chest.

Hayley pursed her lips at herself in the mirror and applied pink lipstick. She pulled her long blond hair over one shoulder, then flipped it to her back, frowning. She half-turned to see herself, smoothing her mini skirt over tights, tugging her midriff-baring tee shirt down. She smiled and then turned her attention to Roxanne. "Wait. Try this one," she said, handing Roxanne a neon green scrunchie.

Not for the first time, Roxanne envied Hayley and her sun-streaked blond hair, honey-golden skin, and brilliant green eyes. She gazed at her own dark, frizzy hair and sighed. At least the scrunchie might hold it in place.

She gamely wound her hair through the scrunchie. She refreshed her lipstick and gazed down sorrowfully at her clothes. Washed jeans—not too bad. But her tee shirt was long, not short, and she didn't own a miniskirt, thanks to Grandmamá.

Since her mother was so out of it most of the time, her grandmother took her shopping, and she was strict. Very strict. Roxanne could hear her voice in her head, 'You might think that miniskirt makes you look cute now, but trust me, years from now, you will look at those photos of yourself and be less than pleased. And remember, how you dress sends a signal to the boys.'

At this, Roxanne always cringed. Send a signal to the boys? Which boys—the ones who ignored her? If only she could send a signal that anyone cared to read.

But Grandmamá never lost an opportunity to lecture. 'You don't want to be the girl the boys think is easy. Be the girl with class, Roxanne, the one who stands apart as different. You're smart. Don't ever hold back your intelligence. Be the girl who no one can take advantage of, ever. The one who is respected and admired.'

"You look adorable!" declared Hayley, looking her up and down and lying as usual. Her best friend always encouraged her, always looked at her with admiration in her eyes, whether she actually believed her own words or not.

"This is perfect," said Hayley. "We can go to the party and stay out as late as we want. My parents won't know since I'm spending the night with you."

They could do whatever they wanted that night, no intervening parental supervision. Roxanne's Mother would be asleep or zoned out on whatever it was she took to help her "nerves." They had the zing of that glorious feeling of freedom that every teenager craves. They giggled conspiratorially.

"Let's roll!" said Hayley.

The party was in full swing when they arrived. Adam, whose parents were away for the night, greeted them at the door. "Hayley," he fairly gushed, gluing his eyes on Roxanne's best friend. She felt a surge of resentment.

Adam was the picture of the worst of adolescence—limp, greasy hair, skinny arms dangling, pants all wrong. Sure, his eyes were nice, but still.

"Take a picture; it lasts longer," she said to Adam, locking her arm into Hayley's and pulling her into the house. Hayley gave Adam a little wave, smiling in her dazzling way, but allowed Roxanne to pull her away. Adam shot a dark look at Roxanne, but she ignored him.

ABOUT ROXANNE

They quickly found the bar—the kitchen counters were loaded with alcohol and mixers. Someone poured some kind of punch-like beverage into large plastic cups, and the two girls wandered around, sipping.

As usual, kids lit up when Hayley approached, eager to connect with the beautiful, popular girl. And, as usual, Roxanne felt almost invisible. Sometimes it hurt to be in the shadow of the sun. But at the same time, she felt the warmth, the cast-off glimmer of being the special friend of the one everyone wanted.

Van Halen's "Jump" started, blasting through the speakers, and reverberating through the whole house. Kids leaped up and began dancing. Someone grabbed Hayley, and she was lost in the throng of gyrating, flailing kids. Roxanne found herself on the edge of the crowd, watching. The sound was deafening.

But even unflappable Roxanne felt the stirrings inside, the excitement of being part of the crowd, part of the wild, untamable teenage energy that permeated the house. She swayed and took a large gulp of her drink. That produced a sense of calm, a sense of being...a part of. She took another gulp. Braver, she got up and joined the melee of dancing kids.

And as the evening progressed, the initial excitement gave way to something else, to the stealthy unfurling of a dark sea change that would sweep away one life and leave the other life forever altered.

In the hospital room, she moaned and twitched in her sleep as her mind traveled from one dreamscape to another.

"Roxanne, wake up." Hayley shook her shoulder, and her eyes popped open. She stretched as she swatted away Hayley's hand. Saturday morning, best day of the week! They would do a little shopping, not

that she had much to spend. Since Grandmamá managed buying her clothes, she had to sock away little bits of cash from babysitting to get a few things that weren't so hopelessly...old.

Malls were a wonderful place to hang out. With loads of discount stores, she could find a few things in her limited budget that were definitely not Grandmamá's taste and squirrel them away. Then there was the movie theater, and with matinee pricing, they could catch something fun. Junk food was plentiful and absolutely required.

She threw off the covers and stood quickly. "Let's get ready and get out of here before your mom thinks of something you have to do." She pulled on jeans and looked around for her bag, which contained her toothbrush and makeup. But Hayley tugged her shoulder again.

"What? Let's go, Hayley." Suddenly it seemed terribly urgent to get out of there...out of...where was she? She looked around, but Hayley's bedroom seemed out of focus.

Slowly, she turned to face her friend. Sunlit hair wafted around her honey-golden face, still so beautiful. And so young. She smiled at Roxanne, whose heart began to thump. Dreaming. She must be having a dream.

Hayley reached out and touched Roxanne's face, smiling sadly. But she couldn't feel her friend's touch. She tried to put her hand on Hayley's but felt nothing.

Wake up, wake up, wake up. If only she could...

Because now, she knew she had to find out more. The sense of guilt, the self-blame for her friend's death had haunted her for so long. She felt jolted out of complacency, unable to think of anything else.

CHAPTER SEVEN

Roxanne's eyes flew open. She was in a hospital bed, and her arms were attached to tubes which were attached to IV drips and medical instruments. A nurse stood at the foot of the bed, tapping on a tablet. She'd been dreaming about her childhood best friend, but this was no dream. "Unh," she croaked.

The nurse looked up abruptly, the shock registering on her face quickly smoothed over into a smile. "Well, hello there. It's about time you joined us," she said pleasantly. "Here, let me get you some water." She poured water into a small cup with a straw and held it to Roxanne's lips.

It tasted so good, the cool liquid sliding down her parched throat. She sighed and tried again to speak, but only a croak emerged. She squirmed, trying to lift her hands and move her feet, but they felt enormous and heavy.

"Give yourself a chance to wake up," the nurse intoned as she moved around Roxanne's bed, checking her vitals on the monitor. "I'm going to have the doctor look you over carefully, and meanwhile, try to take it easy. It's perfectly normal to feel weak."

"Whaa... haa," said Roxanne, her words slurred and almost unrecognizable.

"What happened is you were in a car accident, but you're going to be okay. You've been in a coma for almost two weeks, but the good news is you're back. You've got a bit of work to do to get your strength back, and we'll probably do a full neurological workup, but you are one lucky lady."

Lucky? What was lucky about this? She didn't remember anything about any accident, and that was alarming. "I dooo... re...," she struggled to speak. She moaned in frustration.

"Not surprising you don't remember a lot right now. Let me get the doctor, and then your husband. You're going to feel a lot better with your family." The nurse left swiftly.

Almost immediately, a tall guy in a white lab coat with a stethoscope entered. *Dr. something.* She vaguely registered the stitching on his pocket. He carried himself calmly, an assertiveness apparent in the way he held his shoulders. Someone comfortable giving orders, accustomed to having things put right. But there was something more than that, in the way he looked at her, maybe a depth and a kindness. His eyes flashed at Roxanne as the corners of his mouth curved upward. "Well, Ms. Fairchild, we are all glad to see you back with us."

He moved to Roxanne and began doing things that she found annoying. He held her eyelids open and blasted her with a penlight which she tried to squirm away from, but he spoke soothingly. "It's just a few tests. Try to stay calm; I'll be done in a few minutes."

He tapped her feet with something, and she jerked away. "That's great," he said cheerfully as he continued to irritate her with taps and scrapes on various parts of her body. She couldn't move much, so she couldn't escape, and since her vocal cords weren't working yet, she couldn't tell him to f--- off, which she longed to do.

The door flew open, and Henry rushed to her side, taking her hand and squeezing it. "I'm so sorry I wasn't here when you woke up! We just stepped out for a few minutes to get coffee..."

ABOUT ROXANNE

We? Who was we? Then she registered Jessica, close behind Henry. *Jessica!* Thank God her closest friend was here. "Jethica," she croaked.

"I'm here, Roxanne," said Jessica, smiling but not all the way. Not in the impish, wry way she usually did. "It's okay. In fact, it's great. You're awake now, and we've been waiting for so long."

Did she sound happy? Or something else? Roxanne tried to shake her head, to push away the uncomfortable feeling of having arrived at a place and time without knowing how she'd gotten there. She tried to shrug off the odd emotional pings from her husband and friend. She moaned again and hated herself for sounding so weak, so not herself.

"The girls—," she managed before her voice shut down again.

"The girls are with my parents. They're fine, and you need rest," said Henry soothingly, but she didn't feel comforted. She croaked and squirmed, her eyes opening wider in alarm. "What's happening?" Henry asked the doctor.

"She's waking up, that's what," said Dr. Stevens. "That's good, but it also means she has to find equilibrium. She's going to feel off-balance for a while, not just physically, but emotionally. The coma gave her a break from her life. Now she has to get back into it, and whatever the issues and problems were, she will find them again, right where she left them." He pinned Henry with a look.

Henry's eyes slid away as he thought about Roxanne's blood work, to which he knew the doctor referred.

Jessica looked down.

Roxanne noticed no one held her hand—not Henry, not Jessica, and not even the doctor. Her hands lay like limp noodles on the top of the blanket, fingers twitching and straining. She summoned all her will and directed it at her right hand, sending it flinging to one side. She smiled grimly and did it again, this time deliberately reaching out to take Jessica's hand.

Everyone gasped.

CHAPTER EIGHT

Hours later, her daughters stormed into the room. Rose did, anyway, while Annie hung back and slipped along the wall, eyes wide and staring.

Rose clambered onto the bed, and Roxanne's heart lifted. "Mommy! You're awake!" She threw her arms around Roxanne's neck, and the scent of little girl filled the space between them. "I wanted to bring Biscuit, but Dad wouldn't let me. Annie says there are hospital dogs, and I think they should let us bring ours to come see you, don't you?" She prattled on in her sing-song way.

Roxanne hugged her youngest close. Thankfully, she could. She was weak, but she could move her limbs, her body somewhat. But it had taken all the small degree of energy she had to manage those movements. She was alive, after all, and her family was here. She closed her eyes and let out a slow breath. Her eyes slid to Annie, the daughter who baffled her.

Henry stood beside his oldest, talking to her softly. He nudged her. "Go on. Go hug your mom."

Slowly, Annie pulled away from the wall and walked to the bedside. "Hello, Mom." She sounded almost formal. Her eyes searched the floor, and her cheeks were slightly flushed. She always looked extra rosy when struggling with difficult feelings.

Roxanne reached out and touched her arm. "It's okay, pumpkin. I'm fine, really, I am. I'm a little tired right now, but before you know it, I'll be up and running around and back home. You know that, right?"

Annie's eyes lifted to her mom's. "Of course, I do. Dad explained it all to me. You were in a coma, and today, you woke up. Not everyone does, but you did. Now that you're awake, you will be fine." She spoke flatly, the color intensified in her cheeks, and she looked down again.

Where was the joy? Where was the affection, the warm reunion? Annie was an enigma, but she'd always been that to Roxanne. "What was that? Annie, I can't hear everything you're saying. Can you sit on the bed with me?" She patted the bed next to her. " I want to know all about what you've been doing while I was...away. Come here."

Annie stepped back from the bed.

Henry sighed with exasperation but did nothing.

So much for the touching family reunion. Henry was solicitous but aloof, Rose was herself, and Annie might as well be some other woman's daughter. She was trapped in this bed for now, waiting for physical therapy to start. Meanwhile, she had so much to think about, so much to wonder about and try to understand.

She didn't remember the accident, not even one moment of it. But she'd been reassured that was normal, that those memories would likely reappear, although there was no guarantee. Anyway, it didn't matter, did it? What mattered was what she'd remembered as soon as she had awakened from the coma.

The letter.

And the questions, the memories, and the doubts about what had happened so long ago. And now, the overpowering urge to get up, to do something.

ABOUT ROXANNE

Roxanne's hand, which had been stroking Rose's hair, slowly fell away as utter exhaustion overtook her. A chitter of fear raced through her system. *What if she went back into the coma? What if she never woke up again?* She struggled to open her eyes again, but they were far too heavy. "Henry?"

"What is it, babe? Roxanne?" His voice receded, and she slipped away.

This time, she fell not into a coma but into a restless dream state.

Roxanne bolted awake, her eyes searching for familiarity and not finding it. This wasn't her bedroom, her safe, warm cocoon with the soft comforter and pillow-topped mattress. Her pulse tripped rapidly. Gradually, the room came into focus, and she remembered. *The hospital.*

Every morning, it was the same. She slept, yes, aided by a mild sedative. But she awakened disoriented, taking several minutes to register the truth. After getting her bearings each morning, she dove into exercise with a physical therapist, followed by walking around the hospital, more than advised. But she couldn't shake the deep feeling of urgency that gripped her.

She searched for her cellphone, finding it a few minutes later in the drawer of the nightstand. She pressed call. "Henry, get over here now. I need to go home, and I want you to help me check out," she said as soon as he answered. "No, now. I don't really care what the doctor says. I'm not lying in this bed a minute longer." She bristled as he argued against it. "Well, if you won't help, I'll get someone else to do it." She listened for a minute, then signed off. She felt slightly guilty for the manipulation, but it always worked. Henry couldn't tolerate her abrupt course changes and the invocation of the invisible 'other' who would step in for her.

She struggled to sit up and made it to the side of the bed. Her feet dangled impossibly far from the floor, so she executed a sliding leap and managed to stand. From there, she walked around the room several times, ignoring the weakness and fatigue. She dressed herself and waited. Henry arrived breathless, after an agonizingly long period of time but which was, in reality, less than an hour.

"Roxanne, what are you doing? You're not ready to get up and leave. You can't leave until your doctor sees you and signs off on your release, you know that. Wait, stop it," he said as she opened the small locker in the room and began pulling on her clothes.

"I'm going home, Henry, and no one is going to stand in the way of that. Not you, and certainly not the doctor. Besides, when he sees how I'm doing, it will be a no-brainer to sign me out." She moved to the bed and found the call button again. "Hello, nurse? Send the doctor in here. I'm checking out." As the nurse responded contrary to her wishes, she threw it on the bed and turned to Henry. "Let's get out of here."

Her mother had dubbed it 'Roxanne's Way.' From her senior year of high school forward, her mother held no power over her. They had a few emotional tussles over her so-called curfew and questions about where she was taking the car. One day, Roxanne made her final argument, Grandmamá sitting there as well, rolling her eyes. "Listen, Mother, here's the thing. I'm not getting into trouble. I'm not getting pregnant. I'm not taking drugs. I'm going to school and holding down a part-time job. I'm starting college next fall. You don't have any reason to treat me like a child anymore, so stop it."

Even Grandmamá had conceded defeat, shaking her head while attempting to dole out a few more pearls of wisdom as Roxanne walked out the door leaving the two of them to discuss their favorite subject—*what are we going to do about Roxanne?* If only they knew, but of course, even Roxanne hadn't known the full truth back then.

After that, Mother gave up trying to tell her what to do. Maybe she should have fought harder.

Once home, she threw herself on the sofa. *Finally.* After an argument with hospital staff that included a threat of legal action, she'd signed a stack of papers signifying the release of all liability from the hospital, the doctors, the entire staff, and even the sanitation crew, she was pretty sure. Even she knew that was overkill, and she made her living from litigation.

Henry was gone, and the girls were still at school, so the house was quiet. If she could catch her breath, she'd get a second wind with which to tackle her list. Her cases must be incredibly neglected. It was intolerable to think that Richard might have given them to someone else, especially that reprehensible Cory.

She'd have to figure out how to manage her cases remotely or delegate to Claire so she could get focused on the issue that ate at her insides. She needed to go see Mrs. Strickland as soon as possible and get some answers.

She curled up on her side and pulled a throw over her legs, closing her eyes gratefully. Just a few minutes, a short nap, and she'd be good as new. Biscuit, who'd followed her incessantly since returning home, circled once and dropped into position next to the sofa with a soft doggy sigh. Roxanne drifted off.

Little girl voices, the sounds of backpacks being dropped, and a slamming front door jarred her awake. She pulled herself up as Henry and the girls appeared.

"Mommy!" Rose ran and threw herself into Roxanne's arms. She climbed into her lap and clamped her arms around Roxanne's neck, slathering her with kisses. "You're home!" But too soon, she scrambled down and ran to her room, yelling something about her artwork.

Annie stood on the other side of the room watching Roxanne, who held out her arms. "Annie, can you give your mom a hug?" Her oldest daughter approached slowly, face stoical, no indication that she'd missed her mother. When she got close enough, Roxanne reached out and pulled her onto the sofa, giving her a warm hug. Annie's body relaxed for a moment, and her face softened.

"Hey. How's it going?"

"It's fine, Mom."

"Good. That's good."

Annie's face darkened, all the softness gone. "Yeah, it is good, Mom, and you can thank Dad for that. He takes care of everything."

Henry had the grace to look slightly embarrassed. "Annie, your mom just got home. Maybe you could put off giving her a hard time until she feels a little better, huh?"

Annie pulled away from her mother and headed for her room.

"Uh, bye?" Roxanne called after her sarcastically. "Well, at least my youngest daughter missed me." She glanced at Henry. "What about you, Henry? Miss me?"

Before he could answer, Rose stomped happily into the room, clutching multiple sheets of thick paper covered with brightly painted people and objects. "See, Mommy! I made this for you," she said, climbing into Roxanne's lap, pointing excitedly, and describing each piece of art in detail.

After a few minutes, Henry rescued her. "Peanut, Mom needs her rest. Let's give her a break while you get your homework done."

"I don't have any homework, Daddy," Rose said, wide-eyed. "I'm too little for that." She giggled hysterically as Henry swooped her off of Roxanne's lap.

"No homework? What is this world coming to? In that case, your homework is to brush Biscuit. Plus, I have a list of sixty-five more things for you to do. We don't need any stinking homework, do we? What do you think about that?" He waltzed her around their living room as Rose shrieked happily.

Biscuit's tail went wild as she followed Henry and Rose around the room, her mouth opened in a huge doggy grin, tongue lolling out. She barked once and started panting. The entire room began to spin for Roxanne as she bizarrely juxtaposed this happy domestic scene with the ones she'd observed from the sidelines while in the coma, which swirled up from the fog to cause her heart to thud.

Sweat slicked her chest, and her face flushed as she wobbled to her feet. "Okay, you guys carry on. I have to go to the office."

Henry stopped dancing with Rose and protested, but she brushed him away. "I'm going, Henry." She went to their bedroom, and as she left, Rose's face fell to that little girl look of such utter devastation that never failed to insert shards of guilt in her chest. But she turned away anyway. There were things to take care of, in the forefront of her mind, that couldn't wait.

As she pulled on a jacket, Henry appeared at the bedroom door. "You just got home, you're barely functioning, and *now* you have to go to the office? That's not really a great idea. The girls need to spend time with you—"

"Oh, here we go again," she threw at him as she spun to meet his guilt trip with her glare. "I can't believe I'm barely back, and already you're second-guessing me. Just like old times, huh? I certainly didn't miss that while I was in a coma." Another small wave of dizziness swept over her but didn't stop her.

His mouth fell open for a moment, then his face tightened. "You know, Roxanne, you can't hide behind those snarky comments forever. At some point, your life will demand you face it, and by that, I mean me and the girls." He started to turn away, then faced her again sadly. "But I'm not sure you will understand that in time." He was gone, his words having found a tender spot to bruise. But she shoved that aside.

CHAPTER NINE

1999

Brandon's arms wrap around me, and for a moment, I feel light-headed from his touch. The tingles start in my stomach but go south from there. I wriggle and try to dispel the sensations because I'm pretty sure I know where that leads. He cups my face in his hands and leans in to kiss me as my eyes close.

"Come on, Hayley. It's time to go." It's Roxanne, my best friend. She tugs my arm, and I give her a sloppy grin. We came to the party together after cooking up this plan, one that involved no parental supervision. Someone gave us drinks when we got here. They tasted like fruit punch but with some kind of extra kick. I feel more relaxed than I can ever remember.

"Oh, Roxie, really?" My voice sounds odd to me, slurry, not like me at all. One thing drama has given me is an escape from the East Texas drawl no one else in our small town seems to notice or care about. I hear Mr. Chase's voice, 'World-class actors have no specific accent. They adapt to the needs of the production. They don't walk in with a drawl. Try it again.'

And I do. I work at it. I read out loud every day after school, recording my voice. As much as I dislike hearing it, I listen obsessively for the twang. And I'm getting there. I smile, pleased with myself, though confused at the moment. I do sound strange, even to myself. Plus, Roxanne is still standing there, and apparently, I'm supposed to leave now.

She's amazing, my best friend. She's so smart, smarter than anyone I know. I'm convinced she'll be our class valedictorian, and she'll ace college before taking the business world by storm. No question about it. She scoffs at my predictions, but I know. She's got something special about her, a strength of will. She seems older than the rest of us high school seniors.

And she's always there for me. I know it's not the greatest tragedy in the world, but when Buster, my dog since age ten, died a couple of months ago, and I thought I would never stop crying, Roxanne handed me tissues, fed me Rocky Road ice cream with Oreos, and sat by my side that entire night.

Wobbling to my feet, I sway a bit, giggle, and give my best friend a huge grin. She is not impressed. I know this because of the rolled eyes and the shaking head. I am a student of body language. It's all part of the training.

Brandon tugs my arm. "Hey, baby, don't go."

Brandon is so hot. I've seen him around school, or I used to before he graduated last year, and he was always with one cheerleader or another. I think he noticed me because a couple of times in the hallways, I caught him looking at me with a twinkle and a slight grin. But he passed me by, nevertheless. I still can't believe he's here, at the same party, and now, he's with me!

ABOUT ROXANNE

"I must go now because Roxanne said so," I say, only that's not what I hear coming out of my mouth. Instead, it's something like, 'I gotta go, 'cause Roshie said so,' all precise diction lost, swirled away into whatever I'd drained from that last plastic cup.

"Who is she, your mother?" Bandon challenges.

"No, she's my besht friend," I tell him, failing again to sound composed. A giggle escapes my mouth, then a hiccup. I cover my mouth with my hand. But an errant laugh bubbles up.

"Come on, Hayley, you've had enough," says Roxanne, looking a little off herself. My forehead wrinkles with concern. Someone needs to take care of her, get her home, or something. I'm trying to focus, but instead feel myself sway with indecision, or imbalance, or both.

"I'll get her home," says Brandon, succeeding at tugging me down, this time onto his lap. I giggle as he pulls me into him and kisses my neck, sending tingles all over my body.

Roxanne stands there, unmoved by this display. "No, Hayley. I'm not going to leave you here. Come on," she urges.

"It's okay. I can get back to the house on my own," I tell her, frowning. I always follow Roxanne's lead, always. She's by far the most practical of the two of us, and the most trustworthy. If she says do something, there's always a good reason. If she says don't do something, there's usually a good reason for that, too. But right now, I don't want anyone telling me what to do. I feel stubborn, maybe even a touch rebellious.

This is good. I need the practice at these feelings and the behaviors that go with them. How many movies and plays have been written about rebellion of one kind or another? The rebellious teenager, the pent-up housewife, the bullied nerd, the unleashed college student.

It's a long list. They are often the best, juiciest roles, the ones with the greatest emotional range, with the deepest character development. My drama teacher says stories about rebellion tug at our roots in this country.

"That's right," says Brandon, pulling me closer, shoring up my rebellion. His body heat transfers some of itself to me in a delicious way.

Roxanne shrugs her shoulders. "Are you sure?"

"Yes!" In a wild display of independence, I turn to Brandon and kiss him on the mouth. Vaguely, I register his smirk directed at my best friend as he kisses me back.

Roxanne turns to go, and as she does, I suddenly feel a chill, and it's not because of the spin of attraction I feel for Brandon. Actually, it's more like a shudder, and the small hairs on my arms rise. My grandpa used to say when he felt a chill, 'Someone must be walking on my grave.'

What does that even mean? But recalling that expression gives me another pause.

Roxanne and I do everything together, well, almost everything. There is one exception. But never once, in the history of our friendship, have we separated at an event. No one goes home while the other stays; we always leave together. Socially, she is my rock, my anchor.

People think it's easy for me, but that's because they don't know me. I am in front when I'm on stage, so I am noticed. At those times, I feel the mixture of admiration, envy, and false desire to be close, to have something, whatever it is, rub off. Only Roxie knows what it is all about, understands where I am going with all of this.

ABOUT ROXANNE

Now, she's leaving, and I feel something slipping away. The shiver turns into something more, and now, I feel unaccountably bereft and fearful. Something is happening, something I can't put my finger on, but which scares me.

Brandon puts a plastic cup to my lips, and I drink. The elixir settles into my skin and bones, and I relax again. Silly you, I tell myself, pushing down the fear. He begins kissing me again, and I float away on a tide of pleasure.

CHAPTER TEN

PRESENT DAY

As soon as she walked into the office, Claire rushed to Roxanne, threw her arms around her best friend, and hugged her tightly. "Roxanne! I didn't think you would be out of the hospital so soon. Why didn't you call me? I'd have been there in a flash, you know that."

"Uh, Claire? I can't breathe," said Roxanne, and it was partly true, but she felt instantly warmed, allowing herself to soak up her friend's love.

After letting Roxanne go, Claire stepped back, puzzlement twisting her features. "What are you doing here? Shouldn't you be at home, resting? How are you feeling, Sweetie?"

If people would only stop monitoring her health, she'd actually feel much better. It was suffocating having to constantly answer for how she felt. The rapid-fire questions overwhelmed her, even though she knew Claire meant well. Trying a little patience, she said slowly, "Claire, I'm fine. Now, I need to see my cases, figure out where we are and what needs to be done. Not that you don't have most of it covered," she rushed to add. "But I need to be briefed. And, I have something else I have to take care of for a few days, so..."

She spoke as she marched to her office, Claire trailing behind. Once there, she looked around, puzzled. *Where were her files? Where was the usual chaos, the stacks, and the sticky notes, which she understood like the back of her hand?* "Where is my work, Claire? What happened while I was gone?" Her tone was accusatory and moving rapidly into something worse.

Claire reached out and touched her shoulder, and she jumped. "Sorry, I didn't mean to startle you. But your cases were distributed to the other partners while you were out. It was… uh… Richard's decision. No one knew when you'd be back, so we did the best we could." But her eyes slid away.

What? Her cases, handed out to others? Doled out like it didn't matter who'd been working on them for weeks, months? Clients called and told their case was no longer in Roxanne's capable hands. It was outrageous and uncalled for. She pushed past Claire, who tried to stop her, and barged into Richard's office without knocking.

"What the hell, Richard!"

Richard's eyebrows flew up as he hurriedly disengaged from a call and began to rise. "Roxanne! I didn't expect you back—"

"So soon. I know. Apparently, not much is expected of me around here anymore, Richard. But I am back, and you can get busy getting my cases back from…whoever you gave them to. And it better not have been Cory." Her anger felt sharp again, like needles pressing against her eyelids, almost uncontrollable. It wasn't all Richard's fault, and generally, he was fair with her, but he was here, in her line of fire.

"Sit down, Roxanne," he said calmly.

How could he be so calm at a time like this? Of course, he could be calm. His work was still his, while hers was…*what was hers*? "What is this, Richard? Just cut to the chase, will you?"

"Okay, I will. First, I'm glad you're up and around, and that it appears you're well on your way back to health. That is good. But I'm not going to hide this from you. I know you were driving under the influence that night, Roxanne. I—"

ABOUT ROXANNE

"That is ridiculous, Richard." The denial was second nature, but panic now fluttered like moths in her stomach, threatening to rise up and out of her mouth in an unpleasant, uncontainable way. "Who told you this, this lie?" she asked, choking on her own lie.

"Roxanne, I am aware of the bar you frequent, and I am acquainted with the bartender. I wanted to know what happened that night, so I asked a few questions. I'm sorry, not because I did it, but because I realize this is upsetting to you."

Upsetting? Her privacy, invaded like that? *By her partner?* Not to mention the blather mouth bartender slimeballs who happily poured her drinks and had never once indicated she'd had too many. "Why? Why did you do that, Richard? I thought you cared—" she choked out. How stupid of her to think her partner, her old-enough-to-be-her-father partner, might have those kinds of feelings for her, might have her back, might care.

Stupid of her. It was the good-old-boys club all over again. The same one she'd been excluded from her entire professional life, or least the one she'd had to fight to get into every step of the way.

Richard continued, his voice laced with concern but firm. "You're on leave until you can complete an alcohol abuse program. You may be very angry with me now, but I'm doing this for you. I have tried to talk to you over the past couple of years, but there didn't seem to be any other way to get through to you. Now you're not only risking your life, but the lives of others and the reputation of this firm. You got off lucky because it turned out the other driver was distracted. She caused the accident, not you. Not this time."

It hit her like a punch to the chest. She *had* driven while intoxicated. And she hadn't once asked about the other driver, not at the hospital, and not since going home. She hadn't even bothered to find out if she'd caused the accident.

Thank God she hadn't. But Richard's meaning was clear. He wasn't going to let her off the hook.

A toxic mix of anger and pain boiled out of her mouth, and she didn't even try to contain it. "I never thought I would see this from you, Richard. You guys just couldn't wait to get me out of the way while I was *in a coma*. I feel the knife in my back, and your fingerprints are all over it." She saw him wince at her words. *Good.* "Well, don't think I'm going to just roll over. I know a couple of great labor attorneys, and you will be hearing from one by tomorrow." She stood, glaring, as Richard's face paled.

Then his eyes took on a sad expression. "I'm sorry you feel that way, Roxanne. Please, go home and think about it. I'm not firing you; I'm requiring a treatment program. It's for the best."

"Who are you to decide what's best for me? You have no right." She slammed her palms on his desk, then swiped everything in sight on the floor with an almighty swoosh and clatter. Papers lay strewn as Richard sat frozen in shock. *What a satisfying feeling.* She turned and stalked away, heart hammering and breath short. But head held high.

It wasn't the way she'd planned to take a break, to handle the Hayley situation. But she had the time off, now. First, though, there was a deep thirst to be slaked.

CHAPTER ELEVEN

Roxanne's favorite seat was open. She sat down shakily on the round leather-topped barstool. Dark wood paneling subtly lit by sconces wrapped welcoming arms around her, and she began to breathe more easily. The two bartenders conferred briefly at the other end of the bar, and one slipped into the back after cutting his eyes her way. *Chicken shit*. The other approached and took her order.

As he turned away, she spoke again. "Hey, listen, Stan? Tell your buddy Craig back there that he can run, but he can't hide." Stan rolled his eyes and walked away.

"Nice," said an alto voice nearby. She turned toward the voice, which belonged to a guy who seemed vaguely familiar. The face—sharp-eyed intelligence, small lines betraying fatigue, expressive mouth—she knew that face from somewhere. Definitely a nice-looking face, but she wasn't interested.

"This is a private conversation," she threw at him.

"It's not private in a public bar," he said, and now his mouth curled slightly at the corners.

Wait... of course! Recognition snapped in her brain. It was the attending physician from the hospital. "What are you doing here? Did

NINA ATWOOD

you follow me here, Dr. Stevens? I signed off on everything but my children to get out of there, and as you can see," she spread her arms wide. "I'm perfectly fine."

Her drink landed in front of her on a napkin—frosted glass, ice-cold gin, olives on the side. *Heaven.* She took a delicious sip. Nuts to Richard for thinking she had a drinking problem. She was in complete control.

"Good, huh?" Dr. Stevens again. "Like an old friend you haven't seen in a while, one you can't wait to see again. It's been, what, four, maybe five hours since you were discharged. And this," he pointed his chin at her drink, "is the most important thing in your life right now." He shook his head lightly with a trace of sadness.

Another sip and the cold gin sliding down her throat gave her courage, helped her belly unwrap its knots. Suddenly, Dr. Stevens was no more than a fly, a pesky fly she could swat away. She gave him her most dazzling smile. "Look, Doctor, you don't know me. You don't know anything about me. You have no idea what I'm going through." Another sip, well more than a sip, but who cared? It was just one drink before she went home and faced her judgmental husband. After which, she would make a few calls and unleash the legal hounds of hell on her partner.

Actually, the partner issue could wait for other, more pressing things.

"It's Derek," he said. "And, yes, I do. I know exactly what you're going through." He fished in his pocket and pulled something out, which he placed on the bar, holding it under his fingers for a moment. Then, he slowly slid it over to Roxanne and removed his fingertips.

Curiosity gripped her, and she looked at the object. It was round, flat, and bronze. Her eyes were drawn to the inscription. 'To thine own self be true' was stamped around the outer edge. The center featured a large V.

"Five years," said Dr. Stevens. He turned over the coin to show her the rest. "The serenity prayer," he said.

ABOUT ROXANNE

She gulped down the last of her drink and flagged the bartender, who'd already shaken the second. He poured it into another ice-cold martini glass and placed it in front of her while taking away the empty. She took a large sip and carefully placed it on the napkin while turning to Dr. Intrusive.

He held up one palm, and something radiated from him at that moment, something that pinned her to her seat and closed her mouth, which was all set to blast the guy. "I know. You want to take my head off and get out of here as soon as possible. But I wonder if you have the guts to stay for maybe ten minutes and hear a couple of things from me, a complete stranger who knows you better than you could ever imagine."

"I doubt that." But she stayed, for now. "Maybe you can start with explaining what you're doing in a bar, preaching to me about sobriety." She nodded at his highball glass.

"Have a sip," he said, sliding it toward her.

"No, thanks. I like my gin straight, shaken, not stirred, no fizzy water," she smirked.

"Take. A. Sip."

She rolled her eyes but took a sip and was surprised. Tonic water with lime, no alcohol. She eyed him silently.

"I come here once a year on the anniversary of my sobriety, just to remind myself of what life was like before. And to warn myself. I sat here, on this barstool, every night for almost nine years. And lots of other barstools before that." It was his turn to eye her. "Let me ask you something. What keeps you awake at night? When you're not passed out, that is, on the nights you lie awake, your mind going, your body restless." Somehow, he managed to say it without coming off as judgmental.

Something loosened in her belly. "I try to make sure nothing keeps me awake at night."

"Okay. But when was the last time you were awake at night?"

"It was in the hospital after I woke up from the coma."

"And what was it that kept you awake?"

She flashed to Hayley—the dreams she'd been having. The memories swirling from the past, vividly re-living them. And the letter from her friend's mom.

Dear Roxanne,

It's been a long time. I hope you're doing well. I'm writing because I've been thinking about some things lately, things about Hayley, my beautiful daughter. You were her best friend, and I sometimes wonder if there were things going on that tell a different story. I know that may sound strange, but I discovered some things recently that raised some questions, and I would really like to talk to you about them. I think in person would be best if you can find the time. Please call me so we can arrange something.

"It was about Hayley," but she choked on the next words. It was impossible to continue, incomprehensible to let the rest emerge. A fist grabbed her lungs and squeezed. Oxygen eluded her gasp. Her hand gripped the edge of the bar, and she shook her head, trying desperately to clear her lungs, her head. Sparkles danced at the edges of her vision.

"Whoa. Something has really got you. Here," he said, after flagging down the bartender, who ran to the back and swiftly returned. Dr. Stevens held a small paper bag to her mouth and instructed her to take deep breaths.

She did, her eyes rolling around, but finally, her head began to clear. She pushed the bag away. "I have to get out of here." But her body remained planted on the barstool, voices swirled in the background, and her drink sweated on the napkin. No part of her wanted to sip anymore.

"I know. It's okay, just stay a few minutes. Whoever Hayley is, she's obviously very important to you." The compassion in his voice undid her, and slow tears traced her cheeks. He tucked a wad of napkins in her hand, and she blew her nose into them. "What happened to Hayley?"

ABOUT ROXANNE

"I don't know for sure. It never really made sense back then, but I—"

"You shoved it down. Or, rather, swallowed it."

"Maybe. I have a letter from her mom, and I need to go see her. Find out what she knows or thinks she knows. I don't know where it's all going, but I can't sleep anymore because of the dreams and the…"

"Obsessive thoughts," he offered. "I know. I know what it's like to have something eat at you, keep you awake at night, and how you try to make it disappear. But there weren't enough whiskeys to make mine disappear. The pain—sure, the pain was dulled. But the rest of it was there when I woke up the next day, no matter how hard I tried, and believe me, I really tried hard."

"And what was it that kept you awake at night, Doc?" she asked, recovering some of her spark, hoping to divert this conversation. She blew her nose again and slid her eyes sideways, waiting.

"Name's Derek," he told her for the second time, to which she rolled her eyes. "Anyways, I survived, and he didn't."

"Who didn't survive?"

CHAPTER TWELVE

"Willie, my kid brother. He was five, I was eleven, and I was supposed to be taking care of him. I took my eyes off of him for just a few minutes, and when I turned around, he was gone. I ran all over that mall, the mall where I shouldn't have taken him, but I was bored and wanted to play video games with my friends."

Dear God. "What happened to him?" She asked, afraid of the answer to the most dreaded question a parent can contemplate.

"No one knows. The hunt for Willie went on for months. My parents were interrogated since they were the prime suspects. Investigators tried to get me to acknowledge abuse in the home, but there was never any abuse. Mom and Dad were great—loving, generous with each other, with us. It killed, literally killed my mom. She died of a heart attack two years after Willie went missing."

"And your dad?"

He described the terrible sadness that had emanated from his father, how he'd catch him looking at him with something akin to hatred. That he couldn't get past the knowledge that his remaining son had managed to let his other son get abducted.

"And what happened to you?" she whispered, unable to pull herself away from the horror.

"Me? I stayed away from home as much as possible after Mom died. I worked hard, got into college pre-med, then medical school, and poured myself into the study of how to save human beings from disease and other bad things. It gave me a sense of power, of control. I was a surgeon, one of the best. I was Godlike, and nothing could ever hurt me again."

"Until?" she prompted.

"Until the pain built to an intolerable point. I'd found ways to indulge my love of alcohol starting in middle school. And all the way through college and after residency, and even while I operated on people. I knew when to drink and when not to drink. It worked really well for me. I met and married a beautiful woman who blessed me with two children."

Here he stopped, looked away, his mouth grim, and she waited.

"One night after overindulging, I got myself home… somehow—but when I got there, the house was empty. My wife and children were gone. Most of the furniture was gone. She'd moved out that day, moved across the country to live near her parents so she could have help raising the kids. Because I was worthless as a father. I worked, or I drank. Period. I missed everything—school plays, sports, piano recitals, you name it.

"That, however, wasn't the end of it. The next day, I lost my job as the chief of surgery at the hospital, and that was when I realized that the little game I'd been playing, pretending to myself that no one noticed, was over. Oh, don't worry. I didn't lose my medical license," he said, lips curving again at her shocked expression. "You have to do some truly bad stuff to lose your license."

They sat for a few heartbeats, neither saying a word.

"That night, I got drunker than I'd ever been, so drunk that I ended up in the E.R. because my only friend at the hospital checked on me, knowing that after getting fired, I'd be wasted. My body was at the point of no return, and I was told that if I didn't get sober, I'd be dead within six months. As soon as I got out, I went to my first A.A. meeting."

Electricity traced up and down her spine. It was like looking in a mirror. *The death of someone dear. The guilt, the unshakeable responsibility for what had happened. The thousands of attempts to swallow enough gin to remove it, to no avail.*

She was quiet, then asked him, "How do you live with it? With never knowing what happened to your brother, Willie?" *How had she lived with never knowing what had really happened to Hayley?* The truth was she hadn't, but she wasn't ready to face that reality yet.

"I had to move on. Continue to live my life. But I will tell you this. It never goes away, the unanswered questions, the endless loop of what-ifs." He faced her, and his eyes told the story of depths of pain that should be intolerable but had to be lived with anyway. "You're going to wind up dead, Roxanne, if you don't make another choice. Yeah, I'm a doctor, and everybody dies, but most people don't do it to themselves when they're young and have so much to live for. Your head is corroded, and you don't understand the choices you're making."

He slid off the barstool. "Here. This is someone who can help you figure out what you need to do." He shoved a card into her hand after scribbling something on the back and drained his glass, shaking it and smiling grimly into its depths. "I can't save you. You have to finish whatever it is with Hayley, and you have to save yourself. No one's coming."

Later, she pulled the card out of her bag and fingered it, thinking. *A shrink.* Dr. Derek had opened his life to her, shared his own tragedy. Now, he seemed to think she needed professional help. *Did she?* She pushed the card back in.

And what did he mean by *no one's coming*?

She tucked it back in and pulled out her cell to call for a ride. There was one person who could give her what she needed right now. Perspective. Straight talk. Support, guidance.

A few minutes later, she pulled up in front of a mid-rise condominium complex in the heart of Uptown Dallas, quite posh. Stepping off the elevator, she had a moment of indecision. It was late, and her friend was probably asleep. But she hadn't had a dose of Jessica in far too long. Surely, she was due some leeway after waking up from a coma and losing her job.

Instead of ringing the bell, she knocked softly on Jessica's door. Nothing. She knocked louder and called out. "Jessica! It's me, Roxanne. Open up, girlfriend! I need some advice. I'm sorry it's so late, but it's really important. Jessie?"

The door opened slowly and stopped partway. Jessica stood there, clad in yoga pants and a light sweatshirt. Her characteristically deep red lips were bare, and she wore minimal makeup. But she didn't look like she'd been asleep.

"Oh, thank God! I thought for a minute you were out with some guy, breaking another unsuspecting heart." Roxanne pushed her way in, bubbles of happiness rising, grateful for the friendship and warmth ahead of her, maybe with the added pleasure of another martini...and stopped dead in her tracks. Shock stripped her of words, and disbelief wrapped her in its devastating grip.

Henry rose slowly from the sofa. "Roxanne."

Her head swiveled from one to the other—her husband and her best friend. That was when she registered the flushed skin, the tousled hair, the telltale smell of candles blown out, the wine glasses in the sink, and the incredibly guilty look on Henry's face.

"This isn't what it looks like," Henry began, appeasing her, holding his hands up.

A dragon awoke inside. "Not what it looks like? You're here at my girlfriend's home, drinking wine, with candles and the works? Go ahead. Explain. I have got to hear this."

Henry and Jessica exchanged a look, and that was when the dragon took flight. "You know what? Forget what it looks like. I'll tell you what it is. You're having an affair, and you were probably doing each other while I was in a coma!"

"Roxanne," said Henry, drawing himself together and looking less guilty, "you've been drinking, haven't you? How did you get here? You didn't drive again, did you? And the girls are fine—they're at my parents."

The dragon went on a fire-breathing tear around the room. She picked up the two used wine glasses and threw them at Jessica's beautiful slate fireplace, shattering them into miniscule shards. "No, Henry, I didn't drive, but it wouldn't matter if I did. I'm fine. I'm always fine. You, however, are not going to be fine when I'm finished with you." Tears prickled and threatened to fall.

"Roxanne, please," whispered Jessica, coming toward her with, of all things, some kind of fake compassion.

"Get the hell away from me!" She turned and exited the condo, slamming the door in her wake. A slightly disheveled gray head peered out of a doorway, frowning, and Roxanne glared at the guy as she walked past, stumbling slightly. "What are you looking at?"

As she stalked to the elevator and rode it down to the street level, her face grew hot. Her heart raced, and the shame of it all threatened to engulf her. Visions flashed, of Henry and Jessica entwined, doing things she and Henry hadn't done in months, saying things to each other she hadn't heard in longer than she could remember. Laughing at her, planning their new life together.

Her limbs were numb, her mind blank, as she stood in the lobby. She couldn't focus. Had forgotten why she had come in the first place. But then the elevator behind her dinged, and she bolted out of the door, her heels impeding her escape.

Traffic was thin, both vehicle and pedestrian. She'd stepped into an unfamiliar world, one that she'd traveled many times, but not at this hour. Gone were the twinkling lights in the trees, the laughing singles hanging out in groups, the couples holding hands and beaming as they walked. Restaurant tables were empty, chairs pushed in, no diners to take bites of delectable food and clink wine glasses.

The only people in sight were a couple of faces peering over the tops of coats as they huddled on the ground with stuffed black trash bags by their sides. Homeless. *Her destiny.*

Bile rose, and she stopped, put her hand on the wall of the building. Her breath came in rasps, catching terribly. She heaved. The nearby homeless guy stared at her, dark eyes like marbles, not moving. Just stared. She tried desperately to summon enough saliva to spit but couldn't. The taste made her nauseous again.

She opened the rideshare app on her cell phone, but there weren't any rides within 20 minutes. She cast a wary glance around again, and the shadows rushed toward her as her throat closed up. She struggled to stand up, everything whirling, and vaguely wondered who would find her and when, after she passed out.

With shaking hands, she dug in the outside pocket of her bag and retrieved the card, flipping it over. She punched in the number, spoke a few words, and stood, shaking, until the vehicle pulled up. She stumbled in.

CHAPTER THIRTEEN

Thirty minutes later, she stood at the door of her new home, a modest motel room. "Thanks, Doc, for giving me a ride here." She didn't say, 'thanks for not lecturing me the entire way.' But she was grateful, nonetheless. She began to insert the key as she turned away.

"Please, call me Derek. Can I come in for a few minutes?"

She opened the door and waved him in. They sat at the tiny table in the two uncomfortable chairs in the corner.

"I won't stay long," he told her. "I want to tell you one more story, and it's yours—your typical day." He waited, perhaps to see if she would throw him out. When she didn't, he continued. "You wake up, and you tell yourself, today is going to be different. Today, I'm going to make my kids breakfast, get them off to school with hugs and kisses, and be nice to my husband. Today, I'm going to do my job and feel proud of the work I did at the end of the day. Today, I don't need a drink, so I won't have one, even though it would be okay if I did, and it won't be hard. Today is different.

"But it isn't different. It's like every other day—the same as yesterday, and the day before that, and every day before that. Halfway through the day, you get that first thought. I know I said I wouldn't drink, but...the client was difficult, the judge was unreasonable, the phone rang too many times, and you're stressed out. I don't want to go home like this. I want to be better, mellow when I get home, so I don't bite off my husband's head and yell at my kids. One drink won't hurt. I just need one to take the edge off. I'm still keeping my promise to myself, which was to not get drunk. One drink—that's it, and then I go home."

Ice dropped into her belly. How did he know her deepest thoughts, the ones she had on her worst days? "How do you know—"

"Because I have sat in a chair for hundreds of meetings and heard the same stories, over and over again. And because that was my story." He rose from the chair and stood quietly looking at her. "Get help, Roxanne. What happened tonight was one more example of the self-destructive path you're on."

"Wait. I have a...medical question." He'd stopped, and her words rushed out. "When I was in the coma, I had these vivid dreams, at least I think they were dreams, but they seemed so real. I saw my family and my friends, as if I were there, with them, but I wasn't. I couldn't have been. I feel like I'm going crazy because the most bizarre part was about my high school friend, Hayley, who I can't seem to get out of my head. Am I? Crazy, that is?" Her breath caught in her throat as she waited for the other shoe to drop.

"What happened to Hayley?"

"She...died."

He waited, head cocked skeptically.

"She killed herself."

"That must have been hellish. You've been left with so many questions."

"Yes! I have. But tell me, am I going crazy? I do NOT want to go see a shrink. I just want your medical opinion."

He paused as if weighing his options, and she was worried he would just leave. But then he answered, "Okay...but it's mostly speculation.

ABOUT ROXANNE

I'm not a shrink, and I'm not a neurologist," he caveated. "But, coma patients, the ones who wake up, often talk about vivid experiences that are not explainable. I'm not surprised you had that happen. It's not associated with mental illness, typically. But you still need to see a shrink."

He turned to go as Roxanne rolled her eyes. But there was one more thing. "Wait. One more question. I promise." He turned, waited, hand on the doorknob. "How do you stop? Is there a drug I can take? I'm ready. I'm going to stop now. But how do I do it, from a medical perspective?"

"Under medical supervision, no question. Don't try to do it alone."

"Of course not," she backed up.

"Roxanne. People *die* trying to de-tox on their own." He must have read something in her expression because then he said, "I can get you into a treatment center."

"I know, I'm sure you could. But I'm super tired, and I think the best thing right now is for me to get some sleep. How about we talk about it again tomorrow?"

He looked at her carefully and slowly shook his head. "Don't do it. I can't stop you but don't." He turned and left.

Before she went to bed, she rapidly researched some of the top addiction center websites, gathered the information she needed, and put it to work. She crawled on top of the covers, fully clothed, and fell asleep instantly.

The next two days were hell. Claire brought her laptop, a few necessary clothing items from a nearby discount store, and bags of sundry items. She brushed off her queries, promising to tell her more later and begging off due to exhaustion, which was true.

She paced the room, sipping electrolyte drinks and taking tiny bites of energy bars between bouts of nausea. She drank gallons of water.

Her research had uncovered a roadmap of alcohol detoxification. She fell into the lowest-risk category of drinkers—daily, yes—to excess. But not all day, and not starting in the morning, except on weekends. Mainly in the afternoons and evenings.

She couldn't get herself to acknowledge she was addicted, but she could admit to herself the reality of daily consumption and the toll on her life. But since she didn't drink all day, she wasn't yet in the acute stages of addiction that required hospitalization. Additionally, she'd effectively mostly detoxed while in the hospital in a coma. She was symptomatic, but only mildly.

The worst part of it was the inescapable, endlessly looping mindset with no way to hold it back. Her job, gone for now. Henry and Jessica, a friendship lost and a divorce on the horizon. Her daughters, who she'd been separated from while in the hospital, and who she didn't want to contact now, in this state.

And darkest of all...Hayley. Memories flooded her mind, vivid and irrepressible, threatening to drown her in the tangle of emotions she'd avoided for so many years. The vivid dreams about Hayley, stirring long-buried questions.

Confusion swirled even as a plan began to form. Something tugged, pulling her toward the past. None of it made sense, but the trajectory was in place. Perhaps it had always been there in the dark corners of her mind, waiting for her to notice. And to act.

She pulled out her laptop and went to work, rapidly clicking, creating an online dedication page.

Remembering Hayley

Dedicated to our beloved, lost classmate, Hayley Strickland, 1983—1999, and to all those who gave up on life too soon | Suicide awareness and prevention

It was a bit lame, and she knew it. But someone might find the remembrance page, it might spark a memory, and they might actually post something, and that could be a starting point. Perhaps it would help her understand why...why Haley had cut short her own brilliant life.

Adam Porter stared at the screen, at the newly posted page. *Hayley.* Beautiful, sparkling, irresistible Hayley. There was a photo pulled from their high school yearbook. Sunlit hair and golden skin, the smile of sheltered innocence, hiding the woman-child who'd thrown herself away on a stupid jerk.

He gripped his thighs with his hands as the memories washed over him. Watching them make out on the sofa, *in front of him*. The hands, all over her, touching her, sliding underneath her top, down her jeans. The jealousy he'd felt against his will as he watched.

She'd seemed so sweet at school, giving him homework assignments after he'd missed class. Smiling at him in the hallways while other girls smirked. But also ignoring him, like everyone else, his invisibility at work, again.

Until that night.

He'd never seen her with a steady boyfriend. And that night, when she'd actually shown up, he'd felt a surge of hope, for which he'd punished himself later, after everything that happened.

He remembered it all, how things had gone better later, then gone horribly wrong. *What was it about adolescent memories? Why were they so piercing, with sharp edges so many years later?* He slammed his laptop shut.

CHAPTER FOURTEEN

1999

Brandon's hands slide up my front, his fingers moving under my bra, and I push them away. Meanwhile, his other hand is sliding up my back, and now I feel him fumbling to unhook the lacy item that acts as the only barrier.

We're kissing deeply, and it feels wonderful, but that is all I want. Why don't boys understand the joys of making out, minus the advanced steps that we're not ready for?

His hands having been pushed away from my breasts, he is moving on, down to the real payday. Before I know it, his warm hand is sliding underneath the waist of my jeans, and now, my underwear, and the sensations are almost too much.

Despite the magic elixir still coursing through my veins, though, I preserve my innocence for another day as I yank his hand out of my pants and place it firmly on my...leg.

"Jeez, Hayley, what a tease," he huffs. He sits up and pushes me away, and I feel a small pang of hurt. "What is the point here, anyway?"

I pull his face toward mine, longing for more kissing, but he takes my hands away. "No can do. If we're not going any further, I've got better things to do." He picks up his beer and slugs it down, almost an entire can. "Yeah, you're cute as can be, but so are a lot of other girls." He burps, then stands, rakes a hand through his hair, and walks away.

I feel stung to the core. The truth is this is my first real make-out session. While we were kissing, I pictured him taking me out to the movies, to dinner, and maybe even sitting there in the audience watching me perform, smiling proudly.

'That's my girl,' he'd say to whoever sat nearby. After the performance, he'd hand me a huge bouquet of pink roses, then pick me up off the ground in a hug as he whispered in my ear how proud he was. Everyone would see that I'd snagged one of the cutest guys around for my very own.

What an idiot. I slump on the sofa. What to do now? Roxanne's gone...and in fact, so is most everyone else, I realize, startled. That is when I feel something from the corner of the room, eyes on me. I look up in time to catch an intense look from the guy who greeted us at the door hours ago. Aidan? No, Adam. I'm pretty sure it's Adam.

CHAPTER FIFTEEN

For the first time in two days, Roxanne's heart ticked at a normal rate. She sipped electrolyte-loaded water from the plastic bottle in her hand, steering carefully with the other. Her cell buzzed again, Henry's name and photo popping up. She glanced at it, then pulled her eyes back to the road. He could wait.

She'd texted Henry and informed him she was going out of town. There was no use going into their last encounter and what it meant. Shock and rage had given way to deep sadness.

Jessica. She'd sent Roxanne a flurry of texts, left unanswered, of course. 'It's not what you think. There is no affair. Please talk to me.' Eventually, the texts stopped. She gripped the wheel tighter and turned her thoughts to the journey ahead.

Her Facebook group page, *Remembering Hayley,* was getting a surprising response. After sending it to a handful of high school friends she'd quickly found, another twenty or so of their classmates had joined the online group. It was remarkable hearing their stories, reminders of the generosity, the care Hayley had exuded with everyone.

Hayley helped me study for the SATs... She sneaked makeup to me when my dad wouldn't let me wear any to school... She stayed all night to help finish painting the mural we created for homecoming... She stood up for me the time Mrs. Williams wouldn't let me take a make-up test after I missed because my brother was in the hospital... and on and on.

What would her life have been like? Who would she have married? Would their kids be friends? A life cut short inevitably left the possibilities open and endless.

Now, she had questions, not about what Hayley's life might have been, but about what it actually was. Her suicide had rocked their small East Texas school. There were no questions asked afterward. Tears were shed, heads shook mournfully, and people whispered as Roxanne passed by in the hallways at school. *They were best friends. I never see her cry.* As if Roxanne couldn't hear every word.

But Hayley's death was wrapped up as another baffling teenage tragedy, like so many others. One school counselor pulled her from class one day but met the wall of Roxanne's silence and gave up after one session. Suicide is quickly forgotten, and no one wants to ask why. The counselor told her there was no easy explanation. *Best to get on with your life, put it far behind you, and know that you are not to blame.*

What a lie.

Now that she was sober, the last days of her friend's life wouldn't stop flashing in front of her eyes, awake and while asleep. And that only raised more questions.

ROXANNE, 1999

The party raged on. Later, much later, most of the kids were gone. The house was a wreck—empty plastic cups everywhere, strewn remnants of junk food—bags and bags of chips, some of them emptied on the carpet and crushed by dozens of feet.

ABOUT ROXANNE

Hayley sat on the sofa with a boy Roxanne had never seen before. He wore a form-fitting tee shirt and cutout sleeves that showed off his muscled upper arms. The tee shirt rode high, revealing a flat abdomen. His hair was thick and wavy, shorter on the sides, longer on the top and the back. She couldn't help but see Mel Gibson in Lethal Weapon.

Roxanne rolled her eyes. This guy clearly thought he was God's gift. She walked over. "Come on, Hayley. It's time to go," she said.

"Oh, Roxie, really?" Hayley said in a little girl voice, grinning up at her best friend.

'Mel' tugged Hayley's arm as she tried to stand. "Hey, baby, don't go."

"I gotta go, 'cause Roshie said so," she slurred, wobbling a little on her feet.

"Who is she, your mother?" Mel challenged.

"No, she's my besht friend," slurred Hayley. She giggled, then hiccupped and quickly covered her mouth with her hand. But she laughed again.

Oh, boy. "Come on, Hayley, you've had enough," said Roxanne, feeling a little off herself.

"I'll get her home," said Mel, succeeding at tugging Hayley down, this time onto his lap. She giggled playfully, and he put his arm around her as he kissed her neck.

"No, Hayley. I'm not going to leave you here. Come on," urged Roxanne.

But now, Hayley's smile turned into a frown. "It's okay. I can get back to the house on my own," she said stubbornly.

"That's right," said Mel, pulling her closer.

Roxanne shrugged her shoulders. "Are you sure?"

"Yes!" Hayley turned to Mel and kissed him on the mouth. Mel looked up at Roxanne as he kissed Hayley, triumphant.

Fine. Roxanne turned to go, tight with resentment, but before she did, she glanced at Adam. He radiated anger. Strange, she thought but shrugged it off. Something tickled at the base of her brain, but the alcohol dampened the feeling.

She left and walked back to the house. It was pitch black outside, no moon to shed a little light, and she found herself getting a bit spooked along the way, jumping at every sound. At least Hayley wouldn't have to walk back since she had a ride. Finally, she reached home, let herself in, and tiptoed to her room, where she threw herself into bed and instantly dropped off.

Hours later, Roxanne awakened from a deep sleep and found Hayley hastily packing her things, her back turned. Dawn peeked through the windows. "Hey," she said, yawning. "What time did you get back? Ready for some pancakes?" She was over being mad about Hayley staying behind at the party and ready for some fun and girl talk.

Without turning around, Hayley mumbled something about going shopping and having breakfast with her mom.

"Funny, you didn't say anything about that yesterday when we talked about pancakes for breakfast." The mad surged again.

"I know. I forgot. I'm sorry," she said, again without turning around.

"How did you get home, anyway? Did that Mel Gibson lookalike actually give you a ride?" She couldn't keep the snark out of her voice.

ABOUT ROXANNE

"Yes, of course, I got a ride," she said, not exactly answering the question.

"Hey, what's up with you? Is something wrong? You sound funny," said Roxanne, sitting up in bed, concern overtaking the mad.

"Nothing's wrong. I've got to go," Hayley said and rushed out of the bedroom.

"Really?" said Roxanne to herself, flopping back on the pillows, feeling hurt all over again.

Roxanne called Hayley over the weekend a couple of times, but the phone just went to the answering machine. Monday at school, Hayley avoided her best friend all day, but Roxanne finally trapped her at the lockers. "What's going on? Why have you been avoiding me?" she demanded. Hayley never treated her this way.

But her friend gazed at her with dead eyes. "I'm not avoiding you. I'm just...tired. I've got a lot going on, and then there was Friday night."

"Friday night? That was three days ago! Are you mad at me for leaving? I thought that was what you wanted," said Roxanne. "Did something happen?"

Hayley looked down and shook her head. "No, nothing happened. We just made out, that's all."

But something was terribly off; she wasn't the same with Hayley. Roxanne knew it, could see it. But Hayley wasn't talking. After school, she called, but Hayley didn't answer. Her mother did. "Mrs. S.? Can I talk to Hayley?"

"Hi, Roxanne. I'm sorry, but Hayley isn't feeling well. You know, I'm starting to wonder about that party you kids went to. Was there alcohol involved?"

"Uh, no, Mr. S. No alcohol. Just a bunch of kids, you know, music and dancing, that sort of stuff. Um, can you have Hayley call me when she feels better?"

But it was days before Hayley came back to school. They resumed their friendship as if nothing had happened. Except it wasn't the same. Hayley wasn't the same. Her usually sunny disposition turned dark. She stopped wearing the bright colors that she loved, started dressing in baggy jeans and long tee shirts. No more midriff-baring tops, no more brightly colored miniskirts.

Hayley seemed to be all about covering herself up, which was definitely a complete 180. Roxanne could swear she stopped washing her glorious mane of blond hair. It seemed so stringy and greasy. She quit wearing makeup, and her eyes developed dark smudges underneath. She lost weight, became a little too thin. Her fingernails looked chewed.

At Hayley's house, they played music and studied together, but Hayley seemed to wander off frequently. Roxanne often caught her gazing into the distance, her eyes glazed.

One day, she'd had enough. She slammed shut her book. "What? You've been acting like a zombie for days now, Hayley. What is going on with you?"

But Hayley turned away, wrapped her arms around herself, and mumbled, "Nothing."

After that day, she stopped inviting Roxanne over. But only for a while. Then came the day she did. She greeted Roxanne at the door, smiling. That day, Hayley tried on clothes, having apparently been *shopping the day before. Gone were the plain, dark, baggy clothes, and back were the bright, form-fitting stylish ones. They did each other's hair and makeup, played music, and gossiped about everyone else at school. Roxanne spent the night, and as they were dropping off, Hayley spoke quietly. "Roxanne?"*

"Hunh?" she answered groggily.

"Nothing. Just...I love you."

"Love you, too," said Roxanne, turning over and quickly falling asleep. It was such a relief to have her best friend back.

That was Friday night, and the next morning, Roxanne left after breakfast. At home, she spent the day cleaning the house. Her mother waved and blew a kiss of thanks from her bed. "You are an angel," she said, beaming.

Yeah, right. An angel. But Roxanne couldn't stand the disorder. She'd cleaned the house for herself. She called Hayley but got no answer. She didn't let it bother her, figuring she was out and would call when she returned home.

But Hayley never called the entire weekend. Some best friend. The irritation, and hurt feelings, returned. She retaliated by not bothering to call Hayley again, finding other things to do rather than wonder where she was, whether or not she was hanging out with some other friend.

Monday morning, Roxanne looked for her at school, but she wasn't in the two classes they shared. Guilt set in. Maybe Hayley wasn't feeling well for real this time. Roxanne made a mental note to go to the store after school and get her friend's favorite soup and crackers and leave the bag on her doorstep with a get-well card. And later walked down her street in the last moments of her girlhood, just before all her innocence was stripped away.

PART TWO

CHAPTER SIXTEEN

She pulled her jacket closer and shivered. The park bench was hard and cold, and she'd been waiting for over an hour. It seemed like forever, and part of her wanted to give up, go home, and warm up in her cozy room. But she'd waited forever for this opportunity and wouldn't pass it up for anything, not even the chill of the night air. It was almost too good to be true.

It was time for her unique abilities to be revealed, to shine. She'd wanted this for so long, for as far back as she could remember. The hours upon hours gazing at the screen in rapture. The hours and hours of practice.

A small branch crunched, and her head snapped up. She put on her most dazzling smile, and a flash temporarily blinded her.

"I couldn't resist," said a voice, one that sent a tingle throughout her body. It was him, the one who'd found her out of all the hundreds, no thousands, of others. She couldn't quite see him because the light had blinded her.

"Hey," she said, almost shyly, but then emboldened she half-teased, "That was, like, startling."

"I took your picture. You're going to have to get used to that," he said, a laugh behind his voice.

She giggled. "That's cool."

He sat beside her, and her sight gradually cleared so that she could see him. He was watching her closely, a smile playing on his lips. The way he was dressed, the way he carried himself, his looks, although older, were attractive and altogether reassuring. This was a good idea, she decided. A good decision.

He reached out and took her hands, rubbing them to warm them against the cold. Somehow, it felt right.

"You're shivering. You're not afraid, are you?"

Something about the question sent a trickle of warning down her spine, but she quickly shook it off as he laughed.

"Just kidding." He touched her hair and pulled a strand back. "You have the most beautiful blond hair. Natural? Or enhanced?"

"It's real," she said proudly. Her mother's Norwegian heritage had passed to her, and along with it, blond hair that still shimmered, unlike her 'blond' girlfriends who already had begun resorting to highlights.

He handed her a folded set of papers. "Here you go."

She felt a shiver of nerves but steeled herself against them. She unfolded the pages and quickly scanned them. She looked up at him then, startled. "Isn't it a little—"

"Maybe. But you seem mature enough to handle it."

His words lent her a surge of confidence. Her mother was always telling her she was too immature, that she needed to grow up and be responsible. She chafed a bit, thinking about her mother. She'd soon see how grown up her daughter really was. And anyway, who was the immature one? After that stunt her mother had pulled to get even with one of the losers she'd dated.

She dove in, and within seconds, the park faded, and she was in another place, living a different life, at an older age, and it was everything she'd dreamed of. He responded in kind, and soon, they were totally in sync. Time flew, and she was shocked when they reached the endpoint.

He sat back, then, studying her closely, a finger tapping his lower lip. "It's just..."

"What?" she asked, alarmed. She'd done her absolute best. *Hadn't she?* She'd shone like never before. Maybe it was him. Maybe it was the pathway she'd been given. Whatever it was, she was sure she'd nailed it.

"Nothing. No, there is something. You are..." and he stopped, folded up the papers, and stood, turning to leave.

"What's wrong? You're not leaving, are you?" she asked, her stomach tightening.

He turned back around. "I wonder if you're ready."

"I'm ready, I swear I am! Wait! Let's do it again. I'll be better this time."

"I don't know."

Her heart thudded, and she stood and put her hand on his arm. "No, you have to give me another chance. It's this park and the cold. Can we meet somewhere else, maybe tomorrow, somewhere a little warmer?"

"You know, cold or warm shouldn't matter. You have to adapt. And besides, tomorrow is too late. You know why."

Her shoulders slumped, and she felt herself shrinking inside.

He watched her for a moment, then slowly smiled. "You're not going to give up, are you? You almost had me."

She straightened again and threw him her dazzling smile. "I'll never give up. What do I need to do?"

And he told her, and she did exactly what he asked of her.

She'd gone with him willingly, and she'd never forgive herself for that.

Later, much later—possibly a couple of days, but she couldn't tell, she wrote a note in the shakiest of writing and hid it carefully. At the end of it, she wrote her name in loops, with a tiny heart over the "i." *Daisy*. Then she went back to waiting endlessly, alone, until he showed up again. It was inevitable; she knew that now. And each time, the unimaginable things he did started all over again.

She'd been working on a plan, and the next time he showed up, she tried, with everything she had. "Wait. You don't have to do this. Just let me go. I just want to go home. That's all it is. My mom is bound to be so worried by now. I promise I won't tell anyone—"

"And what exactly would you tell? That you wormed your way into my life and that you begged me to do the things I do to you?" He gazed at her with his reptilian eyes, and she saw that her appeal had no effect.

"You're pathetic," he told her contemptuously.

She saw with a chill that all his initial attraction to her had vanished. She was nothing to him, now.

CHAPTER SEVENTEEN

Roxanne pulled up in front of a modest home on a quiet street filled with mature trees—live oak, sweetgum, and the errant pine. Green leafy shrubs overflowed with azaleas—pink, white, and fuchsia, adding vibrant color to the front of the homes. She sat for a moment before exiting the vehicle. The street seemed so different, the houses much smaller than the way she remembered, in the baffling way childhood memories loom larger than life.

The two-hour drive from Dallas to East Texas had given her a chance to reflect. Her head felt clearer than it had in months, but she attributed that to getting lots of sleep and drinking water. The conversations with Dr. Derek had diminished in her mind, and in their place was a renewed certainty that she wasn't a drunk, that she had this thing in control.

Henry clearly had another agenda, a screenplay of his own writing. One in which her former best friend starred as the new lover and in which Roxanne was cast as the villain. He'd always been her stalwart, her support—there for her and tolerant of her long hours and late nights. He was a wonderful father; she could never deny that.

As a husband? Not so much. He was more like a roommate. A constant presence, but not one with whom she felt the old sparks. *Or did she?* The accident and the coma had interrupted whatever their life had been, and now there was uncertainty laced with fear and resentment.

She'd have to find a way out of her new, unwelcomed role when she got back. Still, no time to think about it now.

The front door opened before she could press the doorbell. Mrs. Strickland beckoned her inside, then pulled her into a warm hug. "It's so good to see you, Roxanne. Oh my, you have grown up!" Her gray eyes, lined with sorrow, still twinkled. She pressed her hand to her throat briefly, as if something fluttered there, then led Roxanne to a sofa that might have been the same one she'd sat on over twenty years ago.

Roxanne tried not to stare, but the house hadn't changed. It was just as she remembered it—dark green velvet sofa and matching chairs, the swooping floral drapes with soft greens and pinks, the brass fixtures. She lived in a time warp. Because of Hayley? "How are you, Mrs. Strickland?"

"I'm fine, dear. I heard you went to law school, and you're a big shot Dallas attorney now." She beamed with pride as though she were speaking to her own daughter.

How did they speak of the girl who never got to graduate and land a big job or a starring role on Broadway? The one who'd never gotten the chance to occupy the second bedroom in their shared apartment in Dallas as carefree singles?

"Are you married? What about children?" She handed Roxanne a tall, sweating glass of iced tea.

Roxanne took a sip and almost choked on the sugar. "I am married, and I have two wonderful daughters." She cringed as the words came out, remembering her last interaction with Annie. "Your letter raised a lot of questions, and I confess, I probably needed this conversation, anyway, so I'm glad you reached out."

Mrs. Strickland looked down, and when she raised her eyes, they were filled with tears. "Thank you for coming to see me. I felt rather bad after I mailed the letter. It's probably just my foolish mind. I'm not sure there's anything to really talk about. You know, Hayley thought the world of you. She used to say to me, 'You know, Mom, Roxanne is so smart. I just know she's going to do something amazing with her life.'"

Right. Amazing things. What had Hayley seen in her? Guilt, remorse, shame, and apprehension swirled in her belly. She needed to stop thinking about herself and focus on Mrs. S, who seemed to be walking down her own painful memory lane.

Was it one of real memories or fantasy? Did her eyes look a bit off? This was her best friend's mom. A woman who'd been a beloved authority figure then, but now, was another adult whom she didn't really know. How does the passage of time, following a tragedy, help or hurt?

Mrs. Strickland pulled out a handful of tissues and dabbed her eyes, softly blowing her nose while she continued to talk. "I've tried so hard to get closure, but it's impossible. She was so happy. She had so much to live for up until those last couple of weeks. But she changed, and it wasn't gradually. It was overnight. I've read a lot of books about suicide, and they all say the same things. 'It's not your fault. They hide it from family and friends. You can't stop it, you're not responsible, and you have to quit feeling guilty.'"

She sniffed and dabbed. "It's stupid, of course, what the books say. No one can ever take the guilt away because it's your child. The number one job of a parent is to protect their children, and I failed. Oh, Roxanne, I'm sorry. I promised myself I wouldn't do this." She blew her nose again.

Roxanne reached out and touched Mrs. Strickland's hand, the heaviness of lingering grief palpable, her own breath shorter. "It's okay. You don't have to do this. I don't want to upset you." *But the letter,* she wanted to say. *What did you mean?*

"No. It's okay. You have no idea what this means to me, your being here. It gives me a chance to talk about Hayley. No one else wants to hear it, not anymore. It's been too long, and most people don't realize that it's never in the past. It's with you every day, forever." She gripped Roxanne's hand like a lifeline. "Let's keep going."

"If you're sure."

"Yes, I am." She blew and wiped one last time and took in a deep breath, sipping her tea with a slightly shaky hand.

Roxanne's guilt bloomed. This wasn't at all the way she'd thought it would be. Hayley's mother looked so fragile, so broken. She'd always been like a tower of parental love and strength. She was the mom-type who'd asked Roxanne to stay for dinner—always amazingly delicious—as if she'd somehow known that the only dinner waiting back home involved canned soup or a stale cheese sandwich. Prepared alone and eaten alone.

It struck her then that someone was missing. "Mrs. S, where is Mr. Strickland?" Immediately, she regretted asking, as her friend's mother's face fell again.

"We divorced three years after Hayley died. It was just too hard for us. He remarried and had two more children." Her face hardened. "How could he do that? It's as if Hayley never existed."

"I'm so sorry."

She sighed. "When a child dies, it's too much for anyone. No one wants to think it could happen to them, so they move on almost with relief. And as for our marriage...every time we looked at each other, we saw the person who was supposed to have prevented it." She sat up straighter and looked determined. "I'm glad we're talking about it, though."

Roxanne launched in. "I might as well say it. I feel guilty, responsible, somehow. I was her best friend. I was supposed to know what was going on with her, but I didn't. No one else can understand what it's like to love someone so much and have that person do...what she did. And to know I was there—every day, hearing all her dreams, and fears, and hopes."

They both sat quietly for a moment. "So, anyway, stop me if I say something that makes you feel uncomfortable." Roxanne paused, unsure how to proceed delicately. So, she didn't even try. "I just wondered what the letter was about."

"You know the worst thing? It's trying so hard to remember everything, and as the years go on, the questioning, the doubts. Was she really as happy as I remember? Did that smile really flash as often as I see in my mind's eye? She was our only child, so maybe we focused too much on her, made too much out of every little thing. Do you remember her smile?" She stared intensely at Roxanne as if trying to read her daughter's friend's memories, seeking confirmation of her own. "The thing that eats away at me is that I can't understand why she would kill herself." Her eyes darkened. "No one gave me adequate answers."

"What about the autopsy?"

"There wasn't one, although later I wished there had been. The medical examiner ruled it suicide from asphyxiation due to hanging herself. At least, that's what he concluded. We didn't push for an autopsy because there didn't seem to be any point."

Out loud, for the first time in twenty-five years, the specific words describing the horrific way Hayley had died felt like a punch to the chest. It was unthinkable. Her mind followed the pathway. First, thinking about killing herself, not as a passing teenage thought, as in, *I wish I were dead* or *what is the use of living after THIS*? Whatever 'this' was to the overly dramatic teenage mind.

No, it wasn't a passing thought. That wasn't Hayley. It wasn't something that could have been quickly tossed aside as soon as a friend called, or another day started with the distraction of classes and teachers and assignments. This was something so dire, so painful, that it had lodged in Hayley's mind like a wave that continued returning to the shore—pulsing, never-ending. And then, like a tsunami, had become overwhelmingly large, eventually so much so that she let it pull her under.

Then, getting a length of cord from somewhere, or a rope, or whatever it was, fashioning it into a noose. And in her parents' home, putting it around her neck and finding some way to anchor it. Perhaps attaching it to her bedroom door and maybe standing on her chair. The chair in which she'd sat doing her homework, preparing for her college days and life after that. Then, shoving it out from under her feet, plunging downward, feeling the rope grab her neck, close off her airway, and cause her own death.

It struck her with a terrible force that she'd never asked questions following Hayley's suicide. She didn't even know the details, other than the fact that she'd hung herself. But sitting here, in her home, she could imagine them.

Roxanne grabbed Mrs. Strickland's hand and clung to it. "I haven't thought about how she died in so long." They held hands for a moment, then let go. "If you're okay, I have a few more questions."

"I'm okay, Roxanne."

"I know this is weird, but can I see her room? I'm sure it's totally changed, but still. We spent so many hours there—"

Mrs. Strickland nodded once, stood, and led the way. The door to Hayley's old bedroom was closed. Roxanne reached out and turned the knob slowly. Then lost her breath for the umpteenth time that day.

Nothing had changed. It was Hayley's room, untouched for all those years. Her favorite posters were still hung, although slightly curled around the edges—the movie poster of "Point Break" with Patrick Swayze and Keanu Reeves, another of Leonardo DiCaprio, blond bangs swooping over intense eyes, and then, the famed poster of Julia Roberts in "Pretty Woman," who Hayley had wanted to be.

The walls still held the lavender print wallpaper, and the bed— neatly made, as though she'd been told to do it right before leaving for school that morning—with the lavender paisley spread and pillows with white eyelet cases.

ABOUT ROXANNE

She choked then. Her friend's presence was everywhere she turned, in every corner of the room. She heard an echo of girlish laughter, caught the flash of twinkling blue eyes and a hand swiftly brushing back golden curls.

And she remembered all of it in a blinding flash of music, dancing, giggling, trying on clothes, and experimenting with wild hairstyles and makeup. Hayley's mother knocking on the door and telling them to 'pipe down. There are other people in the house.' She remembered the quiet conversations with no specific beginning or end, lying on the bed, pinkie fingers entwined.

That was the moment she began to question all of it. The fun, the intimacy, the deep levels of their friendship, and then one day, just up and killing herself with a rope. It made no sense. This wasn't a story with an arc that could be understood.

"Mrs. S, is there anything else about Hayley's death? Anything odd or strange or that didn't make sense? I mean, besides the fact that she killed herself, and I don't think you, or I, really understand that. But anything else?"

"All of it is strange to me. She changed in those last two weeks. I knew my daughter. She was *happy*, Roxanne. You know that. She was full of life, with loads of plans for the future. She was warm and affectionate. She had friends, and all of them loved her. She didn't wear goth makeup and paint her nails black or do drugs. She didn't even smoke. She was a perfectly normal teenager until the last two weeks. And the only change, although unusual but not alarmingly so, was that she was quieter. Much quieter."

Mrs. Strickland's eyes grew wide. "I wish I'd done something when I saw it—saw her go quiet. And she was alone, in her room, all the time. She even stopped inviting you over. I asked her about it, but all she said was that everything was fine, she was just a bit tired. She did have a lot going on. But we figured she asked you over while we were out of town that weekend. We still don't know why she was alone on Monday when she should have been at school. Did she say anything to you about missing school?"

Wait, what? Hayley's parents were out of town that weekend? That made no sense. Hayley would have asked her over if she'd been alone in the house.

And the memories of that weekend came flooding back. Her calling Hayley that weekend and not getting an answer. Then, getting mad and tallying all the slights that had happened since the party, finally deciding that if Hayley didn't care that much about her, then she didn't, either.

But later, on Monday, regretting her uncharacteristic snit and taking soup and crackers to her best friend, who she'd decided had undoubtedly been feeling bad all weekend.

Later, through all the trauma and loss, she'd never stopped to ask for the details, never once questioned the origins of her best friend's apparent descent.

Two weeks, during which Hayley's personality changed dramatically. That's what Mrs. S. had said. It all dated back to the party and the night that she'd left Hayley behind to get a ride home with someone else. And then, she'd mysteriously failed to invite Roxanne over for a weekend alone in the house.

Roxanne's mind spun with memories and questions. "Wait. Maybe there's a way to find out more." She snapped her fingers as it came to her. "Hayley kept a journal, a diary, I'm sure of it. Where is it?"

Mrs. Strickland sighed. "That was one of the first things we thought of. We searched everywhere, but we never found it."

Roxanne went to the bedside table first, then opened all the dresser drawers, rooting through Hayley's underwear, socks, and pajamas—all there, frozen in time, waiting for the teenage girl who would never wear them again. She went to the closet and rummaged through everything, certain she could find what Mr. and Mrs. Strickland could not, her breath hitching as she pulled out familiar tops and dresses Hayley wore.

Mrs. S. waited patiently. "We looked through everything," she said quietly. But she waited until Roxanne satisfied the urge.

ABOUT ROXANNE

Depleted of ideas, she stood in the middle of the room. There was something about the journal she was forgetting. She was sure of it. Her normally razor-sharp memory hadn't fully kicked in. Since the coma, there were small gaps, tiny fractures in her ability to recall everything with photo clarity.

It was maddening, but there wasn't anything else to do here. They made their way back to the living room and stood awkwardly.

"Thanks for letting me do that, Mrs. S. I feel better just knowing I looked for myself." She turned to go, then stopped. "One more thing. You said in the letter that you'd discovered something. What did you mean?"

Mrs. Strickland's face turned pink. "I really just wanted to talk to you. You're the one person who might understand. I don't believe Hayley meant to kill herself. I never believed it, and the counselors all told me that parents of kids who commit suicide always feel this way. They call it denial. But there are things mothers know that no one else can possibly know, and it's deep in your bones and heart where your child lives forever. I know in that part of me that she did not do this awful thing, not on purpose."

And her words resonated for Roxanne. Best friends knew things too, deep in their hearts.

CHAPTER EIGHTEEN

HAYLEY, 1999

I survey the room quickly and take in the carnage of the party, noting the absence of other people. I'd heard the front door slam as Brandon left, and now, it is just Adam and me. Why do I feel my heart rate picking up? I pull myself together, shaking off the silly crush on Brandon. Thoughts of him flick away as I shore myself up.

I am powerful. I hear my coach's voice as I feel myself take on the character of...Elphaba, from Wicked: The Life and Times of the Wicked Witch of the West. No, I am Glinda, in her later best version of herself, a strong force for good. Roxanne is Elphaba and I am Glinda.

My lips twist in a smile as I draw on my friendship with Roxanne and on two of my favorite characters, to whom I'd been introduced by Mr. Chase. 'This book is going to be a play or a movie, and it's going to be a huge hit,' he'd said. He did that—handed me books to read and study the characters, even ones that weren't in theater form. This one is by far my favorite.

I stand and walk casually toward the door.

"Where do you think you're going?" says Adam, crossing the room and arriving at the door before me. "Now that that jerk is gone, maybe you and I can...talk. What do you say?"

It sounds so innocent.... But the warning signals are going off full tilt as I surreptitiously look for an escape route while not showing fear. For some reason, I want to look normal, as if I don't see his aggressiveness, and as if that will ward it off.

He moves toward me, and I stay planted. I will not back up. He will have to invade my space, and to my shock, he does.

Driving back to Dallas, Roxanne thought about Hayley. Standing in her room, frozen in time, her presence had surrounded them. It was almost as if she were there. But it was a delusion of some kind, an artifact of the stirring of things best left unattended, like her mother's death. And her father. *Unfinished business.*

And poor Mrs. Strickland, suspended in 1999, unable to move on from her daughter's suicide. She felt a pang of guilt at having stirred so much both for herself and for Mrs. S.

The worst part was that she hadn't gotten any closure, only more questions.

Her cell rang, and without looking at it, she pushed the button on the wheel. "Hello."

"Roxanne, where are you? Why aren't you answering?" Henry sounded almost breathless. "What the hell."

She heard Rose in the background. "Mommy! Let me talk to Mommy."

"Rose, wait a minute. I need to talk to Mom first," Henry said gently but firmly. As usual, he presented the calm parent to her not-so-much parental portrait.

ABOUT ROXANNE

"Let me talk to her, Henry. I'm on my way to pick them up," she said, ice lacing her tone.

He paused. "No, you're not. Not until you get treatment."

What? "You have no right telling me to get treatment! If I do, it has nothing to do with seeing my daughters. I am on my way home, and I am going to pick them up!" The dragon was awake again, its fiery breath aimed at her so-called husband.

"No, you're not. Rose, Mommy has to go now. You can talk to her later."

"Henry! Put my daughter on the phone. You have no right to—"

But he was gone. He'd never once hung up on her before. She clenched her teeth and tried to ignore the siren call. She pressed her foot to the gas, pushing the speed limit as much as she dared.

An agonizing hour later, she pulled up. At the door, she tried her key. It didn't work. She tried again and again, a sickening feeling slowly descending. She banged on the door. "Henry! Open this door! How dare you change the locks? I will have the police here in two minutes if you don't open this door!" Rage flooded her system, but right behind that stalked fear and sadness. *Her husband locking her out of their home. Her husband, always so caretaking, not only of the girls, but of her, now turning away.* She felt it in her bones. He was leaving her. Her ears buzzed, and she fought the lightheadedness.

She didn't hear the vehicle pull up, barely registered the person moving toward her. "Roxanne Fairchild?"

"Yes, that's me," she mumbled as she turned to the constable, who handed her a thick envelope. Instinctively, she took it, instantly regretting doing so.

"Thanks. You've been served," he said as he held up a phone and took her photo. "You have 30 days to answer this summons. If you do not answer within that timeframe, a default judgment may be rendered against you."

"I know that! I'm an attorney," she said, still in shock.

"Great. You take care now," he said as he walked away.

She tore open the envelope and scanned the papers rapidly. *Petition for divorce...petition for child custody...*Her heart turned to stone as she read about the day she'd passed out while her daughter Rose cut herself and how that meant her children were not safe with her.

It wasn't her fault. Okay, maybe she should have been more attentive. But she'd been working on a brief, sipping her favorite beverage on a Saturday morning—but even as she tried to let herself off the hook for having vodka-infused orange juice, she knew it had been wrong.

She heard Rose's screams replaying in her head and Henry telling her he was taking her to the hospital. She'd passed out again, and later, woke to Henry telling her Rose was all right. It had been a small cut but required stitches. And Annie, pinning her with a cold stare.

Dear God, what had happened to her life? How could this be? How could Henry use that one little incident against her in this way? Her colleagues would read this petition! It was public record now, a permanent, damning indictment of her as a mother.

She threw the papers in the open window of her vehicle and stalked to the front door again, but before she could knock, her cell rang. "What the hell, Henry? Let me in! This is still my home, and I—"

"That is for the court to decide," he said coldly. "The girls are here, Roxanne. If you continue making a scene, you will upset them more than they already are. You need to leave now and respond through your attorney. If you don't, I will follow through on the protective order I had drawn up but would rather not use. Please, *get help*."

Before she could respond, he'd hung up. Again.

CHAPTER NINETEEN

"I honestly don't know why you keep showing up," she said to Dr. Derek as she opened the door, waving him into her tiny motel room. The vibrating inside had climbed to a crescendo and fallen already, leaving behind a trace of itself. She wanted a drink so badly it jumped in every cell of her body.

"I don't know either, except maybe because I see myself in you. Before we get into it, there's one thing I need you to promise. There's a meeting in about twenty minutes, not far from here. Promise me you will go with me."

"A meeting. Now you're negotiating with me?"

"I'm not negotiating. I'm telling you what I'm willing to do and not do. Either you agree to go to the meeting, or you don't."

He didn't say the rest, but she knew what he meant. It was only one meeting, after all, so she agreed to go. "First, though, I want to tell you what happened. I went to see Hayley's mom in East Texas." She described their encounter while he listened closely.

"And how do you feel now?" he managed to ask without sounding like a shrink.

"The same, only I've pulled a thread. It still doesn't feel right somehow, like there's more. A lot more."

He nodded. "What are you thinking?"

Now that was a question people rarely asked. Especially Henry, who seemed terrified of hearing the answer to what she might be thinking. Or feeling. Or planning to do. Before the accident, she'd begun to notice an odd half-turning-away stance he adopted with her, especially at those times when the words boiled inside.

Once, she'd come home after only a couple of drinks, and as soon as she got in the door, Henry turned and walked away. She'd trailed after him and found enough of her voice to begin. *Henry, I think we should talk.* But he'd begged off with a story of exhaustion, and they'd gone to bed again, turned away from each other, their unspoken words so thick she could hardly draw air. After his breathing turned even, she'd slipped out of bed, retrieved one of her stashed bottles, and stayed up for hours, quietly sipping and slipping further away.

"I realize most people think their family member couldn't possibly have done it, couldn't have killed themselves. But the truth is, they do, and it leaves more questions than answers. But when Mrs. S—Hayley's mom—told me she didn't believe her daughter had killed herself, it rang true for me as well. Yes, something changed in those last few weeks of her life. But there's no way I can see her killing herself. Or if she did, it was because of something incomprehensible, something no one else knew about."

"That's your gut talking, right? You feel something deep down about Hayley. It's in there, and it's been in there for years."

"Yes! I swear it's one of the reasons I…" but she wasn't ready to go there. "I've felt it all along, that something wasn't right, something stuck in my brain, buried under years of…but it's about her, about what happened in those last weeks. Maybe about me, too. I just need something to jog it loose. I don't think I'm done with this."

She raked her fingers through her hair. "Maybe I'm wrong, and Mrs. S is stuck in denial or something. And I could be too. But I have to know. If she didn't kill herself, then what really happened? If she did, then why?"

"Sometimes, you can never know why. There's what happened, there's what people said or decided happened, and there's what you conclude about what happened. But *why* is the question that will eat up your guts and make you drink if you can't let it go."

"Maybe so, but I can't stop. And I've got bigger problems. Henry served me with divorce and custody papers. I can't believe it. I think he's cheating on me, but who cares? This is a no-fault divorce state, and that means no recourse for adultery." She looked at Derek intensely. "I want..." but she was too embarrassed to finish the statement. And she didn't have to. He'd been there.

He stood. "Let's go."

"Wait! I'm not ready..."

"You will never be ready. Let's go." And he pulled her to her feet, which placed her close to him and that stirred something. He took the moment to look deeply into her eyes before looking away, and she wished she could read what it meant. Now, however, wasn't the time.

The next hour passed so slowly it was like waiting for concrete to harden. Her entire body vibrated as she strained to remain seated among the other people in the too-small, too-close room. The urge to bolt was so powerful that she dug into her left hand with the nails of her right as hard as she could without making herself bleed.

The biggest shock was recognizing someone. One of the most well-known judges glanced at her as she entered. Her mouth fell open, and Derek leaned in and whispered something about anonymity and confidentiality. Now that she thought about it, she hadn't seen that judge in the bars around the courthouse in months.

They kicked off the meeting with the Serenity Prayer. Then, people told their stories. Wild, crazy stories of people without any semblance of control, acting out their drunken fantasies, destroying their lives and the lives of everyone around them. Roxanne sat still, but inside she quivered with indignation. How the hell did Dr. Derek think she had anything in common with these people? Except maybe the judge.

And where was the part about solutions? No one, not a single person, talked about how they'd fixed their lives, repaired a marriage, or gotten back their job. There were no answers here. Only terrible stories that wrenched her. *Good lord, how could you go to these meetings and not want a drink afterward more than ever?*

She stayed for the entire meeting, but she'd never do that again, not ever.

As they drove away, he cut his eyes to her. "And what you're telling yourself right now is...this is bullshit; I don't know what I'm doing here, these people are losers, and I'm better than all of them." He smiled while she steamed. "Oh, don't worry. That story will still be there, in your head, at your next meeting. And the one after that."

"There won't be another meeting."

"Right."

"No, I'm serious. I can keep myself sober if that's what I choose to do. I don't need a bunch of drunks to tell my sob story to while they sit there bleeding with lives that don't work. Who are they to judge me? Who are you to judge me?" She couldn't stop herself. It was what she did with anyone who dared attempt to pierce the wall of self-sufficiency in which she wrapped herself.

He said nothing further as he drove. A few minutes later, as she opened the door to climb out, he said, "Roxanne. Just one thing. I'm here for you as long as you're working your sobriety program. But don't think I'm going to be here if you start drinking again. I won't." He drove away.

She knew he meant it. And the inevitable question rose up, the one that had been there all along. *Why hadn't Henry ever said that?*

But only a couple of days later, she had no choice about getting help. After some back and forth wrangling with Henry's attorney, she called and made an appointment. It was the only way she had a prayer of seeing her girls anytime soon.

CHAPTER TWENTY

She walked into the waiting room and was greeted by the receptionist, who handed her a form on a clipboard. She quickly filled in her name, cell phone number, and nothing more. She signed at the bottom and gave it back to the receptionist, who pointed out that it was incomplete.

"I'm not writing anything else down about myself until I meet the shrink and decide if this is a good fit." She planted the pen on top of the form, turned, and walked away. Instead of sitting in one of the plush waiting room chairs, she stood scrolling through her phone, tapping her foot.

The last thing she needed was an appearance in family court, with a public spilling of her and Henry's issues. She could fight the custody petition that way, or she could give in to Henry's treatment demands in exchange for visitation. While this was an unnecessary waste of her time, it was a compromise she could live with.

A few minutes later, she looked up impatiently, but the assistant was nowhere to be seen. Five minutes waiting. *I'm on time, and the shrink is late. This is ridiculous.* She turned off her phone, threw it in her bag, and turned to leave.

The door to the inner office opened, and a woman smiled. "Roxanne Fairchild? Please come in. I'm Dr. Jill Rhodes."

Roxanne brushed past the outstretched hand and made her way down a short hallway to the open office door at the end. She did a quick survey of the beautifully appointed room and chose the most comfortable chair, plopping down. She crossed her legs and arms and stared pointedly at the wall.

Dr. Rhodes closed the door and made her way to a seat behind a desk. She was mid-30s with stylish dark hair and wore a dark gray silk jacket over a black skirt, a single strand of pearls, and high-heeled pumps. She had tiny lines next to her grey eyes and smiling seemed to come naturally to her.

The woman was probably far happier personally than most people. Surely a really good psychologist took care of her own inner workings. Then again, she'd once represented a couple of psychologists and found them to be a couple of the biggest sickos she'd ever met.

Dr. Rhodes opened a file, picked up a pen, and slowly made a note, then looked up at her new patient. "I see you took the power seat. Is that something you always do?" she asked, but her lips twitched slightly with humor.

"It looked like the most comfortable," Roxanne shot back.

Dr. Rhodes nodded slowly and made another careful note in the file, smile gone.

Roxanne's annoyance level advanced another notch. "So, Dr. Rhodes, are you going to write down everything I say and do? How is that supposed to help?"

Dr. Rhodes studied the file and spoke without looking at Roxanne. "You can call me Jill or Dr. Jill. You're here because of an alcohol abuse issue." She didn't pull any punches. "Let's see. You had an accident while driving under the influence. You were in a coma for a few days. You were suspended by your law firm, but you went there anyway and caused a scene. At this point, your job is at risk unless you get treatment."

She looked up. "Right now, the deck is stacked against you, or maybe it's for you, and the only way you can get visitation with your daughters is to be here. Unless you want to fight the custody petition in court. I'm guessing you don't want that court appearance if you can avoid it, given the risk to your professional standing."

"You left out the part about my husband," Roxanne spat.

"Right. Your husband, Henry, petitioned for sole custody of your two daughters pending the divorce action he also filed. He says you showed up in a violent rage at a friend's home, disappeared for a day, and showed up, again in a rage, at your own home, where your two daughters are living with him."

"He was carrying on an affair with my former best friend!"

Dr. Rhodes continued as if Roxanne hadn't spoken. "Luckily, you survived your accident, you weren't charged with manslaughter because it turns out the other driver was at fault, and you are sitting here today, in one piece." She gazed at Roxanne steadily. "We know why you were sent here, but tell me, what do you want to do here? Besides act out your anger."

"I don't know." Roxanne squirmed, pushing down the dragon. "Actually, I do have something." She sat forward suddenly. "I'm working on a case, well, it's a personal case, about an old friend of mine who... died."

Dr. Jill looked intrigued. "I'm listening."

It was excruciating opening up to a total stranger. "Look, Dr. Jill, I'm not used to this kind of thing. I've never talked about my... problems... but I'm at a dead-end, and I could use some help with this case."

"Are you asking me to consult with you on a legal case? Because if I do that, I can't sign off on the paperwork that informs Henry's attorney you're in counseling working on your issues. And that means you won't see your daughters anytime soon."

"Well, that's just great. I can't believe this." She fumed for a moment. "How about this. If you'll help me with my case, I'll spill my guts about my personal life."

Dr. Rhodes sat back and laid down her pen. "Fair enough. It's a start. Tell me about your friend."

She did, the whole story—high school friendship, Hayley's sudden change from happy extrovert to withdrawn, then her suicide.

Then the strangest thing happened. As she got to the part about Hayley on a stretcher, face distorted, skin so cold to the touch, she burst into tears. The tide swept over her, a deep-down agony that began in her heart and flowed up her throat and out of her eyes and nose. It was unstoppable, and she was helpless in its grip.

Feeling terribly out of control, with nowhere to go, she stood and wobbled, longing to run but frozen in place. "It. Hurts. So. Bad," she gasped, bending over, snot and tears forming a river, which it turned out wasn't just about Hayley, but also about Henry, and Jessica, and her girls. And her mother and grandmother. And maybe her father.

Dr. Jill stood and moved quietly to her side, stuffing tissues in her hand. She didn't touch Roxanne. She just stood there, breathing softly, and somehow the panic subsided. The river flow gradually slowed to a quiet drip. Roxanne sat down again and recovered her words. "I've never done that before. I don't think I cried at the funeral or later. I didn't even cry when I went to see Mrs. S. the other day."

"Mrs. S?"

"Hayley's mom." She drew a deep breath and felt something unfamiliar. What was the word for it? *Relief.* "God, I feel so strange."

"Maybe a bit lighter?"

"Yes, lighter, that's one word for it." Terrified to look, she braced herself anyway and looked up. Maybe peered up was more accurate, from under her lids, to register the expression on Dr. Jill's face.

Another shock—no evidence of pity, or disgust, or surprise. "I'm not the first person to literally vomit up their emotions in this office, am I?"

"Not by a long shot. But you're probably not used to it. To actually expressing what you feel in this way. It's raw, and it's real."

"But I can't feel this much every day. I'll drown in it."

"You won't. The pipes get flushed now and then if you let it happen. If you don't, you fill with the poison of the unexpressed, and that puts you at risk of drinking and possibly losing your daughters. Not to mention dying young."

Roxanne sat quietly, stunned. Not one part of her wanted a drink, yet this was arguably one of the most painful moments she'd experienced in her life, even though nothing was actually happening. It was pain brought on by remembering the past, but it felt like a storm that had blown through, leaving her refreshed somehow. And maybe brought on by being somewhere...safe.

That was it. This beautiful, professional office somehow felt safe. "I think what I'm feeling now is what I've been drinking away for the past twenty or so years. It feels ridiculous saying that, but it's what I'm imagining—that martini glass that I thought was full of gin was really medicine for this..." She shook her head.

"You started drinking in high school or shortly thereafter, right? And you've never stopped, never questioned the origins. Roxanne, I think maybe your friend's death, and your drinking problem, are connected."

Roxanne's mind flashed to the party with Hayley. Her first drink. All the other drinks, the pushing and striving in school, punctuated by the parties and the alcohol. Getting up the next day and starting the cycle again, over, and over.

She told Dr. Jill about her trip to see Hayley's mom, the strange feeling that there was more to her friend's suicide. "I feel like there's more there, but at the same time, I know what everyone says about suicide. But tell me what you think so far."

"Before I do, what do you believe?"

"I don't believe Hayley wanted to die. That's the bottom line. We were making plans for college right before that. Who talks about college applications and roommates and majors and then does that? My gut says it wasn't her desire to die, even though I know the evidence that day was overwhelming."

"I'm probably not telling you anything new, but you should know that the family and close friends of a suicidal person often are not aware of the inner pain that led to their loved one taking her life. What you and Hayley's mom are feeling is not unusual."

"But why? What makes someone who was so happy, who had so much...*life* in her life, do that?"

"It's not always easy to know. What was happening in Hayley's life at that time? Any new influencers or stressors—a boyfriend, perhaps? Anyone she may have had close contact with leading up to her death?"

"She didn't have a boyfriend, but everyone wanted to date her. She was so beautiful, and so nice, to everyone. She was the most popular girl in school if you measure popularity by how much everyone wanted to be around her. She was in theater, starred in every school play going back to grade school. She was good, too. She could act and sing, and she loved it."

Roxanne thought about the party, about the guy who'd captured Hayley's attention at the end of the evening and whose arms wrapped around her so tightly. "There was a guy at a party who sort of glommed onto her at the end. In fact, I left without her—and we never did that—because she was making out with him and didn't want to leave. She never mentioned him after that, though."

"People keep secrets, even from their closest friends and family. Could she have continued to see the guy but not told you? Maybe she wasn't sure it would last. Maybe she was embarrassed by him while still being attracted to him."

"I don't think so. He was gorgeous, all Mel Gibson. I suppose she might have kept him secret for a while, but that would not have been like her."

"Maybe he had another girlfriend, and she found out later and felt humiliated."

"Maybe. But it was only one night at a party. She'd have told me about him, I'm sure of it if there was anything that affected her."

"Unless something bad happened after you left, something traumatic. People become very secretive following a trauma."

Roxanne's gut clenched. *Had she left her friend in danger?* What if that guy did something, something Hayley didn't want him to do? Date rape was common, and the aftereffects could be devastating, especially for a teenage girl. *Dear God, had she let this happen to Hayley?*

"Roxanne. I see the wheels turning but try to get your mind around this. It is not your fault. If something happened to Hayley, you are not to blame. You were her friend, not her caretaker. Even parents can't be all-seeing, all-knowing, or vigilant enough to protect their children."

"I know that logically, but—"

"You're not going to be able to continue looking into this if you let yourself drown in inappropriate guilt."

"Inappropriate guilt?"

"There are plenty of things to feel remorseful about, but not being able to save another person is one that you have to set down. You aren't that powerful. No one is. Influence is minimal in life, and control is mostly a delusion," Dr. Rhodes explained.

"Wait. Everything I've ever learned, in law school and otherwise, was about taking control of your life." She didn't say it, but her profession was all about helping people take control of situations in which they'd lost it.

"Think about the Serenity Prayer. There are things you can't control in life, things you can, and you have to sort out the difference."

"I'll have to work on that." Surprisingly, she meant it, though she had no clue how to go about it. The other parts—the other things to be remorseful about—she tucked away for now. "I'm going back to East Texas to talk to a few more of our classmates. I'm not sure what I'm looking for, but maybe there's another reason she took her own life, other than…wait, what *are* the usual reasons?"

"Usually, it's depression. If left untreated, it escalates so much that the person can't see a future with anything other than unending pain. Then the idea takes root that others would be better off without them. That is usually the turning point."

No matter how she looked at it, Roxanne couldn't see any way that was Hayley. Except for the last few weeks' withdrawal, she'd always had an innate optimism, and it never seemed fake. But something had happened, something that caused her to turn away from her best friend and her family. *Wait.* There'd been another turning point.

"There's something else. She made another 180 right before she died. All of a sudden, she invited me over again, and she was her old self again. That's a good thing, right? It shows that nothing was that terribly wrong."

Dr. Jill looked serious, not hopeful, at that piece of information. "Unfortunately, it's another sign of suicide. The depression that drives it typically lifts at the moment the decision is made. The suicidal person feels relieved at the thought of ending the pain. It's terrible for friends and family because it appears to them as evidence that the person was happy after all."

Roxanne's face fell.

"There is one more possibility, but it's extremely rare," Dr. Jill continued. "There's a woman whose work I stumbled across a few years ago. She's a professor of medical ethics and a philosopher, and she focuses a lot of her work on assisted dying. One of the concepts she talks about is *manipulated suicide*. She relates it to family members or medical professionals inadvertently pushing a patient toward assisted dying, and since these people are usually suffering intensely, they have little resistance.

"I thought about it, though, in a much more sinister way. What if someone with undue influence over someone vulnerable pushed that person to suicide? This is a long shot, Roxanne. I've never heard of a real case, although you could argue that cyber-bullying fits the bill. But that is group behavior, teenagers being cruel but not really intending to push the person into suicide. So, I'm not sure."

Could Hayley have been that vulnerable? Did someone plant the idea of suicide, bully her in some way, taunt her, and push her over the edge? It didn't seem likely. Hayley wasn't a pushover. And she would have known if someone had bullied her best friend.

Before she left, Dr. Jill gave her one last piece of advice. "I know you believe you've had your last drink, Roxanne, but the relapse rate for alcoholism is high. You're very likely to start drinking again, and the trigger is usually emotional stress in one of the key areas of your life. This case is very intense for you. We haven't even started on your family of origin issues, and I suspect there are many. Plus, you're separated and potentially facing a divorce. *That's far too many stressors*. Be careful. If you feel wobbly with your sobriety, focus on what you really, really want, something you can't have if you take that drink."

Her girls. Roxanne wanted to see her girls. She wouldn't let anything get in the way of that, not ever again.

CHAPTER TWENTY-ONE

Roxanne slid into the booth and greeted the guy waiting there. It was a throwback diner—red vinyl seats, chrome details, soda fountain bar, a real jukebox playing Elvis, and a menu straight out of the 1950s. She was back in East Texas, and after ordering a burger and fries, she took a good look at her companion.

Adam had grown up and filled out. Gone were the pimples, greasy hair, and skinny arms, replaced by evidence of daily workouts. He smiled easily, and his eyes, always a great feature, were even nicer now, fringed in black lashes and catching glints of the sunlight streaming through the windows. The sprinkling of gray somehow didn't overcome his youthful looks.

"Thanks for meeting me," she said. "I know it was short notice, and I see you're in the middle of your workday, at least, I think so." He wore nice jeans, a white shirt, and blazer, but she'd seen the telltale bulge of a sidearm as he sat down.

"No problem. Yeah, it's a workday, but I'm not on anything urgent right now, and besides, it's lunchtime. You know cops—we're all about the food." He smiled, and she relaxed.

"Not exactly a cop, though, are you? I understand you're a detective, homicide, in fact."

"Yep. And you work in criminal law, right? On the other side." His eyes hardened just a bit.

Inwardly, she rolled her eyes. It was always a challenge establishing rapport with cops, knowing her job made their job harder, that in their eyes, she was the enemy. "That's right, although I'm not here professionally. But you know that. Thanks for answering my Facebook message."

"Of course. I was surprised to see the page you set up about Hayley. It's been so long, and now, well, tell me what this is about."

She wasn't sure how much to say. "I recently had a...disturbing personal experience, let's just say. And it made me stop and think back, and I realized that I never felt like things were, I know this sounds lame, but the best word I can think of is *complete*. Things never felt right about Hayley, her suicide. So, I'm taking a look back so I can, " she laughed nervously, "move forward. I know, lame again."

"I think I know what you mean. I didn't know Hayley well, but the little time I spent with her was...," he shifted a bit uncomfortably, "well, it was clear to me she was one of those rare kids who had it all. The most popular girl in school, everyone wanted a shot at being her friend, and all the guys wanted to date her."

"Yes, that was Hayley," she agreed. "Listen, there was a party just a couple of weeks before. And, you were there, weren't you? I know it's been a long time, but what do you remember from that night? I'm trying to get an idea of things that may have happened during the party and after I left."

"Why?" He shifted, looked closed off.

"It seemed like she changed after that night, and I've been thinking about it a lot lately. I can't let go of the idea that something happened that affected her deeply, and may even have triggered her, may have led to her suicide. I know that sounds dramatic," she finished. She tried to underplay the level of urgency she was feeling, hoping he'd want to help and not trigger more defensiveness. "So, what do you remember?"

"I remember her with this guy—"

"Mel Gibson lookalike?"

"If you say so." He scoffed. "They were on the sofa together, making out."

Was that a spark of jealousy? After more than two decades? She kept her face neutral. "Right, and I tried to get her to leave, but he kept pulling her back down onto his lap. He was very possessive of her. Which was ridiculous since they weren't exactly a couple. In fact, I don't think we knew the guy before that night. He was a year ahead of us in school. Anyway, do you know what happened after that?"

"I guess they made out some more. I don't know. I wasn't really paying attention." Though as he said it, Roxanne's attorney radar registered a twinge of mistruth. It didn't feel like a bald-faced lie, but it wasn't an absolute truth either. She remained silent, letting him continue. "But what I remember was right before he left. I saw him push her off of him after he tried to remove half her clothes, and she stopped him."

"Wait, *what?* He tried to take off her clothes in front of everyone?"

"Not like strip her naked, more like lifting her shirt and trying to unbutton her pants. I guess it was a prelude to getting her to go into one of the bedrooms or whatever, but she wouldn't let him go that far. That's when he dumped her off him. He looked pissed, chugged a beer, and left. Total jerk."

Again, that jealous flash. She made a mental note for now but snapped off the next question with urgency. Because it sounded like Hayley hadn't been safely delivered home, that she'd been truly abandoned. "What happened after that? How did Hayley get home?" *Some friend I was, leaving Hayley like that, trusting some random guy to take care of her.* Rocks formed in the pit of her stomach again.

He said nothing.

Her mind filled with possibilities. "I wonder if something more happened between them. Maybe he waited for her after he left. Maybe he came back later, or called her later, or... Wait—*how did she get home?*"

"I'm not sure. Maybe she walked." He looked down, toyed with a fry.

That information sat in her stomach like a rock. All these years, she'd thought Hayley had gotten a ride with someone, but now, it turned out she'd walked. Alone, late at night. Sure, their neighborhood hadn't exactly been a hotbed of crime, but still. She'd been in the legal profession long enough to know how frequently bad things happened to women, even in small-town East Texas.

Her mind whirled. Hayley had never once talked about the party—about the guy she was making out with on the sofa when her best friend walked out the door. And it had definitely been girl-talk-worthy, juicy. *We were making out, and he wanted more than I did, so I stopped him, and he didn't like it. I left and walked home...*

That's where the story lost its thread. First of all, Hayley would have talked about that the next morning. In fact, the Hayley she knew would have made lots of noise coming in that night, deliberately waking up Roxanne, so they could have stayed up for hours analyzing every detail of what had happened at the party.

What did it mean that he'd been all over me, and suddenly not? Why did he book out of there and leave me to walk home? Why did guys do things like that? Did he already have a girlfriend? Was he gay? Ultimately, they'd have laughed it off while making up all kinds of nicknames for 'Mel.'

Unless. Unless an angry, aggressive guy came back that night and waited outside for Hayley. And what happened after that was something so horrible, so traumatic, she couldn't share it with her best friend. Something that changed her life trajectory in a terrible, dark direction. Something that made her lose her natural optimism, sink into depression, and stop seeing her own brilliant future.

"Who is this guy? What is his name?" For once, the dragon had a target for its fiery breath as Roxanne's purpose hardened.

"Brandon Statler. Look, I know the guy. He lives around here, does construction work, and gets into trouble now and then. Drunk-and-disorderly, fighting, stuff like that," he explained. "I can't say I really know him, but the couple of run-ins we've had tells me he's still a jerk. I can look up his record, see if there's anything more serious."

"And how long will that take?" Agitation stirred in her belly, and she needed answers.

"Not long, maybe an hour or so. I'll call you."

"That sounds like too long," she said.

"I know you want answers but don't go find this guy on your own, Roxanne. Let me do my job, and we'll go from there." Again, that hard look in his eyes.

She nodded but fumed inside. It wouldn't pay to get on Adam's bad side, and he might be helpful, but that didn't mean she couldn't continue with her own research. Then she thought of something. "Wait. Are you saying you're opening an official investigation?"

His face twisted in disbelief. "Investigation into what?"

"Look, I know it sounds a bit crazy, but I'm beginning to believe more and more that something happened to Hayley that night, and it was so bad, it set her on a path to suicide. Think about the kinds of things that would be traumatic enough to do that—rape, for instance."

He studied her, revealing nothing. Then, he let out a long breath. "I can see you're going to look into this further, but as for an official investigation, there's not enough to go on at this point." He held up his hands as she opened her mouth to argue. "Hold on. I didn't say I wouldn't help. I'm actually supposed to be taking PTO time starting tomorrow. I was planning on a little fishing excursion with some buddies. But—"

She hadn't expected him to cancel his trip. She wasn't trying to draw that much attention. Just a little help looking into Statler's background was all she needed. "No, it's fine. You've helped enough already. I can take it from here," she said, but his skeptical look confirmed he hadn't bought it.

"I think I'll put off that fishing trip and help you out."

She protested, but he was firm. Reluctantly, she agreed to keep him in the loop. He paid their bill and left while she punched numbers on her cell.

But her eyes slid to his retreating back, boots clicking with precision, his confidence radiating with each step. Adam had grown into a compelling man. *But who was he, really?* He was mostly unknown in high school, and despite how he'd grown up, he was still an unknown.

She didn't need to wait for his call. She pulled up her Facebook page, scrolled, and saw another name, another clue. After a bit more research, she made a call and set up a meeting. *Man, it was easy to find people now.*

It never occurred to her that all the messages posted online back and forth had dropped breadcrumbs that someone else could easily follow.

He watched her leave the diner, pushing her dark hair out of her eyes, long legs striding purposefully. She'd changed a lot over the years. All grown up, mature, and sparkling with confidence, which she'd undoubtedly have achieved. Girls with that rare combination of presence, looks, and charisma had everything handed to them.

How many times had he imagined how Hayley would look today? Never once had he thought about Roxanne, but wow, she'd turned out gorgeous. Her striking features, cobalt blue eyes, riotous dark curls, combined with that sharp intelligence, made her formidable. She crackled with purpose, all of it focused on her now-departed high school best friend, Hayley.

She was asking a lot of questions. Far too curious about things that should be left alone. If she kept poking around, she might uncover notable things, and he couldn't have that. There was too much to lose, too much at stake. The challenge she presented stirred him unexpectedly. Perhaps he could remove the threat while also gaining a little pleasure.

He waited until she'd driven a block away, then followed carefully, periodically glancing at his cell. Suddenly, he peeled off in a new direction. No need to follow her now. He knew where she was going.

As he drove, he indulged in remembrances of Hayley, something he'd done innumerable times over the years.

She was delightfully young and naïve.

No, he corrected himself. She was Lolita, seducing him, fooling everyone else. Their lives intersected in an intense flash of passion and uncontrollable desire.

As he remembered her, time slowed down, dragging out the pleasure of going down memory lane. Then there was the flash-bang at the end. He re-lived it for the thousandth time, relishing it as always.

He turned then to thoughts of, and plans for, the delightful creature waiting for him. *Daisy*. She was no Hayley, but then, none of the others had matched his first.

CHAPTER TWENTY-TWO

Roxanne pulled up at her old high school. The original building had been razed, replaced by a much larger, modern school. In keeping with the trend of lavishing community bond capital on the fixtures of education for today's little darlings, the architecture was impressive. Limestone facades alternated with massive windows and cantilevered rooflines. Beautiful landscaping threaded the parking lots and surrounded the main building. Sprinklers spread a fine mist over the flowering azaleas and various other well-manicured plantings.

When she and Hayley had attended this school, the parking lot was one massive, concrete jungle. The landscaping had consisted of scraggly grass along the outer curbs and the entry to the main building. Then there were the classrooms with rickety chair/desk combinations, blackboards, and overhead projector systems.

She made her way to a reception area, backed by a busy office filled with administrative staff, and was greeted by a woman with a worn expression. "May I help you?" though her tone said she really didn't want to.

After Roxanne made her request, she was told to sit in a waiting area that resembled that of a downtown Dallas office building, with its cushy chairs, end tables, lush plants, and artwork. Instead of sitting, she walked around, checking things out, inwardly wondering how all of the expense that went into this place correlated with the achievement of good education, not to mention preparation for a higher education.

A pleasant tone sounded, not the horrible ear-splitting shrill of the bell from years past, signaling the changeover for classes. Students surged into the hallways, with the typical jostling for social status and locker space. Loud voices seeking dominance echoed while the rest filled the lower register of streaming conversations, laughter, derision, and whatever pent-up exchanges needed to occur to blow off steam before settling down in a classroom again.

She tapped her foot impatiently and headed back to the reception area, but before she got there, a guy appeared. One she immediately recognized. He strode toward her with a huge smile. "Roxanne Grayson! What a wonderful surprise." Instead of offering a hand to shake, he reached out and hugged her, which she accepted stiffly.

"It's Roxanne Fairchild now," she said.

"Of course, you're married."

"Thanks for reaching out, Mr. Chase."

"Russell, please. My kids call me Mr. Chase, and you're no kid." His unusual phrasing and the way he gave her a quick once-over had her slightly taken aback. But it all happened so fast, and his smile was warm; she chalked it up to her slight paranoia given the current circumstances. "Let's go to my classroom. It's empty until the next period."

He guided her to a small seating area in the corner with two plush sitting chairs, not the hard plastic ones for the students. While they settled in, she took a moment to check him out.

He definitely looked older, but not enough to match the passage of so many years. He was just as firmly lean as he'd been, his eyes just as sharp, his jawline just as defined, and he sat with the confidence of a man who knew he was attractive. His hair, chestnut back then, held a tiny sprinkling of gray, which only served to give him gravitas. Twenty-plus years ago, he'd been only a few years older than his students and still had a boyish look, but he'd matured far beyond that.

"I know. I look older. Maybe it's the gray hair," he said. "You, however, look far more beautiful than you did back then. Not that you weren't pretty," he said hastily. "But you were just a kid. Whip-smart, though. Didn't you graduate as valedictorian?"

She bristled at his backhand compliment. "Look, I didn't come here to talk about my academic achievements or how I looked as an ugly-duckling teenager." She sucked in a breath and willed herself to calm down from the flare caused by childhood insecurities. "You saw my Facebook page about Hayley, and I want to ask you a few questions about what you recall." She couldn't help falling back on her courtroom tactics. *Throw the witness off guard and see what shook out.*

He drew back a bit. But he swiftly recovered and smiled sadly. "Of course. It's been a long time, and it was terribly sad. It's tragic when anyone takes their own life, but especially a young life, a promising life."

"You were her drama teacher, so you spent extra-curricular time with her, with all your students who were selected for the school plays. But Hayley was selected pretty much for the lead role in everything, right?"

His sad smile morphed into seriousness. "Yes, she was. She had that rare combination of talent and charisma. She had a bright future ahead." He shook his head. "So tragic."

Was he trying to divert her with all the talk of tragedy? Was he really that sad about Hayley after so many years? Something about his tone seemed slightly off-key. Then again, he was the drama teacher. Maybe he couldn't help himself.

Time to draw him in. "There was a two-week period before Hayley's death that I'm wondering about. It seemed to me like she changed, and I'm trying to understand what that was about."

"What is this really about?" he asked guardedly.

Was he challenging her? Was it genuine curiosity? Was he stalling for time? He was getting harder to read by the minute.

"Through a series of unfortunate personal events, I've come to realize that I never felt complete about Hayley's death, and that's what this is about, what the Facebook page is about. I'm seeking some...emotional closure." She hedged a bit with her answer; no need to explain all her motivations.

That seemed to pique his interest. "I understand. It's hard enough getting through adolescence but losing your friend that way would make it very difficult. We haven't had a suicide since then, but we have had a couple of drug overdoses, and the effects were widespread with the students."

"Right. I'm interested in anything you can remember about Hayley during those last two weeks."

"What do you remember?"

This was going in the wrong direction. He had somehow managed to flip the conversation so that he was the questioner, she the witness on the defense. The old guilt crept in, casting doubt over her motives even now.

She was telling everyone she wanted emotional closure. But why? Because if she didn't find a way out of the heaviness of remorse and self-blame, she would drink again. That meant not seeing her girls for who knew how long.

Her new shrink had said that expressing what she felt was healthy, so why not now. "I remember a best friend who was smart and full of life, who was talented, and who had hopes and dreams. I remember all of that crumbling over the last two weeks of her short life. Apparently, so much so that she killed herself. I'm wondering what you remember about her at that time. After all, you did ping me and ask to meet. I'm interested in your perspective, or you're wasting my time."

He nodded. "You're right. Sorry if I seemed defensive. It's painful to think about because I feel somewhat responsible, too. I do remember things changing with Hayley those last two weeks. She mentioned a party, and she seemed upset about it, so I pressured her to talk. She said there was this guy who had...these were her words...*messed with her.* She wouldn't say anything more, but she was upset to the point of tears. I brushed it off as teenage angst. I confess I didn't take her seriously enough. Then later, when she...well, I felt terrible."

Roxanne flashed back to the party, to the Mel Gibson lookalike, Brandon, his arms around Hayley, his possessiveness, his lack of concern about how much she'd had to drink. His insistence on giving her a ride home, leaving Roxanne with nothing more to do except go home alone. Then, how off Hayley had seemed the next morning, her withdrawal and shutdown.

But Adam had said Brandon left without Hayley. "I don't get it. Brandon left the party before Hayley."

"She told me she saw him again later while she was walking home."

He was very quick with his answer, almost too quick. But Roxanne thought she remembered Hayley saying something about getting a ride. *Was she making that up because she wanted it to be true?* The memories were fuzzy. It was so long ago. But, if Brandon had come back, if he'd given Hayley a ride, and everything cascaded downhill from there, then he may have had something to do with it. She'd told her drama teacher that Brandon messed with her, and maybe that was the source of Hayley's descent into depression.

Had Brandon raped Hayley? Had he picked her up later that night but not taken her home right away. Did they go parking and things went too far? Had he done the worst thing a guy could do to a girl, force her?

It was unthinkable that her best friend had gone through a trauma like that without telling her. It was maddening to find out now, far too many years later, that she might have been able to do something to help her. If only she'd known. If she had tried harder to get Hayley to open up. *If she'd been a real friend to Hayley.*

The siren call of ice-cold gin slithered into her consciousness. She was out of town now, on her own. She could get a room for the night in a hotel with a bar. She could do whatever she wanted. No one would know her; no one who mattered could possibly find out. She could start her sobriety over again tomorrow. *What difference could one more day possibly make?*

Mr. Chase interrupted her thoughts. "I don't know what you're trying to accomplish, but... while it's tragic about Hayley, that was long ago. No one really understands why someone takes their own life, and meanwhile, you have your own life to take care of, don't you?" He gazed at her with something like pity, or maybe it was condescension. Then, he shifted again. "I'm sorry, that sounds cold. It's just that you seem awfully concerned about something that happened over two decades ago, and that can't be undone."

She'd barely registered his last comments, still reeling from her downward spiral. "I have to go. Thanks for the insight about Hayley. I really appreciate it," she said as she stood and left abruptly. She could hardly wait for that hotel room, the downstairs bar, and oblivion.

CHAPTER TWENTY-THREE

As she drove aimlessly, avoiding her destination for now, her phone chimed. She pulled up the text at the next light.

I found out where Statler works. Meet me back at the diner, and we'll go together.

Adam. She'd forgotten about him. She didn't really want to get him any more involved with this. But he'd given her the company name... It only took a moment to find the address and phone number. A quick call, and she was on her way.

She pulled into a parking lot that spanned almost a city block, crammed with pickup trucks, most with the company logo. The business, a civil engineering firm, clearly employed a lot of people in this small town. As she made her way toward the sprawling, one-level building, the front entryway door opened, and a guy stepped out, surveyed the parking lot, and spotted her. He waved her to stay where she was, but she plowed ahead anyway.

"I told you I'd meet you in the parking lot, didn't I?" He stood in front of her with both thumbs hooked through loops on his jeans, his brow furrowed. Brandon Statler hadn't aged quite as well as Mr. Chase, but close. He still showed signs of the chiseled jawline and still sported the thick hair he'd once worn as a mullet, now updated to a classic trim. He presented the typical imagery of a construction worker, his lip bulging with tobacco, and he took this opportunity to spit. Thankfully, not on her shoes.

He was large, muscled, either from the activity of his job or from weightlifting, the kind done by guys who sought to be intimidating rather than healthy. The resulting testosterone overload presented an image that probably attracted many women but never her.

"Thanks for meeting with me, Brandon, and I'm sorry about interrupting your workday." She did her best to turn on a bit of charm with her smile, but he seemed unimpressed. "How about we sit in my car for a couple of minutes?"

He nodded unhappily and followed her, folding himself uncomfortably into her passenger seat. Once they settled in, he asked, "What is this all about? I heard you're an attorney now. Good for you. I don't have much time, so let's get on with it." Even as he said it, his eyes traveled over her body in a way that made her want to shove him out of the car.

She ignored the urge. "Of course. I'm here looking into the death of our classmate, Hayley Strickland. I'm sure you remember her, right?"

"She was the chick in all the school plays, one of those too cute, too nice, girls everyone loved." He said it with a trace of contempt, as though Hayley's popularity, looks, and personality were something to mock. *Interesting*. He seemed to bear some sort of grudge against Hayley, even after all these years.

"There's another reason you might remember her, and it was a party we all attended a couple of weeks before Hayley… died." She couldn't utter the words 'killed herself.' "You and Hayley were making out pretty heavily, and—"

ABOUT ROXANNE

"I made out with lots of girls back then, and a lot more than that," he interrupted, looking cocky and self-important. "How am I supposed to remember one party and one girl?" But it didn't quite ring true.

"The party was at Adam Porter's house. You know him, right? He's in law enforcement now, works as a detective. I understand you and he have had a couple of run-ins over the years." She waited for the light bulb to click on, and it did.

"Oh, yeah. Porter. That little twerp! Yeah, you could say we had a few run-ins. He busted my balls a couple of times when my girlfriend got drunk and called the cops. She dropped the fake charges later, of course. He was always a little narc, even in high school," he smirked.

She let that last comment go, not wanting to waste time on some old high school vendetta. "But you remember the party at his house, right? And making out with Hayley?"

"Yeah, I do, and the only reason is because when Hayley offed herself, they printed her picture in the paper. I told everyone that was the girl I'd made out with just a couple of weeks earlier. She was beautiful, but she was a tease. What a waste."

Roxanne boiled inside. She didn't want to know what he meant by 'waste,' but it was undoubtedly some misogynistic comment for which she longed to verbally remove his head. But that would defeat her purpose.

Right now, she was on a mission. The witness was officially on the stand, the hostile witness. "So, you got pissed-off at the party because she wouldn't do any more than make out. What did you do later, Brandon? Did you follow her? Did you pick her up as she was walking home? Did you drive her somewhere and make your move again? What did you *do* to her?" She bombarded him with questions, giving him no time to think. *Keep the witness off-balance.* People can't help themselves. When rattled in the courtroom, they often blurt out the very things that got them there in the first place.

"Man, are you crazy? The last I saw of that girl was on my way out the door. You got no right showing up here at my work and accusing me of things you don't know nothing about. I don't need this kind of grief." He wrenched opened the door of her vehicle.

"Wait!" she called out. "I'm sorry. Look, I really need to know what you saw that night, after you and Hayley made out, maybe before you left the party. Anything at all would be helpful." She softened her tone and waited.

He still looked offended, but he removed his hand from the door. "That nerd Porter was about to make his move on her. And I don't think she was exactly interested in him—if you know what I mean. Not like she was with me." Back to the self-important smirk which seemed permanently glued to his face.

"What are you talking about?" *Adam—about to make a move on Hayley?* He hadn't told her anything like that. "Adam didn't try anything," she offered, testing him.

"How do you know that?" he asked, raising a brow. "You weren't anywhere around, as I recall." She couldn't refute it, so she remained silent, and he continued. "He made some snide comment as I was leaving to the effect of how Hayley had come to her senses. I told him good luck with that." His expression held some kind of twisted blend of macho pride and deflated ego. Even now, he couldn't admit he'd failed to impress Hayley.

"So, you're telling me you never saw Hayley again after you left the party?"

"That's exactly what I'm saying. I headed out to another party, a little more private. My cousin had some kick-ass weed, and we spent the rest of the night partying together. He was in town for a couple of days, which didn't happen often. He and his parents were staying at our house. You can ask him yourself," he offered.

His story had the ring of truth this time. She took his cousin's information, not intending to use it, and Brandon swung out of her car, then sauntered back to work as though he thought she might be admiring his backside.

ABOUT ROXANNE

As she drove away, she punched Adam's number and set up another meeting. She furrowed her brow as she thought through the ramifications of Statler's claims—true or false, she didn't know. So far, the two versions of Hayley after Roxanne left the party didn't quite line up.

She'd made out with Brandon, then he'd left, and she'd hooked up with Adam in some way.

Or Adam had come on to her, and she'd rebuffed him, then left.

Or, nothing had happened with Adam, and she'd left with Brandon, and he was lying to protect himself.

In any scenario, the hole in the timeline was after Hayley left the party. *Had she walked to Roxanne's house from there?* It would have taken her twenty or thirty minutes, and it was late at night. *Would she have really made that kind of walk on her own?* It was difficult to imagine her doing such a thing, even in small-town East Texas in the 1990s. They were both timid about roaming at night, especially after all the horror movies they'd watched together.

No, someone had to have picked her up, given her a ride. It was the only scenario that made sense.

Then again, perhaps the whole after-the-party theory was wrong, anyway. Maybe there was nothing about that night that connected to Hayley's death, her suicide.

Maybe the problem was with her, Roxanne, making mountains out of molehills, obsessing about her friend instead of dealing with her own life.

As she made her way across town, she wondered about her girls. *Did they miss her? Was Rose crying for her? Did Annie really ever need her?* Or was Henry—Superdad—all they really needed?

Had her slipshod parenting resulted in a loose bond with her daughters, not unlike the way she'd failed to connect with her own mother? Her chest tightened, and again, the desire for a way to dull the pain swept through her as her hands tightened on the wheel of the vehicle like a lifeline.

CHAPTER TWENTY-FOUR

HAYLEY, 1999

Adam moves close to me, and I sidestep him, heading for the door. But he sidesteps and puts himself between me and the door again. "What's the matter, Hayley?" I guess he sees my expression because suddenly, his face softens, and he steps back a bit, shoulders slumping. "I'm sorry. I shouldn't have said that. I can't believe you let that guy feel you up like that. What a jerk."

"I didn't let him do anything, and who are you to say? It's none of your business who I kiss or don't kiss." Indignation is a great defense. "Now, move out of the way." I make myself as tall and as full as I can, the way my cat makes herself bigger when frightened.

There are times you make yourself small for a scene, and there are times you make yourself large. It isn't physical. It's emotional and psychological, or so says my mentor.

"I'm not in your way," Adam says defensively. "I'm just standing here, trying to have a conversation with you. But it's always the *same. No one ever wants to talk to me, especially girls like you. You probably don't even realize this, but I sit right next to you in biology. Like I said,"* he trails off at my puzzled expression.

Now I take a closer look at this guy, Adam. He's about my height, and he's skinny. His jeans hang a bit on his hips, not in a stylish way, but like his mom bought the wrong size. His face looks slightly greasy. His hair is thick and looks a bit greasy too. It would probably be his best feature if he cut it right and washed it. That plus his eyes, which are quite beautiful, fringed by dark lashes.

I remember him from biology. He sits slumped in his seat every day, not making eye contact. It's so easy to slide my vision over and past him when I go sit down. He disappears most of the time, doesn't register. I imagine what that feels like, to be unnoticeable at school, looked past, ignored. I've wished for it at times when I'm tired and irritable and no longer want to feel their eyes on me.

One hand is perched on his hip, fingers in the front pocket of his jeans, awkwardly. He shifts from one foot to the other, and I feel sorry for him.

"Look, Adam—that's your name, right?" He nods curtly. "I'm sorry I didn't remember you right away, but I do now. I would talk to you if you talked to me, you know." I actually mean that. There's something about his eyes. Their color is an unusual shade of greenish-gray, and I enjoy looking into them.

"Sure, you would," he says sarcastically. "Why would you? You're the most popular girl in school, and I'm...not. In fact, I'm the opposite of popular. I'm nobody." He looks at his feet.

I don't know what to say to that. I'm aware of my own popularity. It isn't sought after or wanted, but I benefit from it anyway. Roxanne says I'm like the sun, and everyone wants to warm up in the light. I blow off these comments because they make me feel terribly uncomfortable. A thousand times, I've wished I could be part of the masses.

But I've never thought about what it would feel like to be someone like Adam, someone who people actively ignored, almost shunned. To be so invisible that you wonder if you are real, question if you register in the chaotic social universe of high school.

I move back to the sofa and tilt my head as I sit. He takes my signal and sits a few feet away. His face is flushed. Embarrassment? Something else? "That must feel awful," *I say.* "There must be something you like to do," *I offer, a way to get him to open up.* "What's your favorite subject at school?"

He perks up a bit. "I like history, especially U.S. history. How people traveled here from so far away, set up colonies, and eventually a new government, different from any previous one existing. I like reading about it because the stories are endless and interesting. My dad gave me a biography of Thomas Jefferson. That was so cool. Did you know that besides being the obvious, a statesman, and a lawyer, he was also an architect and spoke five languages? People talk about him being a slave owner, and that part was bad, but there was so much more than that to his life…" *and he is off and running.*

I am sitting stunned. Adam is animated, using his hands to describe the things he reads. His facial expressions lit up with intelligence, joy, and other things I don't have words for. Who knew? Who would ever know that this quiet, shy boy in my biology class is actually a smart, thoughtful person?

He goes on and on, and I'm not sure he realizes I'm still here, except he probably does because he is making eye contact, and his eyes are really nice. So is his voice—resonant somehow, with a hint of authority. I am drawn in and soon lose track of time.

"Sorry. I'm probably boring you." He's wound down and now apologetic.

"No! Not bored at all. It's interesting, the things that interest you. I admit I'm usually not paying a lot of attention in history class, although I really like Mr. Rawlings. He seems like a good teacher, really gets into it, like you!"

"Right. He is good. He's one of the reasons I love history."

We both fall silent and stare at our useless hands in our laps. I'm content and in no hurry to leave. That's before it goes horribly wrong.

Just as I'm beginning to feel truly relaxed, I see Adam slide over into my peripheral vision, invading my space. That's when our nice encounter morphs into anxious awkwardness. What is it with guys who can't read signals?

"You're a really good listener," he says as he leans in. I see the kiss coming. Maybe it's because of Brandon and the way he treated me. Maybe it's because the whole party took a dark turn, and Roxanne isn't here anymore. But in a move that shocks even me, I put both hands on his chest and shove. He lands on the floor in a tangle of elbows and knees and mouth open in surprise. I'm up and running for the door. I've had enough.

Time to go home, or rather, back to Roxanne's. I can't wait to tell her all about my evening, every juicy detail the way we always do. Neither of us can tell a story without delving into every tiny detail, sometimes to the point of ridiculousness. 'Really, Hayley, if you're going to tell me about what happened in third period today, you don't have to start with brushing your teeth this morning,' she'll tell me. 'Can we cut to the chase?'

ABOUT ROXANNE

Only neither of us really wants to cut to the chase. The deliciousness of gossip and stories is all in the ingredients, the inclusion of where and when and what we were wearing and who was there in the background, and the last thing my mom said as I walked out the door into another day of school, another day of adventure.

The last glimpse I have of him, at the house, anyway, is gangly legs sprawled after I shoved him away and him on the floor in a heap, his face flushed, eyes pinwheeling.

CHAPTER TWENTY-FIVE

PRESENT DAY

"I think you left a little something out of your story, Adam. According to Brandon Statler, you made a move on Hayley." This time, they sat in a Starbucks, another harbinger of the loss of the small-town Texas, semi-rural environment in which she'd grown up. Roxanne had passed a Wal-Mart and two strip malls on the way there.

"You went to see Statler? I told you not to do that, not without me." He pinned her with an angry stare.

"Get over yourself, Adam. You said yourself you weren't opening an official investigation, and you're supposed to be on PTO, so I went to see this Brandon Statler guy. *You're welcome.*"

Adam shifted uncomfortably. "You're right. I left out one part of it because it's embarrassing. What's true is I wanted to get to know Hayley. I didn't think she would ever give me even a glance, but after you left and Statler left, she looked so disappointed. We talked, and it was great. I think we actually connected for a few minutes. But then," he stopped there and looked at his clasped hands on the tabletop.

"You just couldn't help yourself, could you? You had to hit on her, just like Brandon did." She couldn't keep the contempt out of her voice.

"No, it wasn't like that," he protested. "But...I did go in for a kiss, I'll admit that." He shrugged as if to say, 'I was only human.' "But she moved out of the way, and somehow, I lost my balance and wound up on the floor. It was one of the most embarrassing moments of my entire humiliating high school experience."

Roxanne sat and watched Adam closely. His neck was slightly flushed, and at that moment, he somehow looked more like his awkward teenage self than the good-looking police detective she'd had breakfast with earlier.

But his eyes didn't meet hers.

"What happened after that?"

"She left in a hurry. Probably to get as far away from me as she could. I offered her a ride, but she just kept going. I'm sorry I didn't tell you before. I didn't think it mattered anyway."

Was the red skin on his neck and face embarrassment? Or residual anger? The wounds of high school experiences for the unpopular ran deep, and the scars never faded. She thought carefully for a moment about what she would say next and decided to take a risk. "Adam, can I tell you something in confidence?"

"Of course, you can." He leaned forward, eager to help now that he'd unburdened himself of his high school social faux pas. If that was what it'd truly been, and nothing more.

But someone had given Hayley a ride home that night. She was sure of it. She'd been conducting this investigation, if you could call it that, all in the hopes of finding resolution for her guilt about Hayley. But it was beginning to feel like an exercise in reinforcement of the feelings of responsibility for her friend's suicide that she'd held and suppressed for so many years. Maybe another perspective would help. And asking for it might reveal more than she was getting so far.

"As you know, I started the Facebook page and came here to talk to people so I could get some emotional closure. I wanted to know why Hayley killed herself, with so much going for her. I wanted to know what could drive someone to that. Someone I thought I knew as well as I knew myself. Someone who was fundamentally happy." She paused, letting that sink in for a moment. Then leaning forward as if they were sharing a secret, she said, "Adam, I don't think my memories of Hayley are wrong. I think the Hayley I knew was incapable of doing what it looked like she did. I'm not the only one who feels this way. Her mother feels the same way."

His face took on a look of sympathy, but she interrupted whatever he was about to say. "I know what you're thinking. Family and close friends often don't see a suicide in the making, don't see the darker side of the person they loved. I get that, but I still feel like I'm missing something in Hayley's story, something important."

"What are you saying here, Roxanne?" He leaned back in the booth. "What is your theory at this point?"

"I don't have a strong theory, but there are some possibilities. One, something happened to her the night of the party. Something so devastating she didn't know how to talk about it or who to tell. She kept it inside, and it ate away at her, plunged her into a deep depression that led her to the ultimate escape from pain."

"And the other possibility?"

This time, she leaned back. Here's where the theory got a little suspect. "Again, something happened to her, and it affected her deeply in a way that made her feel like she couldn't talk about it." She paused, slightly uncomfortable with revealing her other theory. Whether it was because she didn't trust him or her own sanity, she wasn't sure. "But then someone used it against her, pushed her psychologically into a deeper depression, maybe into killing herself."

Adam looked as skeptical as she felt, now that she'd said the words out loud. "Why do you believe something happened that pushed her toward killing herself? Setting aside *how* that might have happened."

"I believe something happened the night of the party because there was a sharp line in the sand with her behavior. Before the party, Hayley was herself in every way. After, she was a shadow of herself."

"What do you think might have happened to her that night?"

"The obvious," she said. "Teenagers, lots of alcohol, and a young girl unsupervised." That last part cost her another stab of pain because she was the reason Hayley had been left on her own to be victimized.

"You're thinking maybe she was raped," he said. "Date rape or otherwise."

"Yes. But she didn't have any visible signs of struggle, at least none that I could see the next morning. That's one reason I still have more questions than answers." But she also knew she hadn't looked closely, would never have dreamed at the time that she needed to check out her friend for evidence of an assault of some kind. "And I hate that expression, by the way. *Date rape*, as if that is a lesser form of the worst thing that can happen, or rather, be done to, a woman."

He nodded, but he seemed to be working something out. "If what you're saying is true, it could be the reason behind Hayley's descent into a suicidal state. But girls who experience rape…typically it leads to substance abuse or promiscuity, not suicide."

"What do you mean?"

"Most teenage suicides are preceded by chronic mental health issues or severe drug abuse. Sometimes, chronic family issues such as being gay with parents who cannot accept them as such."

Impressive. "And where did you gain all this psychological insight?"

"Part of it is from academy training. But I'm taking courses at night. I'd like at some point to get into criminal psychological profiling."

Psychological profiling. Her mind suddenly veered in an impossible direction.

CHAPTER TWENTY-SIX

"I have another, totally different theory. That she was murdered, and somehow it was staged to look like suicide." There, she'd said it, not even knowing where it came from, aware of how ludicrous it sounded.

"*Murdered?* But there was an autopsy, wasn't there? That would have been apparent to the medical examiner." His skeptical look returned.

"First of all, and no insult intended, Adam, but this is small-town East Texas, and we're talking over two decades ago. Was there even a medical examiner back then for this area? Her mother told me there wasn't an autopsy because there didn't seem to be a need. I didn't ask, but I figured the county coroner acted as medical examiner at the scene, took one look at the condition of her body, and checked the box for suicide. From there, it was straight to the funeral home."

"You're probably right, but you realize this is a very unlikely scenario. Even without a medical examiner, there would have been clues that she was murdered. Someone stalking her, someone threatening her, someone who had a grudge. Murder doesn't happen in a vacuum."

"But what if it did happen? So far, suicide looks less likely than ever. To your point, even if she was raped after the party," she winced, "that wouldn't necessarily lead to suicide. Depression, maybe." Pieces came together that hadn't before, and maybe only because the dots she was connecting let her off the hook a bit. "Look, I have a hard time believing that if she was raped, she'd have said nothing to me. I was her best friend. We talked about EVERYTHING."

Now he gazed at her with something like pity, and it took some of the wind out of her sails. "I think you're tilting at windmills. It's terrible what happened, that Hayley gave up on her life. But maybe the scary truth is that she suffered from depression, she covered it up for a long time, and finally, it took over, and that's when you saw her withdraw. You'd be shocked at the number of times family and friends fail to see the signs."

She thrummed the tabletop with her fingernails, her leg bouncing, saying nothing for a moment. Doubt crept in, but she quickly shoved it aside. "What about this, then? I recently talked to a mental health expert, and she mentioned something—she called it *manipulated suicide*. It's when someone intentionally pushes someone to kill themselves."

"You mean like cyber-bullying? Kids ganging up on one kid on social media, taunting, suggesting they're worthless and should just go ahead and kill themselves?" His face took on a mix of disgust and anger. "I've seen it happen, and it's the worst."

"There's that, of course, but this psychologist said it could also be even more diabolical—someone targeting a person and manipulating them over time toward, I'm not sure what, maybe ruminating about something bad, and self-blame." She trailed off, unsure if she was still talking about Hayley. Or herself. Unsure of the entire direction of this conversation.

"I suppose it's possible," Adam said.

This wasn't going anywhere. There wasn't a convincing story to tell, no strong rationale for this *investigation*, or whatever else she might call it. Even to herself, she sounded off, illogical, directionless. And she was never any of those things.

Guilt was her nemesis. It had dogged her for over two decades and didn't intend to let up. She'd be carrying this around forever. Maybe it was time to go back to Dallas, to her non-home, and work toward getting back into her real home.

"Can I ask you something personal?" Adam asked.

"Maybe," she said reluctantly.

"I see your ring. You married? How about kids?"

Her stomach clenched. But it was only fair to answer since she'd drilled him about clearly uncomfortable adolescent memories. "Yes, and two, both girls."

"How does your husband feel about you conducting this… investigation?"

"How is that relevant to anything?" She snapped but immediately cringed at the look on his face. "Sorry. I'm not used to opening up about my personal life. He doesn't know what I'm doing. We're… separated." And as he sat quietly, saying nothing, and not pressuring her, something pulled her open unexpectedly. She heard herself talking. She told him everything—the accident, the coma, the vivid scenes with loved ones while in the coma.

She told him that everyone around her saw her as an alcoholic, but she wasn't sure, and she didn't have time to sort that out at the moment.

But telling her personal story had re-ignited the desire, the *need*, to understand what had really happened to Hayley. "What about you, Adam?" She tilted her head toward his obviously empty ring finger, which nonetheless held a pale outline from what had been there before.

"I'm divorced, months ago. I just took the ring off a couple of weeks ago, but it seems to complicate my job, so I'm thinking about putting it back on. And I have a kid, a son. He's ten."

"How does not wearing a ring complicate your job?" But she already knew the answer. She could picture a woman opening the door of her home to a detective, alone in the house, and she could imagine the false sense of safety conveyed by a wedding ring. How much easier it would be for him to get his questions answered, get a woman to open up to a married man versus a single man. "Never mind, I get it."

"So, what's next?" Adam asked as they closed out the check. "Are you driving back to Dallas after this?"

"Not yet. I need some time to think things over, so I think I'll stay the night. Hopefully, by tomorrow I'll have a sense of direction, or maybe it will be time to put a bow around all of this and go home, deal with some personal issues." She left out the part about the hotel with the bar and the dry, chilled martini with her name on it.

"How about dinner?" he asked, and she actually felt a tiny surge of pleasure. But this wasn't going to turn into a dating situation or a one-night stand. As if he'd read her mind, he hurried to add, "not a date, just two high school friends catching up, nothing more. Things sound complicated for you right now, and I wouldn't want you to feel uncomfortable."

Well played, and he probably meant it. But she'd meant it when she'd said she needed time to think, so she politely declined. They said their goodbyes while promising to talk again. But she doubted it would ever happen.

He watched her drive away, feeling deep displeasure. She was relentless, as he'd surmised already. He'd managed to push off her theories and personal inquiries, but was it enough? Or would she continue to make intrusive inquiries, never letting go of the past?

So far, she hadn't found the trail to him, had no clue what had actually happened. While she'd been sitting there, spinning theories about Hayley, he'd listened closely. It was obvious—her obsessive mind, her will, and determination. Her endless curiosity. She would keep pushing. He knew it.

ABOUT ROXANNE

She was the kind of woman he detested, the kind that noticed too much, asked too many questions, and wasn't easily manipulated. She was the kind of woman who defied the basic laws of nature, who put herself on equal footing with men.

What a worthless exercise, anyway. Hayley, wonderful as she'd been, his first real paramour, was long gone. The past was as dead as the mass of decrepit cells and organs that once was a beautiful high school girl. She was buried, and so should the past. The present was for the living, for life. And now, his life was everything he'd dreamed it could be back then when he'd discovered he could persuade and enchant, and in the process, fulfill his wildest fantasies.

Since then, he'd repeated the exercise, sharpening his skills with each adventure, learning how to use the right tools, to cover up his activities, to charm and fool. He'd been more careful about the final act, though, and only indulged in that most fulfilling fantasy of all when on the road. He couldn't afford to have any suspicions fall here, in his hometown.

Here, he was a pillar of the community. He was admired and respected. He was trusted and even loved. He glanced at his left ring finger. Well, by most people, anyway.

He took a moment to examine himself in the rear-view mirror. His boyish good looks had worked exceedingly well for many years, with only a few mild touch-ups, a little Botox here and there. Soon, though, he'd be the dirty old man trying to hit on them. That wasn't acceptable, either. There was plastic surgery, and he had already begun exploring his options for maximizing a still-youthful appearance.

He pushed a button on the wheel of his vehicle, placing a call carefully as he followed Roxanne. When the person on the other end answered, he spoke, letting honey drip into his voice. "Hey. I was wondering if you might be ready for what we talked about." He listened to her idle chatter, not really paying attention but providing the appropriate responses. "Next week, then? Great. I'll catch up with you later, and we'll arrange a time." He disconnected, feeling satisfied at having already put another conquest in play. He giggled a bit to himself, thinking about how clever it was that the two should overlap.

He thought about Roxanne, frowning, knowing he had to stop her before she became a much bigger issue. *Why was she pursuing this dead girl, dead past? And why now, of all times?*

He had other things to focus on, after all. His current paramour was waiting for him, no doubt anxious for his return by now. While it had been entertaining, the time with Roxanne, it wasn't fulfilling like the time he'd soon have with *her*.

Although, he reflected, that time might be drawing to an end. While she'd been a wonder and a joy for the first day or so, she was changing. Her skin had paled, and she'd developed shadows beneath her eyes. She barely touched her food. She shook when he touched her, averting her eyes from him, and that wasn't any fun. He'd told himself it was excitement, but now he wondered.

Worst of all, she had trouble remembering her lines, her part. And without that, he wasn't sure about what he had or why he should continue.

Irritation rose now, and behind that, rage. *Why did he have to work so hard for a little affection? Why weren't they grateful for all he did for them?*

He gripped the steering wheel and let out a cry of frustration. That felt better. His breathing slowed, and his smile returned. He'd only lost control for a couple of seconds. That was okay. He was back, back in charge. And it was time for the next phase.

With Roxanne, he'd skillfully applied misdirection. Hopefully, it had worked. He'd have to put the next part in motion, though, to fully convince her.

CHAPTER TWENTY-SEVEN

Adam's cell rang as he drove away from the meeting with Roxanne. He glanced at it. "Huh." He hadn't expected that but answered anyway. He was supposed to be on PTO, after all, but when Sergeant Shaw called, he answered. After listening and responding little, he hung up and headed to the reason for the call.

PTO was off the table for now—he had a job to do. This wasn't a homicide case, but his duties went beyond that. Small town, small cadre of experienced detectives.

A few minutes later, he sat in the living room of a modest home with a devastated parent and tried to understand the story of what had happened to her daughter. Gradually, he pieced together the events of the past two days, and a chill ran down his spine.

Daisy, Angela's sixteen-year-old daughter, had gone to school three days earlier but hadn't been seen since. Her mom thought she was on a two-night school trip with her best friend and with chaperones. She'd signed the permission papers. Even helped her pack and had seen her off that morning.

The girl's dad lived in another state and wasn't in the picture.

But after the third night passed and she hadn't shown up, she'd called the school first, then her daughter's friend, and discovered there was no school trip. Daisy's friend was as baffled as she was. She'd been hard on her, grilled her, but ultimately, she'd believed her.

She'd called the police, terrified. Now, she sat with Adam, alternately crying, and blowing her nose. She was young, probably late thirties, and Daisy was her only child. She was visibly shaken, eyes too wide. A pervasive restlessness evidenced in her body perched on the edge of the worn sofa, constant hand wringing, and the fear etched in her worn features.

In response to his questions, there was little information. No, she didn't drink. She didn't do drugs. *Sure.* She didn't have a boyfriend. *Unlikely.* He'd seen her photo, and she was very pretty, with long blond hair and an electric smile.

All the avenues of information-seeking had been explored. She'd disappeared, there were no signs of foul play, and she hadn't shown back up, not yet. Now, he knew he had to deliver a blow. "I know this is hard for you, but most of the time, we find out it's a runaway situation."

That garnered the typical adamant protestations. "She would never do that," Daisy's mom cried. "We're very close, and she knows I would be worried out of my mind. No, there's no way. Something has happened to her. I just know it. You have to do something!"

He nodded carefully, not wanting to discourage her too much. But runaways did so for their own reasons and rarely thought about the heartbreak they'd left behind, often staying out of touch for months, even years.

He wrapped up with promises to look into her daughter's whereabouts and stood to leave. But when he got to the door, he halted and asked one more question. "What was the nature of the school trip?"

ABOUT ROXANNE

"It was supposedly with the other drama students, a Broadway musical in Dallas," Angela shared mournfully. "She loved—*loves* acting. It's her passion. I don't know why she would lie about that."

He thanked her and left, wondering at the naivete of the woman. *Who lets their kid go out of town with a group of students without talking directly to the adults in charge?* But he didn't want to judge her too harshly. He knew from long experience that kids can be brilliant at manipulating their parents.

Odds were good that Daisy had run off on an adventure of some kind. Maybe she had gone to Dallas after all, with a boyfriend, to see a Broadway production, spending a few forbidden nights together. Maybe she figured she'd show back up, all innocent and not understanding her mom's panic. She'd be in trouble for that, sure, but it would have been worth it.

But there was something about the drama students, Daisy's passion, that stuck in his mind.

Hadn't Roxanne mentioned that Hayley's passion was drama? That was undoubtedly why it stuck—the recent coincidental connection between this girl and the girl he'd known so long ago.

He shook it off for now. He had a teenager to find. And on the off chance it was more than an adventure, that maybe something had happened to her, he knew he didn't have much time. In the unlikely scenario of foul play, hours counted.

Since he was back on the clock and had an active investigation, maybe he'd also delve into the questions Roxanne had raised, though he didn't think it would lead anywhere. But if he found out something new, something that might help her accept and move on from the past, maybe that would earn him a dinner out. So far, single life was proving to be a mix of sleepovers, as he called them, with his kid, and the fun that temporarily brought into his life. Followed by long stretches of loneliness.

On the other side of town, Roxanne had found a local hotel, checked in, and now sat in the downstairs bar, waiting for her order.

She used her phone. "Hi, it's me," she said when he picked up.

"Hi," Henry answered.

He sounded so cold, so distant, she could hardly believe this was her husband of twelve plus years, the father of her two daughters, with whom she'd shared the most intimate and important moments of her life. "What a warm greeting," she said, instantly regretting the sarcasm.

He was silent for a beat. "Look, Roxanne, I'm not interested in fighting with you. In fact, I'm not supposed to be communicating with you at all except through our attorneys unless you're representing yourself. In that case, you can call my attorney."

She swallowed her pride, and it almost choked her. "I'm sorry. I didn't call to give you a hard time. I just wanted to ask you a couple of questions." She drew in air quickly, and he was silent. "How are the girls?" She let out the air and waited.

"They're fine. Well, actually, Rose is going through some sort of regression. She's—"

"Wetting the bed?"

"How did you know?"

"It was a logical conclusion when you said regression." So, it was true. Her youngest daughter was regressing to an earlier developmental stage because of her mother's... coma and separation from her father. She was unwilling to look deeper than the surface for the root cause.

But who knew or understood the origins of a child's suffering, often at the unwitting hands of their own parents? Henry was the most loving of parents, by far better for the girls than she, and it hurt deeply to know that. He'd been alone with it for years, struggling to know what to do when the girls got hurt, whether emotionally or physically, figuring out the next parenting steps as they moved through the stages of childhood.

ABOUT ROXANNE

As she reflected on Henry's isolation, things started to fall into place.

"I guess you needed someone to talk to about Rose... and maybe about me."

Silence. "I'm not going to talk about that."

She felt his walls go back up. *How long had he been doing that?* Holding himself together by holding himself inside. Protecting himself from her, from her biting sarcasm, from her obnoxious behavior when drinking, and her emotional distance. "Henry, I don't like this. I know you don't trust me, and I don't blame you right now. I wanted you to know I'm in counseling now. I'm working on some things and working on me. But let's talk, please."

She stopped, squirming inside. *God, this was hard.* She struggled to moderate her tone of voice, soften it. "We used to be best friends, didn't we? I'm not asking you to bare your soul, but let's talk about the girls and maybe a little about us. I want to make things right if I'm not too late. Am I? Too late?" Her stomach tightened unbearably with the unfamiliar vulnerability.

She heard him sigh. "It's not that easy. I don't know if it's too late or not, but you can't call me up and expect me to open the door just like that, just because you want to talk. I tried so hard to reach you. *You don't have any idea*. But you can't call me and throw your cards on the table like this and force me into some kind of answer." His frustration was palpable, and he had a point. "Look, I've got to go."

"Wait." She couldn't let him leave it like this. "You're right." Everything seemed like a negotiation. It was like her second skin—all she'd known for her whole life. With her mother, to appease and gain her freedom. In her job, with every court case. And, not thinking about it, just following her instincts, with Henry, for most of their marriage.

How had life become so transactional? What would it be like if it weren't that way? Once in a while, Roxanne had turned on a feel-good movie and let it run in the background while she worked on her laptop, and she'd marveled at how easily love flowed between fictional characters. But she'd scoffed in the end.

"I withdraw the question." *Oh, jeez.* That was even worse. Talking to her husband like a witness on the stand. She felt the wave of coldness cross the phone line, move into her hand, travel up her arm, and lodge itself in her heart.

"I hope you continue to get help and get your life together. We will always be co-parents to the girls, and I hope you will respect the boundaries I've put in place for now until you get better. Good-bye, Roxanne."

And he was gone.

CHAPTER TWENTY-EIGHT

Her dinner arrived, thin-crust pizza with veggies and cheese. She took a couple of bites and chewed slowly as she worked through what she'd discovered so far about Hayley. It wasn't much.

One, and Mrs. S. agreed with her assessment, it didn't seem at all like Hayley to fall into such a deep depression she'd want to end her life. That she'd never talked to anyone about whatever had so severely troubled her. Not Roxanne, her best friend and someone she undoubtedly knew she could trust. Not her own mom, who was one of the most loving people Roxanne had ever known.

Two, Hayley had been left vulnerable at the end of the party. That brought up the familiar ache. *How could she have been so careless about her best friend? How could she have walked away, leaving her there, without a second thought?* It was her innate selfishness. She'd always been wholly dialed into her own internal radio station, WIIFM, the old *what's-in-it-for-me*, for as far back as she could remember.

Her own mother had been in trouble, gradually sinking into a pit of loneliness, and pills, and ill-health, with no one to pull her out except her self-absorbed daughter, who'd blithely passed her bedroom door every day without ever once asking, 'Mom, are you okay?' Or, 'Mom, do you want to talk? About Dad...'

Dear old Dad. There was a wound she'd probably have to unwrap someday with her shrink. Her father had abandoned the two of them when she was in grade school. He'd packed a bag, hugged her goodbye with no explanation, and left. And that was the last anyone had ever heard from him, at least anyone she knew.

Years later, she'd asked her mother about it, and she'd shrugged it off. After her mother passed, she'd searched high and low but never found divorce papers. Her own legal search online failed to turn up any evidence of their divorce or of the whereabouts of her father.

There had been times when she'd watched Henry with the girls, listened to the tone of his voice as he spoke to them, watched him brush their hair, give them hugs, and she'd marveled. Most girls married men just like their fathers, and hers had walked out on his wife and kid without a care in the world. *How had she managed to marry a guy who turned out to be so devoted to his kids?*

"I can't imagine my life without them," he'd told her once at a party when Rose was a baby and Annie only a toddler. "You can't imagine the depth of the love before the first is born. It takes my breath away." His face had glowed with a lovestruck expression. He'd been unable to stop thinking about them and obsessively checking in with their babysitter the entire time they'd been away that night, which wound up being less than two hours before he couldn't stand it anymore. They'd left, Roxanne reluctantly, after hastily gulping down her third drink.

The two good things—three good things—she'd done in her life were marrying Henry and having her two girls. Maybe it wasn't too late to show up more for them, be more thoughtful of their needs, not so focused on herself. Maybe it wasn't too late for her and Henry.

Unless he was in love with her former best friend, Jessica. *I have to get off of that thought train before I derail myself.*

Returning to thoughts of Hayley pulled her off of the disaster of her marriage. If something had happened to Hayley to cause her to go so far downhill, so quickly, what was it? The rape theory was her strongest inclination. *What else could a teenage girl get into that would pulverize her self-esteem so much that she wouldn't want to live?*

Roxanne pulled out her laptop at the bar and did a quick Google search on the impacts of rape. She focused on articles by social scientists and psychologists. Three concepts jumped out at her—*self-blame, depression, and shame*. Victims of rape tended to blame themselves. *I flirted with him. I made out with him. I let him think we were going to have sex. I wore something that was too revealing. I walked down that dark alley by myself. I brought it on myself.*

Once self-blame took root, depression usually followed. Some saw this kind of situational depression as anger turned inward. The dark cousin of self-blame, shame, could then take root. Over time, the triumvirate of self-blame, shame, and depression could morph into self-destructive behavior.

That was it. She must have been picked up by someone after the party, taken somewhere, and violated. She'd felt so ashamed, blamed herself somehow, that she'd kept it inside, and an insidious depression had taken over her inner world.

One website blog pointed out that a woman who is a virgin at the time of rape might feel shame at a more intense level due to false beliefs about purity, beliefs that are ingrained in some cultures or religions. That sparked a memory of one of her and Hayley's discussions about marriage. They'd routinely discussed their future lives and what they'd hoped and dreamed they'd be, though their dreams had differed somewhat.

1999, ROXANNE

"I want to be a virgin on my wedding night," Hayley said dreamily to Roxanne, who scoffed.

"Are you kidding? Are you planning on being a teenage bride? Because unless you are, you're going to be waiting a mighty long time. Besides, from what I hear, half the fun of college life is dating two or three guys along the way, so you can practice on them, then find your husband after college. I fully intend to enjoy every bit of that action!" She sounded bold, but deep down, she wondered if she'd even have the opportunity to date, given how unappealing guys found her now.

"That's okay for you, Roxanne. But not me. I want it to be special, my first time. I want it to be with someone I'm madly in love with, and he is with me. He will carry me over the threshold of our honeymoon suite, just like in the movies." She sighed, gazing into space at her imaginary future husband.

"You're a hopeless romantic," Roxanne said, throwing a pillow hitting Hayley on the head. "Better watch out at the party next week. You might meet your future husband and get married before graduation." They both giggled at the ludicrousness of that thought. Hayley reminded her they'd pledged to go to college together, hadn't they? College first, then marriage, and babies after that. It was their pact.

But Roxanne just wanted to get to the next, independent steps of moving away for college. Number one priority: make sure you can always financially take care of yourself. Her mother's example had taught her the value of that. She would never be dependent on a guy for anything, especially money.

Roxanne's heart sank with the memory. That conversation had taken place only a short time before the landmark party, after which all of Hayley's dreams for her life had been derailed. And their dreams together... college, husbands, babies, living close to each other and taking kids to school, swapping parenting duties to give each other a break. Dreams that had ended for her friend before she could even begin to make them come true.

What had happened to Hayley? And who had sparked the downward spiral? Was it Brandon Statler? He hadn't exactly turned out for the better. He had a history of violent altercations. Could there be more in his background, maybe things he'd done but never been arrested for? He'd been aggressive sexually with Hayley. Didn't that only get worse as a guy aged? Heavy petting as a teenager, not respecting a girl's boundaries. Later, force? Rape?

If not Brandon, then who? The only other possible perpetrator she knew of was Adam. What if the appearance of helping her investigation was, in fact, an attempt to stay close by so he could monitor her activities?

Criminals sometimes stalked those who investigated their misdeeds, secretly wondering how clever they've been covering up their tracks, a part of them wanting to be found out. Another part watching closely so they could intervene and derail the investigation.

What if Adam had been the one to follow Hayley, pick her up, take her somewhere and assault her? He'd already lied by omission about his little move on Hayley at the party. *What if he was covering up a lot more than that?* He seemed so well put together, so kind and helpful. It would be horrifying to find out he was the one who'd done the unthinkable to Hayley.

From that unwelcome thought, she pulled up to a different view of her investigation, if you could call it that. The truth was it could be anyone. Just because she'd been focusing on Brandon and Adam, it didn't mean there wasn't another guy on the scene that night. It could have been a random stranger out driving around, looking for an opportunity. And he'd found it in Hayley.

She felt like something hovered in the air, something she was supposed to know already, a key to the mystery of Hayley's short life. Maybe that one martini she'd promised herself would help loosen the mental gears, bring back a clarifying memory, illuminate a clue, or at the very least, help her relax.

I want to tell you one more story, and it's yours—your typical day. You wake up, and you tell yourself, today is going to be different. But it isn't different. It's like every other day—the same as yesterday, and the day before that, and every day before that. One drink won't hurt. I just need one to take the edge off...

Dr. Derek. He wasn't even here, but he'd somehow managed to pull her back from the fragile edge of her newfound sobriety. She paid the bill and took a couple of slices of pizza to her room to get away from the bar.

Once there, the bed drew her eye. She looked at the way the sheets and comforter were tucked, all around the sides and foot, tight. *Hospital corners*, that's what Hayley called it. Her mom, Mrs. S, loved to do hospital corners when she made the bed, very meticulously, and she'd taught her daughter.

And then it hit her. Excitedly, she dialed Mrs. Strickland. "Hi, Mrs. S, it's Roxanne. I think I figured something out." And she told her but made her promise to wait for Roxanne before taking it a step further.

Smiling, she climbed into bed, and as she drifted off, she could swear she heard Hayley reward her with soft laughter and a high-five.

Tomorrow morning she'd finally have the answers, and maybe then, she could let go of the past and focus on fixing the future.

CHAPTER TWENTY-NINE

1999

As I slowly cruise the neighborhood, my headlights pick up a small figure walking along the side of the road. Someone out partying, no doubt, and trying to sneak back home. As I get closer, familiarity washes over me. I pull alongside.

"Hi," I say. "Where are you going?"

She's surprised but also pleased. "I, uh, I'm walking back to...back home. What are you doing? I can't believe you're out this way."

"I know. I've just been driving around. Come on, I'll give you a ride. It's not safe for you to walk by yourself this late at night."

"No, thanks," she says, walking forward again, but I know she doesn't mean it. A crack sounds nearby, and she jumps. But she keeps going, determined to conquer her anxiety.

"If you say so," I tell her, driving slowly alongside her. "But you're just being stubborn."

She keeps walking, and I begin thinking about the possibilities with which I have just been presented. I pull ahead of her as if to drive away, but slowly.

Suddenly, we hear an owl, its cry unearthly, and she jumps again. She picks up her pace, trying to catch up with me.

I laugh as I stop the car. "Get in, silly. Come on."

She pauses only an instant, then jumps in.

Of course, she does. I realize this was probably contrived, her walking alone, waiting for me to come along. Anticipation races through me.

CHAPTER THIRTY

PRESENT DAY

Adam began with a deeper dive into Brandon's legal history. What he found confirmed what he already suspected. A guy who hadn't done much with his life, who took out his frustration on others, getting into fights, drinking too much, and occasionally punching women.

He reached for his third cup of coffee, taking a swallow. He'd found sleep challenging. Twice he'd reached for his cell phone with the thought of calling Roxanne. But he couldn't figure out what he'd say, and all his half-formed questions and statements, in his head, sounded far too lame. After rolling over several times and punching his pillow, he'd finally gotten up and started the research he wanted to do on his own time anyway.

Tomorrow, he had a missing person case, and he'd have to focus on that primarily. But he still had tonight.

He continued the probe into Statler's life. Twice divorced. Bad credit. Bankruptcy.

Did that profile point to a guy who rapes teenage girls, starting in his late teens? Brandon Statler was a guy who hadn't achieved anything notable, who was barely holding onto his looks and charm, and who had financial issues. Not that construction workers didn't make good money; they did.

But in Statler's case, his periodic clashes with the law pointed to poor impulse control, and that often coincided with poor financial decision-making, as evidenced by the bankruptcy on record.

What about a serial rapist? The perpetrator of Hayley's rape, if that was what happened, likely wouldn't have stopped victimizing. The guy could be anyone, but more than likely, he'd have been a contemporary of theirs. Someone they knew, that Hayley knew. A high school student with them, or maybe a nearby college student.

She would have been comfortable with a guy at or near her age. Highly unlikely she'd have trusted an older guy.

Something had driven Hayley into deep despair, so much so that she'd killed herself. Since it appeared that it stemmed from the night of the party, it was a good theory to imagine she'd let someone drive her home, someone who'd made a stop along the way and assaulted her.

But now, he was in a long chain of theories and assumptions. Was he making the classic error? He'd identified a potential suspect, Statler, and now he searched for evidence that it was true. But Statler was one of many guys at the party that night, any one of which could have followed and picked up Hayley.

Adam shook his head in frustration. He was trying to find evidence against one guy while trying to build a criminal profile, all without any evidence of a crime, with no facts other than Hayley's suicide.

At this point, it was all supposition. It was shoddy police work, but it was all he had.

Still, it was a serious case if it did exist. Hayley was sixteen at the time of the alleged assault. That meant there was no statute of limitations. If he found real evidence, he had a shot at getting the D.A. to file charges.

Adam believed in gut instinct, especially during the phase of an investigation when facts and evidence were few. His gut told him that the current chain of theories about Hayley was right. Better to decide that and follow the evidence as it was gathered, leading to confirmation or denial, rather than freeze in indecision or self-doubt. He plunged on, even though it was getting later and later.

But he stopped at one point, frustrated and no longer believing his own theories. Statler was a check-kiting, womanizing, occasionally abusive jerk, but beyond that, it was pointless to pursue his history.

As he dropped off, he resolved to focus on the case of the missing girl. If Roxanne wanted to keep searching for answers to Hayley's suicide, that was okay.

The next morning, after managing to drag himself out of bed and gulp two cups of coffee, Adam sat down with the high school drama teacher. A familiar face from the past, Russell Chase. "Thanks for meeting. I'm looking into a missing girl, and I found out she's into drama, so I thought of you."

That sounded lame, but he wasn't sure where to start. He briefly told Chase about Daisy, how she'd given a story to her parents about a trip to go see a Broadway production in Dallas, then disappeared. He'd discovered that there wasn't any such production going on in Dallas at that time, that the schedule for the summer musicals wasn't starting for another three weeks.

Chase looked genuinely puzzled. "That is strange, but you know, I don't recognize her name. She's not a student here, as far as I know."

"Right. She goes to school in the next town over. But since her story was about drama, and we have a connection, I thought I'd ask you if you know of anyone taking kids on extra-curricular activities like that. Is that something you do with your students?"

"Sure, I do. But it's been weeks since the last one, and there are always a couple of parents that go along as well. You can check with school administration." Chase just smiled calmly and waited patiently.

"I'm sure that won't be necessary." This was feeling like a dead end. Then he thought of something else. "While I'm here, and we're talking about kids and drama, I saw Roxanne Fairchild yesterday. She reminded me about Hayley, the girl who committed suicide when we were all classmates. She was into drama, too, and you were her teacher then, right?"

Chase's face fell into an appropriately sad expression. "Yes, I talked with her as well. I'm afraid she's having a hard time letting go of the past. Water under the bridge, so to speak. But yes, I do remember Hayley. She was one of the most talented girls I ever had the pleasure of teaching. So sad."

"So, since you remember her, do you have any idea why she would have killed herself?"

Chase shook his head slowly. "No clue, really. Unless it was maybe that boy, Brandon Statler, who I think she maybe had some kind of relationship with." It was said as supposition, but his expression was as if there was a bad taste in his mouth. "I think she rejected him, and maybe he didn't like that. Teenage boys don't handle rejection well, you know."

Adam did know.

"I think he still lives here," Chase continued. "You might want to check with him. Maybe he knows something about Hayley."

Statler's name, cropping up again, in conjunction with Hayley's. Maybe it was time to pay him a visit. He thanked Chase and got up to leave.

"Let me know if I can help again in any way," Chase told him as he left.

As he headed for Statler's location, he decided to check in with Roxanne, so he called her but got voice mail. "Hey, it's Adam. I'm still doing some research. Call me when you get a minute." He hung up and, a moment later, received her text.

Hi Adam— running down a new lead, will call you in 30.

CHAPTER THIRTY-ONE

It had taken a bit of persuasion, but he'd finally succeeded in getting Statler to meet with him. They sat eating fast food, Statler complaining the entire time. But the promise of free lunch had been all it had taken.

"What's this about?" he asked around mouthfuls of burger and fries, not bothering to wipe the food off, eyes wary. "I gotta get back to work."

"I know Roxanne came to see you already, and I—"

"That again? Look, I already told her I don't know anything about that chick who offed herself back in high school. She was hot, though," he said offhandedly.

Adam's eyes grew cold as ice as Brandon carelessly tossed out the only contribution he had to the tragedy of Hayley's death, *that she'd been hot*.

"She committed suicide," Adam said slowly.

"So, what does that have to do with me?"

He ignored Statler's question. "What happened after you left the party?"

"Nothing, dude. I left. End of story. Now, I gotta get back to work. Thanks for lunch," he said sarcastically as he rose, throwing down his napkin and turned to leave.

"We're not done yet, Statler. Sit. Down."

"Or what?" He laughed at Adam.

"There's the little matter of a series of parking and moving violations and your court date coming up. I might be able to do something to help out with that—if you help me out."

That got his attention. "Man, I can't turn around without hearing that *whoop-whoop*. Some dumb cop always trying to make his quota hassling me about driving five over the speed limit. And as for the parking stuff—where else am I supposed to put my truck when I'm trying to get to a job?" He went on, but Adam stopped him.

"I get it. I have a couple more questions," he told Statler as he settled back into the booth. "What was Hayley doing before you left the party?"

"We were making out. She was all over me, man, and I was starting to get somewhere, but all of a sudden, she got cold on me. What is it with chicks who turn on the green light and then slam on the brakes? Anyway, I had better things to do, so I left to go find my cousin and smoke some weed."

What a loser. "And after you left? When did you see her again?" Presumptive questions sometimes hit the target.

"I never saw her again, at least, not for real. Just her picture in the paper after she hung herself. Who does that, anyway? She was messed up." He shook his head at the bafflement of another person wanting to end their life.

"Someone gave her a ride home that night," presumptive again, "and we're trying to figure out who. Was it you?"

"Nope." Spoken with a pop of his lips. "Like I said, I never saw her again. But you were there when I left, weren't you? I saw how you looked at her, dude. You wanted in her pants, too. Why are you grilling me when you're the one who was still there at the end?" He looked slyly at Adam as if they were co-conspirators in the grand scheme to remove panties from girls.

"You and I are nothing alike, *dude*," Adam said, cringing inside as the arrow hit its mark. He'd wanted Hayley, too. But not *that* bad. He'd hit a brick wall with Statler. The guy was a jerk, but he had nothing on him.

Wait. A vague memory floated up. A sarcastic comment thrown his direction by another cop, startling him out of his focused work that day. 'Hey, Porter! Remember that loser guy we went to high school with? Brandon Statler. Just got picked up for statutory rape. Can you believe it?'

And he hadn't been terribly surprised. But he'd gone back to work, never giving it another thought… *until now*. "You know, I seem to remember something. Didn't you get charged with having sex with an underage girl just a few months ago?"

Statler's face turned purple. "That never happened! This chick I was dating got pissed at me because I broke up with her, and she got her daughter to lie about me. She was psycho, man, but her daughter 'fessed up' about the lies, and the charges were dropped."

"The daughter was fifteen, right?" Adam recalled the details of the case. "Did you intimidate her into dropping the charges?"

"Man, you are outta your mind. You can forget about fixing the tickets; I'm done with this. Screw you," he threw over his shoulder as he stalked out of the diner, almost knocking over a server carrying a tray full of food.

Interesting. He'd hit a hot button, for sure. *What was the real story about the girl who'd accused Statler?* It wasn't unusual for a victim to back out of the criminal process at some point, refuse to testify, recant earlier statements. How difficult would it have been for Statler to approach her, threaten her?

He ordered more iced tea and pulled out his laptop. Logging into the system, he quickly pulled up Statler's history, and this time, he found the statutory rape charges. It was true that the charges had been dropped. That's why he hadn't found them in the first search. He'd only been looking for convictions.

As he continued to read the notes, his eyes almost popped out of his head.

A teenage girl, into drama and acting. With a single mom struggling to make ends meet, looking for someone to take care of her, and hooking up with guys who would never be good partners. Someone breaking up with her, the anger and rage, wanting payback.

A teenage girl...one who was also into drama...one with a single mom. Daisy. The details were just too close to be a coincidence.

He threw down enough cash to pay the bill plus tip and hurried out of the diner.

A few minutes later, he knocked on the door. He heard someone inside. "Open up, Angela. Detective Porter here again. I have some questions about you and your daughter."

The door remained shut.

"I know what you did." Still nothing. "If you don't talk to me now, it won't look good for you later down at the station." He moderated his voice as much as he could. "Look, I understand what you wanted. Statler is a complete jerk. But now you have to think about Daisy."

More silence then, slowly, the door opened.

They sat again in her worn living room. "What happened?"

And Daisy's mother, swollen eyes rimmed in red, tears dripping, told him. How Statler had promised her the world. He had a good job in construction, made three times her tiny paychecks, and would build a house for her and her daughter. How she'd believed him, had thought they were in love, and had planned her future with him.

The humiliation of catching him with another woman because she'd gone to his place without telling him first, planning to surprise him with a bottle of wine she'd splurged on and bought to celebrate their one-year anniversary.

ABOUT ROXANNE

Caught in bed with someone else, he'd been the opposite of remorseful. He'd gone defensive, laughing at her for thinking they had something exclusive. Humiliation had turned to rage.

"This is all my fault," she sobbed. "I talked Daisy into making up the story that he'd had sex with her. I just wanted him to feel bad, to regret what he'd done to me, to us. I didn't want it to go that far, but once we started, it was hard to stop."

Daisy had eventually had enough. She'd balked at testifying, clammed up, and refused to explain why to the District Attorney. There had never been a rape kit done because there was no allegation of force, so there was no evidence other than her testimony. Charges were dropped.

As far as Angela knew, Statler hadn't forced Daisy to drop the charges. She'd done it on her own, tired of their game and wanting it to stop.

"Do you think he's done something to her? Oh, God, I can't imagine that! He's a cheater and a liar, but I don't think he would actually hurt Daisy. Would he?" Her eyes spun crazily as she imagined the worst possible scenarios perpetrated by the man she'd once loved.

"Did he ever threaten you or Daisy after he was accused?" Adam asked.

"Not me, but maybe her. She seemed to get a kick out of concocting the story, acting the part. She's really good, you know. Fake tears that you'd swear are for real. But then, she decided it was too much and wanted out. Was she afraid of him? I didn't see that, but she's a good little actress. Maybe she was afraid of him and couldn't tell anyone. Oh, God, what if she was terrified? What if he threatened her with…something terrible?"

And Adam thought, *what if he wanted to get even for the false charges? What if he'd really wanted Daisy more than her mother?* He'd seen more than one case of pedophiles who dated women with pubescent daughters for the purpose of getting to the child. Had Daisy and Angela unknowingly concocted a story that was actually not far from the truth of what might have been?

And then there was Hayley. Statler was the connection to both girls. *What if Hayley was merely the start of a pattern that had extended over the past two decades? Was he a predator of opportunity only, or could there be more victims?*

He'd like to bring Statler in for more questioning. But he wasn't sure he had enough yet.

CHAPTER THIRTY-TWO

He started with an assumption. It might be wrong, but if it was right, he stood a chance of finding Daisy before it was too late. It was worth the risk of going down rabbit trails.

Assumption one. Statler picked up Hayley for a ride home and assaulted her. A crime of opportunity, but one that set off an emotional tsunami that had resulted in her suicide.

That led to assumption two. Statler abducted Daisy, maybe a revenge scheme gone out of control or another crime of opportunity. Or maybe... another girl in a pattern that had started with Hayley and escalated over the years to abduction, and maybe more.

Going off of assumption one, his instincts prompted him to investigate that angle. If rapists typically don't stop at one assault— they typically don't—then he could reasonably assume additional rapes. Since serial rapists do so in patterns unique to themselves, like fingerprints, he might be able to discover a link to Hayley.

Using the FBI's Violent Criminal Apprehension Program (ViCAP), he began searching, using assumptive criteria based on what he knew about Hayley. He began with unsolved sexual assaults in East Texas over the past twenty-five years. He assumed Hayley had been the first based on Brandon's age at that time. There were too many to look at individually, so he narrowed the criteria to teenage victims.

That brought the number down, but something Roxanne had said came to mind. *What if Hayley's assailant hadn't stopped at rape?*

What if she didn't commit suicide but instead was murdered? Roxanne had theorized as much, though reluctantly, and he'd quickly brushed it aside.

He sat back and listened to his instincts and felt that familiar ping in his gut, the one that often led him in a direction that eventually resulted in a case solved. It wasn't infallible, but he'd learned it was valuable.

Time stood still as he narrowed criteria and searched, reading cases, until finally, he discovered there were at least nine female abductions over the past couple of decades that hadn't been solved, five of whose bodies were found. Four vanished without a trace. But as he read over the cases, he found a couple of striking similarities.

One, they all shared the same physical characteristics, including race. They were all white, in their mid-teens, and were blond-haired and blue-eyed. Looking at their photos, they were all attractive girls, although none quite as beautiful as Hayley had been. But maybe that was his prejudice. He couldn't help but notice how similar they were in appearance.

He looked up high school yearbook and social media information on each of the victims, easier for the ones that had occurred more recently, more difficult with the older cases when social media hadn't been invented. They were all heavily involved in a specific school activity.

That was far more than a coincidence. Adam didn't believe in coincidences much anyway. Usually, if there was a correlation of some kind, information that lined up with a high degree of similarity, it formed the proverbial smoke that meant there was definitely a fire somewhere.

ABOUT ROXANNE

But the victims were all from different high schools and communities. Spread all across Texas, from Austin to Houston, to San Antonio, and into West Texas. The fact that they were into the same after-school activity didn't necessarily mean their paths had crossed with the same killer.

If they were in different communities, how could they have had a person in common? Different schools in the same community, he could explain, but not with victims so geographically diverse. Not to mention that the person who had theoretically raped Hayley, even if a fellow student in 1999, would be much older today. *How did a thirty or forty-something guy cross paths with teenage girls on a regular basis? And go unnoticed?*

It didn't add up. *Who could have traveled all over the state of Texas, finding victims, committing the crimes, and covering up evidence, all while avoiding suspicion?* Unlike Hayley, if these girls were abducted and/or murdered by the same person, it wasn't a fellow student, not after the first couple of girls. The killer had to have grown up, become an adult. Yet was somehow able to continue preying on young girls.

What if the perpetrator was an older guy who somehow inspired trust, yet who was also viewed as a contemporary?

Was Brandon Statler more than he appeared to be? Under that exterior that screamed loser, was he a cunning and vicious hunter of girls? Grudgingly, Adam had to admit Brandon still had the kind of looks that would appeal to women. But high school and college girls? Perhaps.

It didn't feel right. A cunning serial killer, a sociopath of the highest order, typically avoided contact with law enforcement. Brandon Statler often got into trouble and was well-known to the local cops.

But maybe that was his brilliance. He was hiding in plain sight, secretly thumbing his nose at them each time he came across their radar, knowing they'd never suspect him of anything as far-reaching and complicated as this.

He thought of something that might tie Statler to the other crimes, calling his company. After getting through to the main construction supervisor and introducing himself, he got to the point of the call.

"Listen, I'm working on a case, and while I don't think it has anything to do with your company, there is someone who works for you that we're looking at. Can you tell me where you do business? Do your guys work primarily in the immediate area, or do they travel elsewhere in the state for projects?"

He listened, jotting down notes, thanked the guy, and ended the call, sitting back in puzzlement. As he'd suspected, the company's projects were spread throughout the state. They'd been around for at least the past twenty-five years or so, and most of the cities matched his previous list. But not all of them.

Even more alarming was the newfound knowledge that Statler held a position at the company that required a high level of skill. He wasn't the low-level blue-collar worker Adam had envisioned, but rather, a project manager who managed others.

The person he was wasn't how he presented himself, at least not how he'd presented himself to Adam, who'd made it clear that he was digging into Statler's history and current circumstances. Digging that may have given Statler a reason to shroud himself in one of his personas for Adam's benefit.

Another marker of a cunning sociopath was the ability to act in a chameleon-like way, fashioning a personality for each circumstance, to be pulled out and exhibited when needed. The average person had little innate ability to discern the difference between charm, often a façade, and an authentic, engaging personality, thus enabling the most dangerous predators to prowl through society undetected for years.

John Wayne Gacy lived an average suburban life as an independent construction contractor, was married, and quite sociable. He performed as a clown for charitable events and children's parties, all while systematically luring and killing 33 boys and young men over a period of around ten years. He was so persuasive that he convinced houseguests and his wife that the foul stench emanating from beneath their home was nothing more than a moisture issue.

Statler's looks, combined with a modicum of charm, might be enough to gain him access to women and their daughters, all while looking fairly harmless with his jeans, his truck, and his chewing tobacco—the staples of all good ole Texas boys. *Flag-waving, churchgoing, good ole boys.*

And how easy would it be to pull out his good-old-boy persona when encountering local law enforcement? And later, laughing at their ineptitude, their inability to see the killer right in front of them.

Sociopathic killers often found creative ways to put themselves close to law enforcement, gaining tremendous pleasure in their ability to baffle the police. A bar fight here, a traffic violation there, and he regularly basked in fooling them, diverting them.

It wasn't foolproof, but it was enough to raise his suspicions about Statler far higher.

Especially now that there was Daisy, a clear link to her mother's former boyfriend. A guy who could be a predator hiding without hiding, gloating with superiority as he repeatedly fooled everyone. *A guy who was with Hayley, who'd slid downhill after her one encounter with him.*

Time to rattle his tree, see what fell out.

Adam found him on a job site. As he approached, Statler shook his head and called out aggressively. "What the hell are you doing here, man? I'm at work." He spat chewing tobacco, managed to spew some of it on Adam's shoes, then delivered a fake apology. "Sorry 'bout that," he smirked.

He noticed how big Statler was, his muscles straining his shirt. *How easy would it be for him to overpower a teenage girl?* He had a couple of inches on Adam and a temper he'd seen the guy use over the years. He could end up on the wrong side of a vicious fight, but it was time to take some risks.

"Sorry is one word for you."

Statler's face turned red, and he lunged at Adam, who side-stepped and used Statler's forward momentum to push him in the small of his back, so he toppled and fell. Before he could react, Adam had flipped him over and cuffed him.

"What the hell?! I'll have your badge for this!" Statler fumed while Adam stood over him. It gave him no pleasure to do it.

"Calm down. You came at me first, and I stopped you. Now, you have two choices. I can haul you down to the station and charge you with attempted assault on a police officer," stretching it a bit here, "or… you can go voluntarily to the station and talk."

"If this is about that high school girl I dumped, you're barking up the wrong tree. Take these off, now!"

Adam really didn't have much cause to detain him, but he didn't need to know that. "I'll take them off if you'll play nice. What's it going to be?"

"Don't worry, I won't do anything. Just get these off." He strained to hold back his anger, his face taking on the mottled look of nice plastered over rage. Under the right circumstances, charm wasn't always available, and the true persona showed through.

Adam uncuffed Statler and hauled him up, then put him in the back of his vehicle.

Statler sat quietly in the interview room, uncharacteristically mute, but the wheels were clearly turning. "What is this about?" he asked, no longer resorting to his typical slang.

Now, how to get him to share the right information without seeing the trap?

Going from memory, Adam asked, "When did you start working for this company? I'm asking because we're looking at someone who may or may not have traveled around the state with the business, doing work, over the past twenty years or so."

Statler reacted quickly. "I've only been at the company for the last nine years. You can check with the office if you don't believe me."

"What about travel?"

"Everyone travels in this business. So what?"

Adam read from his notes, reciting the cities where he's seen the cases he'd connected by their similarities. He said nothing of the victims, choosing not to reveal the information about the girls, saving that for later. Statler shrugged, refusing to acknowledge that he'd been to those specific places, pretending to not remember.

"How can you not remember where you've traveled for work?"

"It's easy when you're on the road all the time. And I'm not the only one. We go as a team. Are you hassling any of those guys?" He challenged Adam.

Time to switch directions, try to throw him off balance. "What did you do to Hayley? And where is Daisy?"

Statler ground his teeth. "Nothing. I answered those ridiculous questions already."

Adam peppered him with more questions about Hayley and Daisy, switching back and forth between the two girls, hoping to penetrate Statler's defenses. But Statler didn't react. He answered without hesitation as Adam hit him with more questions. He'd calmed down, no easy feat for someone wired for defensiveness and action.

He was in his project manager persona—a man in charge, not someone who could be easily rattled. He seemed to grow more resolute as Adam drew out the questioning. Finally, he drew a line. "I know my rights. If you're not going to charge me with anything, you have to let me go. If you don't release me now, I want my attorney here."

Reluctantly, Adam had to admit to himself that he couldn't break through Statler's defenses, and he had no reason to hold him.

Later, disappointed, he felt the pinch of failure. He'd reached the end of the road for now. Questions still remained unanswered. *Who, if anyone, might have started with Hayley and advanced to nine other girls? Was it Statler? Or was he, as Brandon had said, barking up the wrong tree?*

CHAPTER THIRTY-THREE

Adam called Roxanne again, and the call went instantly to voice mail, indicating her phone was completely off. That was odd. *Why would she turn off her phone after saying she'd get back to him?*

Where was she? Maybe she was in her motel room doing research or just resting. He didn't have anything better to do, so he'd head over that way. But she'd acted funny when he suggested dinner, so she might not welcome his presence.

If that was the case, so be it. He needed to talk to her about what he'd found out. But first, he wanted to look into something else, something Roxanne had said in one of her texts. He read it again. *Checking on a new lead with Mrs. S.* What did that mean?

He headed to Mrs. Strickland's home. A few minutes later, he greeted her at the door and explained who he was and his mission. She led him to Hayley's bedroom but let him know that Roxanne's tip hadn't paid off.

"She called and said she was certain Haley kept a journal. She said to look under the bed. At least, I think that's what she said. But we've searched this entire room numerous times, hoping to find something, anything that would explain how our daughter could have committed suicide."

Adam's eyes scanned the room, the onetime sanctuary of the girl he'd briefly known. He took in the posters of the musicians and teen stars she'd loved—the indicators of her passion and aspirations.

The comforter had been pulled back. "Okay if I look?" he asked Mrs. Strickland, who nodded. He ran his hands over the sheets, feeling for anything hard, or even soft, that seemed out of place. He did what she'd undoubtedly done just a few minutes earlier, getting on his knees, pulling his duty flashlight, and searching under the bed. Then under the dresser and nightstands.

He pulled out every drawer completely, searching under the bottoms, behind the backs, as if he was looking for drugs. *Nothing.* "Can you tell me exactly what Roxanne told you?"

"Look for a journal, and she said it was under the bed. She kept saying something about hospital corners."

"Hospital corners?"

"Yes, it's what my mother taught me and her mother before her. You tuck everything in this way." And she demonstrated, first with the sheets, then with the bedspread.

What did hospital corners have to do with Hayley's journal? Clearly, nothing. There was no evidence that Hayley had kept one, and all the searching over the many years hadn't changed that fact.

Disappointment sank in his belly. This was another blind alley that led nowhere. It was probably time to pull himself off of this so-called case and get back to his real job, back to finding Daisy.

As much as he wanted to help Roxanne, he wondered if her supposition about her friend was entirely wrong, no more than an attempt to allay her own guilt. She wasn't guilty of anything, the way he saw it. But he knew that friends and family always carried an irrational sense of responsibility when a loved one committed suicide. And he probably wasn't helping things by trying to find ties to Hayley's suicide with the disappearance of Daisy.

Still, the thing that nagged at him now was the string of disappearances and murders of girls who looked almost identical to Hayley. Maybe they weren't connected to Hayley's suicide, but maybe they were. He'd talk to the lieutenant about it tomorrow, brainstorm about it, and get his perspective. Perhaps they'd open a cold case file.

He could run that investigation alongside the search for Daisy, whose disappearance he still felt had some kind of connection, a thread that wound between the girl from two decades ago and the events of today. Plus, there was Statler, still on his radar.

"What was that?" Mrs. S. had been talking, and he'd missed most of it, but his unconscious had caught it and tugged on his sleeve.

"I said, if my daughter kept a journal, I didn't know it. But if she had, she probably wouldn't have wanted anyone to read it. She would have hidden it someplace no one would think to look." She laughed gently, sadly, her eyes wandering off. "But we've looked everywhere."

Of course. A teenage girl's journal wouldn't have been tucked under the comforter or placed in a dresser drawer or under the bed where her mom could easily find it.

She'd put it far out of reach. Hospital corners were the decoy. A tightly made-up bed meant nothing hidden. But underneath, under the mattress...

It was a King-sized bed, the mattress far too large for a woman the size of Mrs. S to lift. She'd only have been able to pull up the corners, and those not far. Also, most people didn't search diligently for lost objects, especially when they weren't certain those objects existed.

Searching for contraband over the years in the homes of suspects, he'd experienced how difficult it was to find things that the owner didn't want found. Sure, there were the ones who hastily hid their drugs, and those were easy. But the ones who had something truly incriminating, those people could squirrel things away in the most obscure places.

He lifted the mattress, raising it as high as he could.

"What are you doing?" She sounded alarmed.

"There," he said, holding the mattress with two hands, breathing heavily with exertion. "Grab it," he told her.

She hesitated, but then peered under the mattress and gasped.

Hayley had placed her journal in the exact center underneath the mattress. If her parents had searched, they might have checked under the edges, but never think to lift the entire thing high enough to see all the way to the middle. *What teenage girl could have lifted a mattress that size?*

And indeed, she couldn't have lifted it. But she could have snaked her arm underneath, put it there, and, knowing exactly where it was placed, snake it out again each time.

In all those years, no one had thought to look there.

"It's a little heavy, so if you could hurry," he said, straining and trying to breathe. She scurried and grabbed it, and he dropped the mattress a moment later.

They stood together in wonder, staring at the small journal in her hands. It was decorated on the outside with sparkly paint, covered in flowers, hearts, suns, and moons. *Property of Hayley Strickland – do not read!* Was written in cursive with a purple marker.

She looked up at him with wide eyes, her skin drawn and pale, as she held it out to Adam. "Read it first, please."

But why wouldn't she want to read her daughter's journal first?

Then he got it. *What if it contained the ramblings of a girl who'd been angry with her mom one day?* A girl who'd maybe written things that would be agonizing for a mother to read decades later. Things she'd have later regretted writing and had never really meant. A typical teenage girl blowing off steam, but a knife to a mother's heart, especially in this situation.

Adam opened it and began reading. He flipped the pages faster, skipping over the short notations about next to nothing. *Roxanne's coming over tonight. It's movie night!*

ABOUT ROXANNE

Notations about various classmates and the funny things they did. Sometimes the things they did that she didn't approve of, like instances of ridiculing a fellow student.

Then, he began seeing notations about a specific person. Benign at first, then a change in tone. Indications that she found his behavior odd. A trace of concern.

Then, reading the last two pages, Adam's brows shot up, and his heart began to thud.

There was someone who'd aroused Hayley's suspicions, someone who she'd felt anxious around, someone she'd previously felt safe with.

One of her last entries stirred Adam's interest.

Still feel bad from the night of the party. Something happened, something bad. I'm sure of it. I feel different. And I can't remember all of it.

And then, the reference, the name, and Adam almost dropped the journal. Because he knew that name, and it tied the loose ends together in an unexpected way.

This was it. Confirmation, at last. About Hayley, and possibly about the other girls over the years.

Probably confirmation about what may have happened to Daisy too, and that thought pierced him. The common thread wasn't the location of job sites for Statler's team, as he'd previously theorized. It was something entirely different. And now, he wondered about a particular person, not Statler, but someone else who could be the chameleon he sought.

He closed the journal and looked at Mrs. Strickland. "I think you'll want to read this later. Everything in it proves what a wonderful mom you were. For now, though, I'll need it for my investigation, which has just taken a different turn."

Her eyes filled with tears as she looked at the journal.

He left as quickly as he could. His mind racing.

Daisy... he had to find the trail to her. There was a slim chance that she could still be alive. But he'd been on the wrong trail all along and wasted precious time.

Roxanne. She'd been to see the person now on Adam's radar.

And he hadn't heard from her in hours...

CHAPTER THIRTY-FOUR

The caller gave Roxanne his best, most charming low laugh. "I thought about Hayley after you left, and I remembered something. A few years ago, the school was about to be renovated, and they told me to throw out as much stage stuff as I could. I didn't want to, so I boxed a lot of it and put it in storage. Hayley used to love going through the costumes and props after school. I wondered if there might be something in all that stuff that would tell you more about her, remind you of her, or maybe give you more peace of mind. You're welcome to any of it."

"That's very kind of you. I'm on my way back to Hayley's mom's house to pursue another angle, but I can meet with you later to look at the stuff."

"Oh, shoot. I have classes later, and after that, I have plans for the weekend. I know you mentioned only being in town for another day. The only time I have is right now, but I understand if that doesn't work for you. Probably a long shot, anyway..." He held his breath, waiting for the hook to sink.

"Um, let me see. I guess I can go see Mrs. Strickland later. I'll call her and let her know I'll be late and text you when I'm on the way."

He gave her the location, ending the call with anticipation humming in his veins. How easy it was to lure, to charm, to crook an imaginary finger and pull even someone like Roxanne in the direction he wanted.

Roxanne passed down several streets in a warehouse district, making first one turn and then another, trying to follow the directions Chase had given her. It was a quiet part of town. No traffic coming in or out.

She found the unit he'd told her about, on the end of a long building on the very last row. Nothing beyond it but a small gravel area and an open field. She parked and waited. Only a couple of minutes passed before she saw him drive up in a black late-model SUV. She got out and met him at the storage unit door.

"I have no idea if there's anything useful in here, so this may be a waste of time," he told her as he unlocked two padlocks and pulled up the rolling door. He stood aside and waved her in.

It was dark inside. There were no windows and no skylight. The only light came from the open door. But because it was deep and not wide, not much light penetrated the darkness. She vaguely registered stacks of boxes, all neatly taped and labeled. There was a tripod with a video camera on top. *Odd.* She turned to find him smiling at her. "Where should I start?"

He ambled over to one of the stacks and pulled off the top box, sealed with masking tape. She was just about to ask how she could open it when he pulled out a pocketknife and sliced open the tape. "I don't know, but how about this one?"

She opened it and saw hats, all kinds of hats from various periods. There were a couple of bowlers, women's hats with huge feathers, and there was a sequined hat that looked like it fit the flapper period. There was a small cowboy hat, and she flashed to Hayley starring in "Annie Get Your Gun." Her heart lurched.

Soon, she was lost in her memories. Flashes of sitting in the school auditorium, heart swelling with pride as her best friend stole every single scene in which she appeared. Hayley had a glow about her, a sense of magic that transferred itself to the audience. At the end of each production, when the cast took their bows, the auditorium always thundered with applause for her.

Hayley would bow, her brilliant smile lighting her face and her skin flushed. Afterward, they celebrated with ice cream sundaes and overnights, and she listened to Hayley spin her Hollywood and Broadway dreams.

She could see Hayley on a Broadway stage, and the loss of her bright and beautiful spirit seemed too much to bear. *Was the pain of regret ever going away?* She gasped, returning to the dark and dank storage space. *Why was she here—to lay claim to the ragged memorabilia of her friend's most treasured aspiration? For what purpose?*

While Chase cut open another box, he began asking her questions. "So, what were you hoping to find out from Mrs. Strickland?"

As she dug through a box of old yellowed playbills, she answered. "I remembered where Hayley kept her journal. I'm hoping maybe she wrote something in it that will help me understand why she was suicidal. She's probably found it by now, but just waiting until I get there to read it."

He pulled something out of a box, whatever it was clanked together. Turning, she saw it was handcuffs. Theatrical ones, no doubt, with a built-in breakaway lock. She saw the grin. *Oh boy.* No wonder he's still teaching theater decades later. He's still an immature kid.

"What do you think is in Hayley's journal?" He'd moved closer to her, still dangling the handcuffs.

"I don't know. Probably things about school, maybe her parents, I'd guess. But something drove her to suicide, and the most likely place to find out what it was, is in her journal." She continued pulling things out of boxes, but now nothing reminded her of Hayley. It was just old junk from past school plays, going back for decades. Apparently, Chase took everything. It was an archeological record of the school's plays for the past two or three generations of kids.

This was a hopeless quest, anyway. It was time to wrap it up with Hayley's journal entries. She could do that. She could read her friend's thoughts. And no matter what she found there, she would decide to be okay with it, to let the past go. Something settled in her stomach, and she felt calmer. But she continued opening boxes, only looking half-heartedly.

Then, she found something odd. It was a make-up kit for a guy with various fake eyebrows, mustaches, and beards. *Were those fake contact lenses with different eye colors?* The case looked fairly new, and it wasn't sealed, as if it had been used recently. She frowned. *What would this be doing in the storage room?* Wouldn't it be at the school, accessible for use in the school's current productions?

"Maybe she wasn't suicidal," he said, his tone odd.

She turned around, noting how close he stood, still holding the handcuffs. "What are you talking about?" As she spoke the words, the sounds of someone approaching caught both their attention.

Adam's instinctual ping grew louder as he thought about the girls who'd disappeared and about an older perpetrator—not a fellow student, but someone with authority. Someone who appeared trustworthy, someone Hayley, or any teenage girl, wouldn't hesitate to go along with. *They were all drama students.*

Hadn't Roxanne told him she'd spoken with one of Hayley's teachers yesterday, the same guy who'd taught at their school when they were all students together? The same person whose name had turned up in Hayley's journal, not with a definitive finger point, but certainly strong implications combined with doubt and strong reservations. He thought about one of her final journal entries.

Something is wrong with me, and there's something strange about Mr. Chase. I tried to talk to him, but he wouldn't listen. I've been having dreams about him, too. I feel bad about those dreams. I wish I could talk to Roxanne.

He went online and searched the name. Russell Chase. A quick background and criminal records search turned up zero. The guy was clean. But a deeper dive into Google revealed a website touting his skills as a drama coach. There were loads of reviews by former students, almost all girls, as well as references to the ones who'd gone on to get roles on Broadway or in soap operas. No big names, though.

He looked perfectly respectable, but his years as a cop told him that meant nothing.

He could be the common denominator to all the missing and murdered girls' cases. He may have had something to do with Hayley's suicide.

Or maybe it wasn't suicide...

Didn't most teenage girls dream of being famous? Wasn't it typical for them to get into acting in high school, banking on their winning looks combined with a modicum of talent and hope for more later? Only to find out that getting chosen for any kind of significant role professionally was like winning the lottery.

But someone who understood that could easily use their fantasies and dreams as a lure. Someone who appeared safe and legitimate, who encouraged them and built their egos. Someone who knew precisely how to lay the trap, how to groom them.

Sociopaths groomed their victims—with attention, with affirmation, with time spent catering to them, and even with gifts, all designed to instill trust and create vulnerability. Then, at the maximum moment of psychological safety, when the victim expected nothing more than the continuation of the same attention and affirmation, the final steps of the long-planned assault were launched.

Grooming was so diabolical that sometimes the victim could be persuaded to stay quiet afterward and even to doubt their own senses.

How could someone who'd been so kind previously do anything harmful?

I must have imagined it, must have exaggerated it in my mind.

I asked for it, provoked him. It was my fault.

He didn't mean to hurt me.

There may have been other girls who he'd lured away. One's that he'd done whatever he wanted with them and let go, having sufficiently threatened them. Or persuaded them, brainwashed them even into thinking nothing had really happened or that it had been with their consent.

He checked the time again. It had been far too long since he'd heard from Roxanne.

CHAPTER THIRTY-FIVE

A few minutes later, he stood outside the door to Roxanne's room and knocked for the third time. He put his ear to the door but heard nothing, no rustling around, no television playing. Nothing.

He went to the manager's office. The guy behind the counter, tattooed, skinny, wearing a name badge that said 'Glenn,' was completely absorbed in his cell phone and ignored him. "Hey!" Adam said, snapping his fingers to get the dude's attention. "I could use some help here, Glenn."

When the guy looked up, Adam's badge was in his face, and his eyes went big. "Uh, sorry, officer. What's up? Did I do something wrong?"

"I don't know. Did you?"

"Uh...," he mumbled as his face lost its color.

Now Adam felt bad about scaring the guy. "Just messing with you, Glenn. I'm actually a detective, and I need to confirm who is checked into Room 208."

"We're not supposed to give out that information," said Glenn, recovering his sense of self and now puffing up with indignation.

"You're allowed to give the information to an officer of the law. Which I am. But if you won't, then I'll be forced to run a check on you and find out if there are any outstanding warrants or tickets with your name on them."

Bingo. Glenn's face turned red. "That won't be necessary. Let me look." He tapped keys on the computer and turned back to Adam with a name. Roxanne Fairchild.

This next part was dicey, but he did it anyway. "I'm concerned about her welfare as she hasn't responded to family members in hours. You can go with me, but I want to make sure she's not in the room in need of help."

Glenn looked undecided, but finally caved. "That's okay, you can go without me. Just bring back the key card when you're done." He pulled a card, ran it, and handed it to Adam, who quickly made his way to Roxanne's room.

In the room, he first stood and looked around. She wasn't there, but he'd already surmised that. Her clothes were strewn a bit, but it wasn't that messy. Her purse was gone, but her suitcase was next to the dresser, and her laptop sat closed on the small desk. She hadn't left town.

Next to the laptop was a notepad and pen. He picked up the notepad and saw notes. Mrs. S... journal... meet today.

But she'd never made it to the Strickland's home. He tore off the top sheet of the notepad and put it in his pocket.

Roxanne slowly returned to consciousness. She lay on her side, hands bound by handcuffs and not the breakaway kind. Her mouth was taped shut with duct tape, but her feet were free. She registered the motion of the vehicle with a plunging sense of dread. *Dear God, where was she being taken?* She could see bits of light at the edges of the trunk lid, so it was still daylight.

This was the absolute worst-case scenario for anyone—man, woman, or child—abduction followed by travel to a remote location. That never ended well for the victim, and her heart began to race.

ABOUT ROXANNE

No! Anxiety right now was not her friend. She inhaled deeply, drawing air through her nostrils, and willed herself to calm down. She couldn't afford to work herself into an emotional state. Crying would just plug her nostrils, and she knew where that would lead. Instead of panicking, she needed a clear head. *What did she know so far?*

She knew her abductor, or so she'd thought. He hadn't seemed like a threat, in fact, the complete opposite. He seemed charming, mild-mannered, and had even offered helpful suggestions.

But was Russell Chase really her abductor? Or, had someone else—Brandon Statler or some other person—followed them to the warehouse, afraid they'd find something incriminating?

She tried to remember what had happened, but her memory was foggy.

Whoever it was, *why go to this extreme?*

Someone felt so threatened that he'd kidnapped her to shut down her prying into the past, but it seemed over the top. This was a rape case, most likely, and yes, it was serious. He could be prosecuted for that, but what was the evidence? Hayley had been cremated, so there wasn't any DNA evidence that would point to Chase, or Statler, or anyone else.

Wait. Chase had asked her about Mrs. S at the warehouse and why she was going to see her.

And she'd told him about Hayley's journal. *Hayley's journal.* Now, finally, she understood the importance of it. It was evidence. And if she found the journal, it would almost certainly have references to the perpetrator, rapist, or otherwise. Someone had approached the storage facility, and that person may have overheard their conversation, deciding to act against her, and perhaps, against Russell Chase.

What had she written there, in the last two weeks of her life? What private agony had she documented, rather than sharing it with her best friend? A journal could be a refuge, a place to inscribe secrets, hopes, dreams, and thoughts of life and death. Maybe a wish for death because life had become untenable.

And she'd been on her way to find it, to read it when someone stopped her. Whoever he was, he knew about the journal, so he'd come up with an abduction scenario to stop her, and there was no worse scenario.

Maybe it wasn't too late. Maybe Adam had somehow picked up on her references about Mrs. Strickland and gone to see her. Maybe he was there now, and they'd found the journal. Maybe in those scribbled pages was the evidence leading to her abductor.

But she knew that was a terribly long shot. Even if they found the journal, how would Adam know she was on her way to a remote location, trapped inside a moving vehicle?

She scanned the dark interior of the vehicle trunk, searching for the emergency release pull that all newer model cars were required to have now. Their specific purpose to help someone in her exact situation escape or to help those who inadvertently locked themselves in get back out.

It was no use. She couldn't find it, and even if she did, how would she get it with her hands bound so tightly?

Maybe she could kick out a taillight. Hadn't she read somewhere about that, in a story about someone who'd been trapped in a trunk, had kicked out a taillight and stuck out a hand, alerting another driver to contact the police?

Or was that one of those urban myths?

She wriggled around, trying desperately to find the location of a taillight, but it was so dark, and she was so constricted that she finally stopped, exhausted with the effort.

There would be other opportunities to escape. He couldn't drive forever. He'd have to stop, whether to gas up the vehicle or because they'd arrived at their destination. *But what kind of destination? Where does someone take a gagged and bound woman to unload her from a vehicle?*

To dump a body, of course. Remote locations were ideal for concealing bodies.

She shook inside.

CHAPTER THIRTY-SIX

Detective Adam Porter sat at his computer again, searching online, vibrating anxiously. *Was he wasting valuable time doing this?* He still hadn't heard from Roxanne. Who knew where she was or what was happening? She might be perfectly fine, but then again...he had no idea, and he couldn't take the chance.

First, he called the school and quickly found out Chase wasn't there. He'd taken a PTO day. No surprise there. He asked a few more questions and hung up, puzzled. Chase had been at the school, teaching every day, for the past few weeks. That meant he couldn't have taken Daisy on a drama trip at the time she'd disappeared. If she'd actually gone on a drama excursion, which was looking very doubtful.

He found another reference he needed, and a few minutes later, he rang the doorbell, holding his badge up to the video monitoring lens. After a long moment passed, a woman answered, looking puzzled. She carried a toddler on her hip and looked exhausted.

The sounds of television and child laughter in another room wafted through the door. *A family guy.* That was unexpected.

Doing his best to appear calm, he introduced himself. Most people were leery of law enforcement, and an unexpected visit to their home could be frightening. Most went to the worst-case scenario, and he needed her to be open and willing, not feel threatened.

Unfortunately, he felt he'd have to manipulate her to get her to invite him in and get the answers he needed.

"Is your husband Russell Chase, and does he work as a drama teacher at the high school?"

"Yes, he is, and he does. What is this about?" She'd put the toddler on the floor. The little girl chewed on a plastic toy she'd picked up, drooling a bit, and stared at Adam with huge blue eyes.

"A...student has gone missing," he improvised. "And we need to speak with him as soon as possible because we think he can help us find her. We're canvassing all the teachers. He's not at the school, so we need your help locating him."

"That's impossible. He left the house this morning for the school. There's been some mistake." But her eyes were wide, her breathing a bit shallow. She was afraid, uncertain, and now, suddenly vulnerable in a way no one likes to find themselves.

The scariest things in life always come out of the blue at the least expected times.

"Ma'am, we know for a fact he's not working today. He used PTO. When he takes time off, where does he usually go?"

"He doesn't go anywhere without me and the kids." But she licked her lips and touched her face. The tells would probably go unnoticed by most, but not a seasoned cop.

"What about his drama trips?" He took a stab in the dark.

"Sometimes, he takes his students on trips to see regional professional theater performances. He's a drama coach in his spare time."

Russell Chase had the means to move around the state, protected by the legitimate cover of extra-curricular trips. And while there, after the students left, what did he do? Find or meet with girls he'd lured prior to the trips, maybe using the internet, maybe other ways?

Daisy had told her mother she was on a drama trip, but the timing was off. Chase hadn't been out of town. If he had her, if he'd abducted her, he'd taken her somewhere nearby. "Besides those trips, where else does he go when he has time off?"

Now she looked defensive, closed. "Nowhere, like I said. If there's any other travel, we do it together as a family."

But her eyes darted unconsciously to the desk along the wall nearby. Envelopes, some with 'Past-Due' stamped in big red letters, lay strewn across the top, some torn open, some not. An open checkbook lay in the stack.

He leaned toward her just a bit, enough to convey urgency. Hopefully not so much that it frightened her into clamming up. "I think he has someplace he does go without you, somewhere you don't enjoy going or don't want to bring the kids."

"The kids and I don't like it. It's rather… rustic. He goes there to write. He's a playwright," she finished, lifting her chin.

"Where is it?"

"It's nothing. It's a broken-down piece of property his parents left him, out in the country. I don't even know the address. But he's not there. He always tells me when he's going there." But she swallowed nervously as her eyes darted to the desk again.

"I think you do know the address. You pay the bills. There must be utility bills for the property." He stood and moved toward the desk, and she sprang up, trying to get there before Adam.

He picked up an envelope with a utility company address and turned to her.

She snatched it out of his hand, but at his look, quickly caved.

Two minutes later, he walked out with an address and with the fervent hope that he'd get there in time. It was over an hour away.

As he drove away, Adam thought about Chase's wife, about her blind trust, and the shattered look on her face. Deep down, she'd known something, knew instinctively that this day would eventually come. The day of no longer having the luxury of denial. Of facing who her husband really was, who she'd really married.

It's impossible, really, that a wife wouldn't know, wouldn't suspect something about a sociopathic husband. We're hard-wired for connection, and sociopaths are incapable of real connection. They are cold and calculating. Unless his wife kept herself drunk or high all the time, she'd sense Chase's true nature.

And now, it was getting clearer. He was the charming drama coach who preyed on girls with big dreams. He was the common element between whatever had happened to Hayley, whatever had happened to all those girls, and whatever might have happened, or was still happening, to Daisy.

He pressed harder on the gas.

He watched from down the street, shaking with rage. That meddling cop had gone to his house, spoken to his wife! What had she told him? Surely, there wasn't anything. She didn't know anything.

She'd never known anything.

When he'd met her, she was working as a waitress, nineteen, gorgeous, and looked thirteen. *Perfect.* She'd been completely impressionable, so in awe of him, her senior by more than fifteen years. The plan had been to enjoy her for a few months, then move on.

But pregnancy and the unpleasant confrontation one day by her father and older brother had squashed that. Country hicks, but persuasive, he'd give them that.

After marrying her, he'd realized the advantages of having a wife and children as cover. After all, up until that point, he'd been the only single teacher his age. He spent a lot of time with his drama students, and maybe some people had thought it was odd. Overnight, he'd become the handsome, charismatic teacher with the pretty wife and kids. Became someone who fit in with the rest of the faculty, someone who was far above any kind of suspicion.

Then, his dad had died, leaving the property to him. It was perfect, easy to get to. It enabled him to do what he did more often and closer to home. *Going there to write, for entire weekends, and long stretches of summer break.*

She'd swallowed all his stories easily. She was a guppy. He fed her with a nice home, enough income, so she didn't have to work, and his sperm so she could continue to reproduce. She responded by providing him with home-cooked meals, not that he valued that especially, and sex, not that he found her all that enticing.

Best of all, she met him with silence at his long absences, no questions.

But what had she said or done, now?

He watched as the cop left the house and drove away, his hands clenched. Then, he pulled in front of his home, leaving his cargo in the trunk for now.

Moments later, he confronted her. She pleaded with the terrifying stranger who she'd mistaken for a loving husband. Swore she hadn't told the cop anything. Only revealing the betrayal after he threatened her. He made her swear on her life and the life of her children that she would say nothing to no one, go along with his plans. He promised terrible things if she didn't. Taking custody of her children. The freedom to do whatever he wanted with them, including moving away. Or worse. He let that primal fear sink in.

He had all the resources, control of their money. What a fool she'd been, turning over her life that way. Subjugating herself, never asking questions, just content with more babies and a life of denial. Now she regretted letting him isolate her from her family. Allowing herself to be set up for this day, for the humiliation and pain.

But she had no choice at this moment except to comply. She promised to do what he instructed her to do, and she knew she would.

Roxanne tried to track time, but since she had no idea how long she'd been trussed up, it was impossible. At one point, they'd stopped, and she heard the unmistakable sounds of the driver's door opening and closing. *What was he doing? Buying a pack of cigarettes? Getting gas?* How bizarre to stop and shop during an abduction.

But this was her chance. She tried to scream, but only a faint mumble emerged through the duct tape. She struggled mightily, but all she was able to accomplish was tiring herself and raising her heart rate. Minutes or hours later, impossible to tell, she heard the door opening and closing again, followed by the movement of the vehicle.

She lay in defeat, unable to stop the swirl of fear and striving to think of a way to escape. If he stopped once, he might again. His arrogance might override caution, as he figured she had no chance to fight or free herself. That lack of caution could work against him and in her favor.

She drifted with the sway of the vehicle and the rhythmic lull of the tires on pavement. At first, it sounded like they were on a freeway. She could hear the other cars on the road with them. Later, it became quieter. They no longer traveled the freeway system. Country roads, most likely, heading into the middle of nowhere. *Great.*

She did her best to formulate a strategy while time drifted.

The vehicle slowed, and she felt her body sling around as it turned, then drove straight, but now with considerable ups and downs. A bumpier road, gravel, off of the main road. After what seemed like an eternity, the vehicle stopped, and she registered the sounds of the door opening, then closing, and footsteps approaching the back. She took several deep breaths then willed herself into stillness.

The trunk opened, and strong arms gripped beneath her armpits, trying to drag her out of the vehicle. Though it hurt like hell, she made her body a dead weight. Her abductor grunted and mumbled something, then swore as the handcuffs caught on the trunk latch.

He turned her around and took off the cuffs. *Good.* He picked her up and began walking, and she kept her limbs loose and floppy, along with her head. She tried to quell the rising fear of injury. He wasn't exactly careful.

Soon, her body was lowered, and then there was contact with a hard surface. Footsteps receded. She lay still for a moment, then slit open her eyes. It was a small, rustic room, probably the living room of a cabin. Footsteps approached again, and she lay still, struggling to still her breath, which had accelerated with the anxiety.

The sudden slap against the side of her face made her teeth rattle, and her eyes flew open instinctively.

"I figured you were faking it. Time to wake up." He hauled her into a sitting position. "Be good and I'll let you live another hour. Try to escape and, well, you won't see those adorable little girls ever again."

"Don't you dare mention my daughters! You can do whatever you like to me, but they are off limits!" The dragon roared, and she didn't really care what happened to her.

He pulled her up to her feet and frog-marched her into another room, a room like none she'd ever seen before. No furniture except for a mattress on the floor, dust bunnies scattered. He pushed her onto the bed, and she tried to prepare herself mentally for the inevitable.

"Oh, don't worry," he said, his lips curling cruelly. "I'm not going to rape you. You're too old." He rapidly sorted through her handbag, pulling out items, and finally, her cell.

She tried to distract him. "Just don't destroy my cell, okay?"

"Like you'll need it again," he said, scrolling through her texts. *Why hadn't she password or fingerprint protected her phone?* It was fairly new, and she'd never taken the time.

"What have we here? Looks like that Dudley Do-right old high school pal of yours thinks he's onto something about Hayley." A nasty smile played on his lips. He slid her phone into his back pocket. Then he spoke the words that planted a deep dread in her stomach. "But don't worry. He's headed to the storage unit, and so am I."

He stopped at the door, looking her over. "Remember, if you try to escape, that older daughter of yours is mine. She is a tasty morsel, for sure." He turned and left as she screamed at him with impotent rage. She heard him lock the door. Then, silence.

And she thought about Russell Chase, Hayley's drama teacher and mentor, how much contact he'd had with her friend.

CHAPTER THIRTY-SEVEN

Adam's cell rang. It was Russell Chase's wife. He answered and listened, then thanked her. He changed directions and drove toward a warehouse district. She'd informed him that there was one other place her husband frequently visited. It was far closer than the other address, so he headed there first.

A short time later, he found the unit wide open but with no cars or people in sight. He approached carefully, with his service weapon drawn, but held loosely at his side for now.

Had something happened here? Was Roxanne inside? Was he too late?

He moved to the side and slipped into the opening, quickly scanning the dark interior, weapon raised. Slowly he lowered it as he realized there was no one there, only him.

As his eyes adjusted to the low light, he stood and stared at the stacked boxes, some open, most not. He pulled out some of the detritus of old school plays, wondering why this unit was significant to Chase. Even more concerning, why had his wife thought it was important enough to tell Adam about it? *And why now?*

A chill rolled down his spine as he replayed her voice on the phone a few minutes ago. *Had she sounded frightened?*

Was this a game to lure him away from going to the other property, the one that sat far out in the country away from prying eyes?

Or was Chase's wife genuinely trying to help him, maybe now that she'd realized there might be a huge problem with her husband? He couldn't tell if she was his stooge, just a young, hopelessly naïve woman. Or was she his accomplice? Or perhaps she just wanted to save her husband. Was she savvy enough to see the direction all of this was headed, with Chase in the sights of law enforcement and his sick games about to end forever?

Adam stood indecisively, trying to work out the confusing mix of what he felt, what he'd heard on the phone, and what his instincts were telling him now.

He felt the presence of someone else as he spun around.

It wasn't his preferred way to roll, but he couldn't let that cop destroy his life. His wife, groveling pitifully, had quickly agreed to call the detective and lure him here to the storage unit, which he'd strategically left open.

He crept carefully along the side of the building, moving steadily toward the doorway of the storage unit, out of sight for now.

One of the reasons he'd chosen this unit was its proximity to the very back of the property, which was next to an empty field. It was isolated and quiet. He paid the lease annually, well in advance, so there would never be a reason for management to open or look in his unit.

Not that he actually conducted his *relationships* here. But he did keep certain items on hand, which he periodically spent time with.

No one was ever around, except for earlier today. Just before he'd incapacitated Roxanne, a maintenance person had strolled nearby, footsteps crunching loudly on the gravel, telegraphing his presence. But that unexpected surprise had actually worked in his favor. Her eyes had gone to the sound outside the unit and not to him. She wasn't prepared when he knocked her out. Luck had been on his side again because the maintenance man had been focused on his phone and never looked up as he walked by. Never saw Chase as he rolled down the door of the unit and waited until he was gone.

He smiled at the thought of how so many people presented themselves as easy prey today, always buried in a screen, never dialed into situational awareness. Everyone convinced of their invulnerability due to thousands of likes on social media. Though his profile of the right girl hadn't changed from a physical appearance standpoint, he'd refined his criteria to focus on the social media-obsessed, as those were the most naïve, the easiest to groom, and the easiest to lure. *Piece of cake.*

Lately, he'd been restless. It had been only a few weeks since the last girl, the one before his current amor. He tried not to think about the shrinking timelines between relationships, as he liked to fondly think of them. But he'd been grooming a new girl recently. He felt a small thrill. First, though, he'd have to take care of the girl whose charms had fallen away, replaced by reticence, a wan and pale expression, too many tears, and too much passivity.

If only this Dudley Do-Right hadn't gotten into the middle of things. But he had, and now, things were about to get messier. Ultimately, it would only be a small hitch in his plans, but it had to be done. He shrugged at the thought.

He'd taken off his shoes, and yes, the gravel hurt, but he was getting closer and still hadn't made a sound. He took one painful step, paused, then took another.

He was almost at the endpoint of the side of the building and could sense the yawning opening just ahead, around the corner. He paused, getting ready.

He swung rapidly around the corner and into the opening, raising his weapon of choice, a Glock 9mm handgun, normally kept at his cabin in the country.

Just as the detective turned, he pumped two rounds directly into the center of his body and watched with satisfaction as he fell. He stood still for a moment, allowing a small smile to play on his face, his heart rate quickly decelerating.

After making sure no one had heard or responded to the reverberating sounds of the gunshots, he pulled down the storage unit door and padlocked it from the outside. He could deal with that mess later.

It was time to take care of the other meddler, Roxanne. And then, the sad, pitiful girl he'd thought would be so much fun.

The room, and the house, had fallen silent. He was gone, but her thoughts spun about where she might be, where he was going, and what he might do. *Annie, Rose*...she had to get to them, or at least warn Henry.

She prayed for Adam's safety, her mind spinning on the possibilities. Had he allowed himself to be lured to the storage center? Was he carrying his service weapon, and would he be ready for Chase?

If only she hadn't been so suspicious of Adam, pushing him aside to pursue her own theories, setting off on her own so-called investigation. If she'd included him, maybe things would have been different.

If only she'd seen the reality of Russell Chase, his place in Hayley's life, the uncharacteristic lessening of her friend's interest in drama in the last couple of weeks of her life. If she'd paid attention back then, she could have done something, and her friend would be alive today.

If she'd thought of others more and of herself less, these things wouldn't have happened. She wouldn't be here now, and Adam would be safe. Her daughters wouldn't be threatened.

She looked around the barren room desperately. She searched every square inch, but there was no other way out. The room had only one exit, the double-bolted door, which appeared to be solid core.

ABOUT ROXANNE

There was no egress to a washroom or anywhere else. The ceiling was solid. Had it been a dropped ceiling to an attic, perhaps.

The only dingy window was reinforced with wire mesh, and there was nothing she could use to hit it, to try to break it. Plus, it had iron bars covering it on the outside.

She pounded on the door, knowing it was no use. Silence descended as slow tears traced her cheeks. She sat on the mattress because there was nothing else to do. Her throat was unbelievably dry, and she tried to swallow.

Her mind wandered.

What was Henry doing with the girls? Were they home? Home. It once was hers, too, a place where she'd felt safe and loved when she'd allowed herself to feel. It should have been her sanctuary, the place she couldn't wait to get to at the end of the day.

But she'd rarely rushed home with anticipation. She flashed to their family room, on their girls—watching television, giggling, or arguing briefly over some perceived injury, perhaps a toy misappropriated, or a room transgressed. Always blown over quickly, thanks to Annie's prescient way of dealing with her sister prior to any significant eruption.

To Henry patiently preparing dinner while refereeing. Why hadn't that been enough? She thought of her kids.

Rose—so sweet still, the way she followed her big sister around, always trying to gain her attention. Her flyaway gold curls and the way she brushed them aside with her plump, tiny hands. The way she bent with concentration over her artwork and the pride with which she displayed it afterward.

Annie—so bright, so complex, and so out of her reach. Already pushing away from her mother, the way Roxanne had pushed away from her own mother early, in her pre-teen years. Gone was the look of love and adoration Annie had held for her mom when she was little. Slipping away was the bond that Roxanne had taken for granted. The fantasies of shopping, lunches, and settling her into the dorm her first semester of college, with laughter and fond reminiscences, a little motherly advice given and accepted—not likely.

Lately, her vision of a sweet relationship had been replaced by the perpetual expression of doubt with which Annie regarded her mother, coupled with emotional distance. Her precocious older daughter seemed almost to read her mind, to understand things a child her age shouldn't even be aware of. *What are we going to do about mom?*

Indeed, what about her, what about Roxanne?

A deep yearning rolled up from her chest. She ached inside with longing, with wanting so badly, so desperately.

But she longed not for Henry. Or for Annie, or Rose.

No, the yearning was for her only true relationship, the one she'd given up everything for. The longing that clutched her now was for gin. For that ice-cold slide in her throat that led to peace and oblivion.

No, she didn't ache to return to her husband and daughters. Why yearn for something she so clearly and deeply didn't deserve? They weren't really hers to claim. She'd blown that immeasurably.

It served her right that Henry was with Jessica. Anger toward them, the pointing finger of blame, now aimed square at herself. Gin now the only hope for relief.

When you feel yourself slipping, think of the one thing you want, more than anything, that you will lose if you take that drink.

Dr. Jill, her words echoing in her mind. She had no idea how undeserving Roxanne was. How little she'd done to endear herself to her own family, how terribly messed up she was. She was so messed up; even her flaws had blemishes on them. She grinned wryly at that thought.

It's a day in your life…when you promise yourself you won't drink…but you do, anyway. And it's not just one day…it's every day.

The ache spread without restraint, and she bent over, clutching her stomach, struggling for breath. The ragged breaths she struggled to pull in stretched endlessly, punctuated by darkness that threatened to close in.

She curled up on the filthy mattress. Time passed, her mind in a dark fog.

Then, out of the dredges of her memory came something else, something she'd heard once, maybe during church, on a rare occasion when she'd actually paid attention, or perhaps read in a book. How did it go?

When you feel like you aren't worthy of love, try loving someone else instead.

Could she do that? Could she love her husband again, love her daughters by devoting her time and attention?

Could she win Henry back, or maybe, let him go and wish him well?

The vision of ice-cold gin receded. At least for now. The blanket of pain over her chest eased a bit, but the grief remained.

Roxanne's head dipped as tears dripped onto the dirty mattress.

She spotted something white, stuck between the mattress and the wall. She scrambled to pull it out. A note. She held the tattered piece of paper in her hand, and her heart fell away as she read the scrawl of a terrified girl who'd known she was going to die. It was signed with large, loopy letters. Daisy. It held information about her captor, information that only a victim could reveal. And it had a date, just a few days back.

What kind of a monster had held Daisy here? What had he done to her? And to whom else? Dear God, was she in the very room where he'd done terrible things to this girl, maybe even murdered her?

If he'd done to Daisy what she'd written, what had he done to Hayley all those years ago? How many times, how many subsequent victims? She shuddered, feeling a cold wave wash over her entire body.

Something terrible had happened to Daisy. She couldn't do anything about that.

She hadn't been able to save Hayley.

Her situation was hopeless. An ache spread without restraint, and she bent over, clutching her stomach, struggling for breath. The ragged breaths she struggled to pull in stretched endlessly, punctuated by the darkness that threatened to close in. One sob escaped, then another, and soon, she was wailing.

Eventually, the sobs turned to dry heaves and finally faded. She curled up on the filthy mattress, left with only the sound of her sniffling. Time passed, her mind a dark fog.

Then, she heard the faint sounds of scratching coming from the room next to hers.

Was that a whisper?

She jumped up and ran to the wall, putting her hands on it, her ear against it. "Hello?" she shouted. "Is someone there? *Daisy, is that you?*"

And with a combination of relief and horror, she heard the hoarse whispers of a desperate girl, heard her crying, begging for help.

CHAPTER THIRTY-EIGHT

The brief whispers on the other side of the wall had fallen away. "Can you talk louder?" she pleaded. "He's gone. He can't hear you."

She waited while the silence stretched. "Daisy? If that's your name, knock once on the wall." *One knock*. Daisy must be having trouble speaking, her throat dry, perhaps, from dehydration. Predators didn't exactly attend to the wellbeing of their victims, didn't lavish them with delicious meals and an abundance of water.

Daisy might not be able to talk, but Roxanne could speak. "If you can hear my words clearly, knock once again for yes." *Yes*. "Daisy? Knock once for how many nights you think you've been here?" *One, two, three*. "Are you okay? I mean, knock once for yes if you're not severely injured, if you think you might be able to walk out of here. Because I'm going to get us out of here." *Yes*.

Daisy was alive; she wasn't incapacitated. This teenage girl had no doubt been abducted or lured here. She'd been here for a while, her parents devasted by the fear of what might be happening to her. *What if it were Annie?* She shuddered.

Roxanne got up again, swept every square inch of the room, examined the door all over again. Stood still, thinking. Breaking out wasn't possible. But there had to be another way.

Then, her eyes fell on her handbag, contents strewn. Her mind worked frantically on the problem of getting herself, or at least, getting Daisy out of here. Alive.

There might be a way, but it was risky, a long shot. A plan slowly unfurled. It was sketchy, full of risks, and unlikely to work. But it was the only plan she had. She only needed a little time to set things up.

Then, her breath caught as she heard the unmistakable sounds of someone entering the house. She was out of time.

The key turned in the two deadbolts, and the door swung open. He looked slightly flushed. He spied her in the corner and moved in, closing the door behind him. "Good girl," he said. "Now that Dudley is no more, you and I have some things to sort out."

Her heart sank, but she held her expression neutral. "What did you do?" She stayed where she was across the room, trying to appear non-threatening.

She could see him now, the chameleon who'd pretended to be a charming high school teacher, someone who helped his students learn and grow. The predator slithered behind his outward appearance, and she knew he was dangerous, more so now than ever. After all, he'd been spotted by at least one adult. That meant the shelf life of his behind-the-scenes activities had been shortened. He was smart enough to sense that and to be ready for whatever he'd planned for his final act in a play that might include her. Or worse, Daisy.

She had to keep him engaged for as long as possible while she looked for a way out. His energy was that of a tightly coiled spring, ready to go off at any moment, so her first priority had to be avoiding any kind of emotional explosion.

"Why do you care? He's out of the way, with two bullets in the heart, and now, there's only you to deal with. Unless—" he paused, regarding her closely. "What exactly happened to Hayley's journal?" He advanced on her. "You will tell me, you know. It's just a question of how much it hurts before you do."

"I don't even know if there is a journal. It was just a theory." She shrugged noncommittedly, deliberately slumping her shoulders and looking down dejectedly. "But people are going to miss me and are tracking me right now," she tried. She thought of Adam. *Had she led this monster to the one person who had tried to help her? Was he even still alive?*

"Right!" He cackled. "You didn't miss your calling, that's for sure. What a pitiful performance. Your phone is far from here, pinging cell towers miles away. And by the time anyone finds it, I'll be long gone, while you? Well, let's just say there won't be anything to find." He shrugged his shoulders theatrically, holding his palms up as if to say, *look, nothing here.* "Anyway, Mrs. Strickland will be easy to take care of later if need be."

Oh, God. Had she endangered Mrs. S.? *Keep him talking.* "How did you know about Adam, anyway?"

"You never saw me, sitting right next to your booth, did you? It's amazing what a few simple touches can do, a mustache, a hat, glasses, and different posture." He looked pleased with himself.

"What about Hayley?" She had to buy herself more time. "What did you do to her? I know you were the person who picked her up after the party," she said, hoping that was true.

He paced the room, talking and gesturing. "She was walking alone at night. What was I supposed to do? I'm a teacher, after all, and she was being stupid. Sure, I picked her up. We went back to my place. And why not? We had so much in common. It was wonderful, what we shared." He stopped and glared at Roxanne as if daring her to contradict his sick version of the truth.

Her stomach roiled as she searched for the right words. "You shared something. Something special." It made her sick to say the words, but she forced them out.

"Yes, we did. And it would have all been okay if she'd just calmed down. Her parents were gone, and we were reading lines together. It was perfect." His eyes gazed into the distance as he talked, drawn into his own twisted memories, those he'd crafted out of the monstrous reality of what he'd actually done. He talked in snippets, enough to tell her what had really happened to Hayley, though he seemed to be reliving every detail.

CHAPTER THIRTY-NINE

1999

She opened the front door cautiously and let him in. A shaft of sunlight lit her hair and set off a sparkle in her eyes. She was beautiful, of course, but that was easy to find. She had charisma, a rare commodity. And talent. She had a good, possibly great, career ahead of her, in theater and elsewhere. With him by her side, the sky was the limit.

She hesitated, informing him her parents were out of town and a friend might be coming over later. It took a little gentle manipulation, but soon they made their way to her room. They began reading out loud.

He watched her carefully as she read, noting her expressions, so poignant, so perfectly mirroring the tone and depth of the story. It was his first play, inspired by Hayley herself, written feverishly late at night. Not finished, of course. He didn't need all of it written at this point, only the critical parts for today.

She wouldn't know and didn't need to know that piece of information. The secrecy of the writing, the anticipation of Hayley, all of it created a crescendo of pleasure.

Even better to his psyche was the memory of her from the first time. How she'd let him use her body however he'd wanted, more than once. Her doll-like features in repose, her wonderment later. She'd no doubt re-lived it as he had since then. But maybe not, since she'd seemed confused afterward, and that had suited his purposes then.

The evening stretched before him, and he felt full, almost bursting from the promises of pleasure, the excitement building, overpowering him with anticipation. He'd never taken things this far before, but he'd fantasized about it many times.

By now, she'd no doubt recalled what had happened that night. Remembered his role, as evidenced by the invitation to her bedroom today, he assured himself. She wouldn't have let him into the house unless she was ready for him again. It had been an amazing experience, their first time. He indulged in the memories briefly.

While she read her lines from the play he'd written, he remembered her waking up the next morning, his anticipation of more passion. Then, the confusion, the bewilderment, his desire flattened by the slow realization that she didn't remember what had transpired the night before. That she wanted only to leave. He'd sensed it wasn't the time to re-enact their erotic acts.

Instead, he'd brought her water and driven her home, or, more precisely, to a friend's home, though she wouldn't tell him whose. A tiny trickle of concern had wormed its way into his belly that morning over that.

That concern washed over him again as he sat on her bed, but he brushed it aside. If she'd talked to a friend, after all, things would be very different for him now. The thought of being exposed to those who wouldn't understand gave him a trill of fear which only enhanced the current moment.

He drank in the sight of her. She held herself in the way he most loved, an enchanting combination of innocent girlhood and blossoming womanhood. He reveled in her high-toned voice, pouring over him like honey.

They read his brilliant fragment of a play, the first of many. Would he ever finish this one and release it? Maybe...but it might be too risky. No problem, though, because he had endless creativity. It wouldn't be long before his big break, no matter what happened with this one. And this one had brought him to these moments with her.

INT. LOCATION #1 - NIGHT

Caroline sits on the bed in her room, her eyes gazing into a non-existent distance, in a state of rapture, cocking her head to listen

GHOST BILLY

I miss you so much. I wish I could hold you again, kiss you. I wish we were heading off to college together. But I know you are ready, ready to join me here. It's not so bad, Caroline, really not so bad. In fact, it's good, and it will be so much better when you're here with me. And we will be together, forever.

CAROLINE

This night, this perfect night is my farewell. The stars are shining for me and for my life. And for you, Billy, and your too-short life. But I will be with you soon, and that is the most I can hope for. No one, not my parents, not my friends, or my teachers, can possibly understand how much we love each other. There will never be anyone else for me again, never.

She stands, walks over, and places the chair by the closet door.

GHOST BILLY

Before you make the transition, I want to feel you in my arms. You may not feel me, but I can touch you.

She approaches the bed where ghost Billy sits. He reaches up and pulls her onto the bed, taking out a silken cord.

She seemed a bit uncomfortable but surrendered to his touch as he pulled her onto the bed. He kissed her passionately as he slipped the rope around her neck. She started to protest, but he assured her it was part of the play. He tightened it, and she gasped and began to struggle. He tried to continue the kiss, but she moved her lips away, thrashing.

This wasn't going at all as planned, and anger rose, coloring his perception. How were they supposed to share this passionate moment, the heightened pleasure of sex with the restriction of oxygen? He'd studied it at length, knew exactly how it was supposed to go. But this was his first attempt at it. He loosened the cord, anticipating a return to submission, and Hayley began gasping.

"What are you doing? You're hurting me! Let me go, get this off of me!" She tried to pull the cord off, but he saw his error. She wasn't going to cooperate as easily as he'd thought. She needed more persuasion. He pulled the rope tight again while holding her hands. After a few minutes of struggle, she lay still, skin flushed, eyes closed. He checked her pulse. Still strong. Perfect.

ABOUT ROXANNE

This wasn't so different from the first time, he reflected. It should have been with her fully awake, her blue eyes fixed on him in rapture. But he had a vivid imagination, and so he began removing her clothes as he pictured her begging him to do so. He prepared for their lovemaking, but suddenly, she began to awaken.

She struggled again and fought him. "What are you doing? Oh, God, let me go! I remember now. You were the one the night of the party! Stop it!" She shoved at him, but he was too strong for her. Her eyes took on a sheen of fear. "Look, just leave. My parents will be back any minute. I won't tell anyone, I promise. Things can just go back to normal."

This wasn't how it was supposed to be. The rosy romance disappeared, and the anger rose. His pleasure and hers were supposed to be the perfect blend. Now, she'd threatened him.

Despite her words, he knew she'd talk, and that couldn't happen. But maybe it wasn't too late. He pulled the cord tight again, and she fought and struggled, but he was far stronger. This time, she remained still. He quickly dressed himself and her. This could still work out.

Gently, almost reverently, he moved her body to the closet door. After wedging the cord securely over the top of the door, he allowed her body to drop, pulling the cord impossibly tight, so much that anyone who wasn't already dead would be asphyxiated. She revived momentarily and struggled faintly again, but he pushed her shoulders downward. After a few minutes, she was permanently still. He checked her breathing and pulse repeatedly, making sure.

Unfortunately, her beauty had been destroyed. But she'd brought it on herself. They could have been great together, this teenage beauty and he, her mentor.

He spent time in the house wiping down all the surfaces he might have touched, removing the manuscripts, and finally, exiting the back of the house just in case. He felt high, intoxicated. He'd easily brushed aside any regret. He couldn't wait to get back to writing.

CHAPTER FORTY

Roxanne tried to process the bizarre story of Chase believing he had some sort of romance going on with Hayley all those years ago. A *romance* that had ended in her death. Her *murder*. Which he somehow brushed off and blamed on Hayley.

She felt nauseated, sickened unimaginably as she considered the truth of her friend's death. *Not suicide. Not self-inflicted.*

Murder perpetrated by a trusted authority figure. The killer, currently lost in his fantasies at the moment, perhaps thinking of how he'd soon dispatch Roxanne and poor Daisy in a similar fashion.

Chase's eyes were dilated as he gazed into the psychotic past, a world tilted to fulfill his sick fantasies, untethered to the care and warmth of real relationships. She saw with crystal clarity the complete absence of humanity, how he was completely devoid of compassion.

She stared at the narcissistic beast in front of her, and she wondered if she beheld a reflection of herself. Not the psychotic murder part, but the ego-centrism. *How selfish had she been, long ago with Hayley, and now?* How many of her waking hours were consumed with self-pity and self-absorption, as she sought, lived for, and anticipated the next drowning of herself in gin.

How many of her conversations with colleagues, partners, and her own husband, had been laced with deflection, lies, and blame of others, of anyone but herself.

Had she ever taken responsibility for her own behavior?

For her...she could say it to herself now...*addiction*.

She'd failed Hayley, and now, herself. Her killer would not fail. Adam was dead, his life cut short because of her carelessness, and now, *no one* was coming to save her. Just as Dr. Derek had said to her before she set out on this impossible quest.

"Hayley wasn't your only...your last. Was she?"

His eyes jerked back to hers. He'd seemed lost in his fantasies, mumbling something about the other girls, and she sensed who they had been. Girls like Daisy, who'd never return home, and whose families waited endlessly for the phone call or the knock at the door that would someday confirm their worst fears.

No one should die with their family never knowing what really happened to them.

Hayley's mom should finally know peace—that her daughter hadn't committed suicide because she'd somehow let her down. She deserved to be absolved of the guilt and the belief that despite her devotion as a mom, she'd missed the signs of a suicidal depression. She should have that small shred of solace about her daughter.

And in between Hayley and Daisy, there had been others. It made no sense that he'd systematically lured and killed Hayley, then abducted Daisy, and been law-abiding in between. Or, lured them here and later, let them go. No, she'd seen enough true crime to know that she now faced a serial killer.

The families of the girls Chase had brought here deserved to know what had happened to their daughters, their sisters, their nieces. The lost girls, as she thought of them now, deserved to have their story told, to have their killer brought to justice.

Though she'd never met them, never even seen their photos, she could almost see their faces like a slideshow in her mind—fresh-faced high school girls, smiling brightly, eyes filled with promise, blond hair flowing. Somehow, she knew they'd all be blond. Just like Hayley.

Something stirred inside, something to do with making a difference. A tiny seedling of purpose. She wasn't done, not yet. Not while she had breath left in her body and a vision of her two girls in her heart.

She thought of the sad, loopy note stuffed deep in her back pocket. Hoped Daisy remained quiet now, on the other side of the wall. It wouldn't do for him to divert his focus from Roxanne and on to the girl who now waited for her to get them both free.

She had to distract him. "What else did you do? You were saying something about the other girls."

He paused, seeming torn between answering her and whatever else it was he'd planned to do to her next, in this house of painful secrets and unimaginable terrors.

"You might as well tell me since I'll never get a chance to repeat it," she said in a louder voice, hoping to dominate his focus. "Let me be your last audience," she said, playing to his theatrical delusions.

He stopped pacing and glared at her, a strange smile crawling. "You're right. You're never getting out of here. The only person who knew you might be here is in a permanent sleep." He struck a pose as if he stood on stage.

And he talked, rambling coherently and incoherently at points. He swung between a braggadocios tone of voice and one of confusion, as though he couldn't quite put his finger on reality.

He'd learned over time how to subdue girls. First, the slow seduction, the flattery, the confirmation, and the inflation of their fantasies of Broadway and Hollywood. He was their coach, an expert voice, a persuasive authority figure. He drew them into his own fantasies, and they became his because there really wasn't any other choice.

For most of them, it was easy to manipulate and terrorize them into submission, for his purposes. The ones he couldn't subdue, who screamed and cried, or who lashed out in anger and threatened to reveal him—those he'd been forced to silence, permanently. Far too quickly, though. It wasn't his fault. It was theirs. They might have gone on with their lives, but they'd blown that chance.

He shook his head at that point as if expressing regret. But he went on, and she realized it wasn't regret for killing them. It was for not getting all the fun he'd wanted with them because he'd been forced to cut short their lives, and thus, the extension of his pleasure.

He hated blood, which she found odd given his pension for death. But apparently, he was a clean-freak, meticulously so. That's why the drugs, and the ropes, were so ideal. Of course, with Adam, he'd been forced to take bold, pre-emptive action. The guy would have shot him, he knew that, and he blithely justified it to Roxanne. *It was his fault for sticking his nose into Chase's affairs, going to his house, daring to speak to his wife.*

But his wife, spoken with contempt, *had come through, had misdirected Adam to the storage facility.* Where he now lay dead of gunshot wounds.

Roxanne absorbed that in silent shock. *His wife.* This creep had a wife. And Adam had gone to see her, been lured to his death by her. *What kind of woman marries a man like that?* She stayed very still, not allowing her face to reflect the revulsion. Instinctively, she knew he'd draw energy and power from her emotions, like a vampire.

A shadow passed the window. *Was it a trick of the light?* A tree limb whipped by a sudden wind burst, casting a momentary shadow?

She kept her eyes glued on Chase. "You killed Hayley and made it look like suicide. She didn't kill herself." It was obvious, but she needed him to keep talking.

"Of course, she didn't kill herself. She didn't have that much spine."

She clenched her fists, wanting desperately to punch him for that comment. "You'll never get away with this. I'm a well-known attorney and a wife and mother. People will look for me. I've left loads of clues about what I was doing here, including notes about you."

His eyes gleamed, and a sinister smile played on his lips. "You have no idea what I'm capable of. I'm in theater. A master showman. I have a hundred ways to disguise myself. I'll be out of here, and thousands of miles away before these hick cops have a clue. I'm pretty much done with this town, anyway. And no one knows you're here."

It was true. It could be months, years even, before she was tracked here. By then, her body would be desiccated.

He was grandiose, convinced of his own invulnerability.

Yet no one was invulnerable. Eventually, something altered the balance of power. And now, she felt the shift as she prayed that it was so.

There it was again, the shadow. Was it a brushing of something against the window or a person interrupting the sun's unrelenting glare on the window? Then she heard a faint sound, and she caught her breath in surprise. It was definitely not a tree. *Or was it?* In her desperation, was she seeing phantoms, hearing things like unlikely rescuers?

She watched the window in her peripheral vision, keeping her eyes fixed on his. Hoping he wouldn't notice, wouldn't turn, wouldn't see what she'd seen, or perhaps imagined.

Hope warred against a growing sense of doom.

He was so mesmerized by his own voice, by the telling of his sordid tale, that he apparently hadn't noticed what she'd heard. Or, more accurately, felt.

There's something so compelling, and so exigent about the presence of other human beings that their complete absence sets off a unique, uncomfortable awareness, tiny alarms, raised hairs.

When Chase had first dropped her onto the floor inside the front door of this house, she'd felt that distinct absence of presence, not just at that moment, but ongoingly. A house was supposed to feel occupied, filled with the rustlings of people. This house felt vacant, and if occupied, it certainly hadn't been filled with joyful voices, with laughter, with the comforting sounds and smells of mealtimes and playtimes.

No, this house had been a house of pain, of sadness, and suffering. And devastating quiet for long periods of time. She'd felt it immediately.

Even after hearing Daisy and their halting communication through the wall, this structure that had once been a home stood eerily silent, as if the evils that had transpired here had snuffed out all vitality.

CHAPTER FORTY-ONE

"Tell me something." She had to stall, even if there was only a small glimmer of hope that help was on the way. "How is it with all your... talents... you can't write a screenplay worth anything? I mean, it's been over twenty years, and you're crawling around like a venomous cockroach preying on young women like that's some kind of accomplishment." The dragon reached out and provoked him.

"Shut up!" His face mottled.

As he spoke, she heard a faint noise in the house. *Was it the telltale pop of a loose floorboard, the auditory trace of a foot treading carefully?*

She believed beyond a shadow of a doubt that there was someone else—someone beside her and Chase, besides Daisy. She prayed they were here for her.

She had one chance, and it wouldn't last long. She briefly eyed the double-bolted, solid core door. Unless the people outside this room had brought a huge battering ram, there was a chance he'd kill her before they got into the room.

She couldn't physically fight him off, at least not for long. But maybe she could slow him down, get out, run away. Or, if she wasn't delusional, run into the arms of help, taking Daisy with her.

Unless, of course, the sounds she thought she heard were anything but help. *What if he had an accomplice?*

The wife. It was a chilling thought, but not enough to stop her from trying.

"It won't hurt, I promise you," he said as he tightened the cord between his two fists. "It can actually be pleasurable, the oxygen cutting off, you know. Some people report seeing beautiful visions, feeling euphoric."

Hayley flashed in her mind, and she wondered how her friend had felt when she'd faced him, understood he'd meant to kill her. *Had she fought him? Had she struggled, tried to escape?*

Was it painful?

Roxanne wasn't going to wait to find out. Her decision made, she reached behind her, sliding her secret weapon out of her back pocket, holding it tight. She'd had it forever, as a fail-safe when walking alone to her vehicle after late nights at the office in downtown Dallas.

Or when walking alone to her vehicle from the bar.

He'd seen it earlier when he ransacked her bag, even handled it. A lipstick tube, small, innocuous. He'd thrown it on the floor with all her other make-up and the random contents of her bag. She'd held her breath at the time, praying he'd missed it, been fooled by its disguise.

She aimed the lipstick at Chase, depressing the hidden button, and sent a stream of oleoresin capsicum—pepper spray—directly into his face.

He screamed in rage and pain but still managed to lunge blindly at her.

She danced out of the way, continuing to spray him while yelling for help.

"Stand back from the door!" shouted a deep voice.

Knowing what was coming, she dove to the side, throwing herself on the mattress, trying to get as far away from the door as possible. One gunshot, then another, and the door burst open. Chase was thrown on the floor, his hands jerked behind his back, and handcuffs applied.

Her throat burned from the back spray as she lay stunned. Strong hands picked her up and carried her out of the room and out of the cabin. They laid her gently on the ground, and she felt grass under her hands. "Are you okay?" asked a familiar voice.

Her eyes still watered, but she was finally able to take in a deep breath. Calmer, she allowed the person to pull her to a standing position, her legs still shaking from adrenaline. "Adam!" she yelled when she realized who her rescuer was. "How did you? I thought...but he said he'd killed you." Uncharacteristically, she burst into tears.

"I'm very much alive, but I wouldn't be if I hadn't had some help. I had a feeling things could get dicey, so I wore my vest." He showed her the bullet-proof vest, with two rounds buried deep, around the location of his heart. "I'm afraid it knocked me out cold, temporarily." He moved his shoulders around a bit, wincing.

"Are you hurt?" she asked, swiping at tears.

"Just sore. But the real obstacle was the padlocked door on the storage unit. If it hadn't been for—"

"Wait, Adam. There's someone else here." She rushed back into the cabin and down the hall to the other deadbolted door. "Daisy! It's okay," she called through the door. "We're getting you out. These people are here to help you."

The tactical team broke down the door, and Roxanne waved them aside. "Let me see her first—she'll feel safer with a woman." She stepped slowly into the room.

Daisy sat on the floor in the corner, her arms wrapped around her knees, and slowly raised her head. Her eyes moved toward the vicinity of Roxanne with a thousand-yard stare.

Roxanne approached slowly, gently, noticing the shake of Daisy's shoulders, the stark fear in her striking blue eyes, eyes that had lost the twinkle of innocence permanently. She lowered herself onto the floor next to Daisy, who whispered something.

"It's okay, Daisy. We're safe now. You're safe."

"Are you an angel?" Daisy asked in childlike wonder.

"Nope, not an angel. Just someone who needed someone to save. And maybe, save herself at the same time. And you know what? I bet there's someone who loves you and is waiting for you."

"My mom," Daisy said. Now looking at Roxanne, tears beginning to slide.

Paramedics took over then, and Roxanne held Daisy's hand the entire time until she was tucked into the rescue vehicle.

"Wait. Are you going to come see me later?" Daisy asked.

And Roxanne promised she would.

Roxanne sat with Adam in his vehicle, suddenly wondering how it was that he sat there with her. "How did you get out of the storage facility if it was padlocked?"

He told her the rest of the story of Russell Chase's wife. How she'd not been so easily cowed by his threats. "Apparently, he underestimated her. When she called 911, she ranted about how he'd threatened to take her kids, and she wasn't ever going to let that happen. Plus, she'd expressed her shock at learning he might have lethal intentions toward a police officer. She said something about how she hadn't grown up on a ranch in West Texas for nothing, and if the police didn't do something, she'd get her two brothers to go after him." Adam smiled grimly. "I think there was also something about a shotgun, but I'm not sure.

"I think, at first, they thought she was a nutcase, but she did a good job of persuading them. She gave them my name and badge number, which I'd given her, and when they couldn't reach me on my cell, they mobilized a SWAT team. I had the address of this property, so after they found me, we got here as fast as we could."

"Thank God," she said fervently. "But Adam, I think there's more going on here than Daisy." She told him about her conversation with Chase, showed him the note Daisy had written. "I think he's been bringing girls here for years, and I think he killed more than one."

That sparked the launch of a full CSI team, including cadaver dogs. But Roxanne wasn't allowed to stay for the rest of the investigation.

Adam pulled her aside before she left. "Roxanne. Mrs. Strickland and I found Hayley's journal. I think it contains evidence, though not as definitive as what I suspect we'll find in this house. You may want to read it later. I hope you can find some peace..." he looked abashed. "I know that sounds terrible."

"No, it doesn't," she assured him. "It's why I came here in the first place, to find out what really happened. Adam, can you copy the pages for me?"

"Sure, I'll do that. And Roxanne. What you did for Hayley. Looking into her death, putting yourself at risk. It was stupid beyond belief. And incredibly brave. Because of you, Daisy is going home to her family. Thank you."

They hugged tightly, and now her chest hitched with something wonderful. *Friendship*.

EPILOGUE

She slipped quietly into the room and found a seat. Ten, maybe twelve or so, people sat in a circle. Some held takeout cups of coffee.

Some were very young. The girl with wiry hair and tattoos on her neck looked around sixteen but was probably a few years older. The guy in the chinos and golf shirt was probably in his forties.

Some were much older. The woman in faded jeans and tee-shirt, who'd probably never seen the inside of a gym, let alone a hair colorist, was probably late fifties, with the ragged look of having lived a difficult life. But she was one of the most alert, eyes shining, and a slight smile playing on her lips.

The judge was back, but she carefully averted her eyes from him, as did he from her.

One other recognizable face sat three seats to her left. Her stomach tightened, and she fought the urge to leave.

Everyone stood and recited the serenity prayer, and she managed not to roll her eyes or huff out a sigh of exasperation. In fact, she allowed herself to take it in.

God grant me the serenity to accept the things I cannot change...

"Roxanne, wait."

Damn. She'd almost made it to her car. She turned slowly and faced Dr. Derek. "Hey."

"Hey. Um, where are you headed in such a hurry? I'm glad you showed up. I thought maybe we'd get a cup of coffee." He gave her a quizzical look. "Unless, of course, you don't have time, and if so, maybe some other time."

"It's okay. You don't have to, you know. I'm fine."

Now he looked really puzzled. "Don't have to...what?"

"You know. Look out for me. Rescue me from myself. I really appreciate all you did for me before, really. But I'm good now. You can check me off your patient list."

Now he smiled knowingly, and that irritated her. She turned and headed to her car, but his voice followed her.

"Okay. I get it. You need to prove something about being strong and independent. But when you're done proving that to yourself, let me know, and we'll get coffee. Just two regular human beings. Uh, two regular addicts."

She turned in time to see his smile and hear his chuckle, see the sparkle in his eyes as he stood there watching her, with that confident stance. Not one sign of pity. She sighed. "Do we have to actually use the *term* addicts all the time? I mean, isn't that just a little bit too much? We know we're addicts, and all the other people in that room know it, but does the rest of the world need to know it? Is there a sign, or a logo, that we're supposed to stick on our shirts or something?"

He laughed, and she loved the sound of it, maybe too much. They made their way to the coffee place a couple of blocks away.

After settling in, he led the conversation. "So, how are you really doing?"

There was no escape with this man. He had her dead to rights and would spot any amount of dissembling instantly. She didn't even try to side-step. "I'm shaky, still, but determined. I've been clean. It's not much, but…"

"It is what it is. It's a start, and one day builds on another." He sipped his coffee, never taking his eyes off of her. "What happened with your friend, the one who died in high school? Did you find out anything new?"

She told him everything, including the horror of what they'd found later, at the house belonging to Russell Chase. The girls, five of them total, now in the process of being identified, if possible. Some of their remains were so far gone it would take some time to work through the various missing persons databases, find likely families, obtain dental records, and so on.

They'd offered him a plea deal—life without parole, and considering this was Texas, he was getting off easy with that. In exchange, he offered them information about a half dozen other girls he'd killed in other places. The grim work of notifying families had already begun, and the media had obsessed about the case, giving the monster his longed-for moment of fame.

Mrs. Strickland, though horrified that her daughter had been abused and murdered by her high school drama teacher, had gained solace knowing that her instincts about her daughter were true. She hadn't committed suicide.

Daisy's mom was endlessly grateful. When Roxanne had gone to see them, Daisy had hugged her until she'd had to push her away gently, protesting laughingly.

"And how are you doing with all of it?"

How was she doing? It was foreign to her, this checking inward, asking herself how she felt. She'd been numb for so long it was like breathing air—unconscious and completely normal. Checking out her own feelings felt bizarre, completely unfamiliar. "I guess I'm ok. I'm still processing it." She made air quotes on the word *processing*, another term that felt alien.

"Processing. That's one way to put it. Knowing you and your history, I wonder if you've lightened any of your guilt load by now."

Her stomach tightened. He'd hit the nail on the head. Guilt was the constant follower in her life, always there, just over her shoulder, waiting to pounce. For any reason. Or for no reason. "Not much. I mean, some. I realize, or let's say I'm playing around with the idea that maybe I wasn't responsible for all of it. But I'm still holding onto the idea that if I'd been paying more attention, I could have pulled it out of her, found out what happened the night of the party."

He nodded. "Right. And if you were God, you would have prevented the whole thing." He lifted an eyebrow.

What to say to that? She pushed her coffee cup around, staring at the tabletop. Finally, she looked up. "I guess I have some more work to do on that."

He watched her closely. "There's something else, isn't there? Something else eating at you."

She sighed, then squared her shoulders and looked him in the eyes. "Yes, there is. It's my family. I had this moment while I was, uh, being held captive..." He winced, but she continued. "I thought about my family, my husband, and my daughters. I realized I don't deserve them, their love."

She held up her hand as his mouth opened. "No, you can't talk me out of this one. I did everything possible to push them away, especially Henry. I treated him terribly. No wonder he and my... former best friend, Jessica, have grown close." Her heart dropped, and so did her shoulders. Pain bloomed in her chest, but not the kind a cardiologist would be concerned about. It was the kind that she'd spent most of her adult life numbing.

He nodded slowly. "I get it. It's the narcissism of the addict. We think of ourselves morning, noon, and night. And the people who love us eventually realize we're not thinking of them. Alcoholics are convinced they are the ones who are suffering. They don't see the suffering they cause. *We*. We don't see it. We act like we're the victims, constantly on the defense. Nothing short of a nuclear weapon can get through those kinds of defenses."

They sat silently. She stared into her coffee cup as if the swirling mocha liquid held the answer to the mess of her life, the secrets to winning back the hearts of those she loved.

"It was too late for me, but it may not be too late for you."

"What?"

"I destroyed my marriage and lost my kids for years. Eventually, I got visitation, and I've managed to get my kids to speak to me. My ex still thinks I'm the devil himself. I don't think I can ever fix that. But maybe, and I don't want to give you false hope, but you might be able to repair some of the damage in your own family."

How could she do that? Henry was barely speaking to her. Rose wanted to see her, but Annie had declined the last two attempts at visitation.

She hadn't yet reached out to Jessica. It was too painful, but maybe someday. Claire, she'd spoken to by phone, but it had felt stilted, not nearly as warm as the friendship they'd shared before.

Before she'd awakened from a coma, gotten herself placed on indefinite leave from her job, and ran off to solve a decades-old personal mystery. "If you have something, tell me. I'm listening."

But he backed up. "Actually, one of the things we try not to do in the twelve-step program is give advice. It's important for addicts to figure out their own solutions. While staying sober."

"Wait. What? I thought that's what sponsors did…give advice. I mean, why bother having one if you can't count on them to help you with things like this."

"Well, I'm not your sponsor."

"Well, I *need* a sponsor."

"Well, I'm not sure I should be your sponsor. We have a… friendship."

"That's right. I mean, maybe it's friendship, or—" She thought about Henry. Did she still love him? Was there any chance he still loved her? Could she get her family back, all of them? Or was she headed for single motherhood?

She thought about Derek's eyes, the way he looked at her, really saw her. How her stomach relaxed when she was near him. His hands, the long fingers, *surgeon's hands*...and for one moment, she imagined those hands around her waist, pulling her in.

But now, he said something about sobriety and relationships. "Roxanne. There's a part of me that wishes for something more with you. But the priorities are clear, especially now, while your sobriety is so new. One, you have to figure out what's right for you and Henry and your girls. Two, you need at least one year of sobriety before even thinking about a new relationship."

Now he fiddled with the coffee cup. "I can't tell you how much I didn't want to say that to you." He raised his eyes to hers, an expression of regret flashing briefly. "But it's the right thing for you." He drained his cup and stood.

"Wait. What about being my sponsor?"

"I'll think about it. It's a big commitment, and it means we'd talk pretty often. Sometimes at odd hours. You're still married, and if you patch things up with your husband, he might not want you having me as your sponsor. A woman would be better. There was someone at the meeting today I can get you to talk to."

She thought about the fifty-something woman. "No, I want you. Don't think about it. Just tell me."

He sighed. "I have a feeling I'm going to regret this. But okay, I'll be your sponsor. For now."

"I'll make sure you don't regret it." She gave him a smile, stood, and they walked out together.

ABOUT ROXANNE

She sat again in the office that resembled a cozy living room. After rudimentary greetings, she did what she'd come to do. "You're fired."

Dr. Jill Rhodes looked momentarily puzzled, then nodded with that enigmatic 'ah-ha' expression.

Before she could speak, Roxanne continued. "It's not what you think. This isn't about your very timely help the last time we met. It was exactly what I needed, but now I need something different. I'm working on getting into marital counseling with Henry, and I'll see that person individually if needed." She shared briefly about her Twelve-Step program.

Dr. Jill spoke. "I'm glad you're working a sobriety program. I think it's the right step to get into counseling with Henry, and I'll add this. The goal should be healing in your relationship, regardless of whether or not you decide to continue the marriage. I don't need to tell you this, but your daughters need two parents who are not at war, who treat each other with basic kindness and respect. It's a tall order sometimes, but it's the one thing that gives them the brightest future."

They spent the rest of the time with the story of solving Hayley's murder, along with the harrowing details of her abduction and rescue. It helped to recount it, and when she was done, Dr. Jill encouraged her to write in a journal to continue to work through all of the old and new emotions about Hayley and all that had happened.

Inwardly, Roxanne rolled her eyes. *Journaling.* Didn't she see the irony of that? They wrapped up, and she looked at the next item on her list.

Early in her career in litigation, going to court had been exciting, the ultimate adventure. Butterflies in the belly, yes, lots of them, but an overriding thrill at finally getting to do what she'd been training to do for years. Later, after a couple of losses, excitement morphed into anxiety. But it had served her well because anxiety was the signal to prepare more, deeper, and harder for her cases before court appearances.

Now, she faced something that instilled a level of anxiety she'd rarely felt before, in her career or otherwise. There is a risk level, a sense of deep emotional exposure, with broken relationships that surpasses most other challenging life experiences.

What if I'm rejected? What if it's too late? What if I am forced to face all my transgressions, and it still doesn't matter?

What if I find out that I am truly unlovable, unredeemable, and, therefore, doomed to be alone?

But it was time. A few minutes later, with shaking hands, she pressed the button. At his cautious answer, she said, "Henry? Please, let's talk. I'm not asking for anything from you or the girls, just to talk. I promise it won't be about me. It's about you. And Rose and Annie."

THE END

NOTE TO READERS

Thank you so much for reading *About Roxanne*! It is my latest book in three stand-alone books, with more to come. Keep reading below for all the information on my books and for VIP Reader access.

Did you like the brief cameo with Dr. Jill Rhodes? If so, check out my next book, *The Expert Witness*, book one in the brand-new mystery/thriller series I am launching, with Dr. Jill as the central character throughout. Also, you'll see Roxanne make an appearance and maybe become a central secondary character.

I am an independent author. I don't have a huge publishing house behind me, with a massive marketing machine. I write, publish, and market my own books. I rely heavily on my readers' reviews because that is the best way for independent authors to gain promotion for their books. I would be very grateful if you could add your review on Amazon. Written reviews are the best, but I'd be very grateful for a simple starred rating. Thank you in advance!

- Nina Atwood

OTHER TITLES BY NINA ATWOOD

Unlikely Return: A Novel, is available on Amazon.

Free Fall: A Psychological Thriller, is available on Amazon.

Nina's next full-length novel, book one of the electrifying Jill Rhodes mystery/thriller series, is scheduled for release in 2022. (See excerpt at the end of this book.)

Get Nina's FREE Novellas when you join her VIP Reader Club. Go to:

> www.ninaatwoodauthor.com/freenovella

Reward Special note: If you introduce me to someone in the moviemaking industry [big screen, streaming content, etc.] that results in a signed contract and paid advance on <u>any of my books</u>, I will pay you a reward of $10,000!

– Nina Atwood

Contact: nina@ninaatwoodauthor.com

Keep reading for an excerpt from *The Expert Witness*.

THE EXPERT WITNESS

by Nina Atwood

[Working title, book one of the Jill Rhodes mystery/thriller series]

PREVIEW

Copyright 2021, Nina Atwood Enterprises, LLC

PROLOGUE

She almost fell over tree roots along the way a couple of times, but finally made her way to the designated meeting spot. It was late afternoon, and the autumn sun was making its way quickly to the horizon, golden light peeking through the leaves here and there as it drifted downward.

She glanced at the time on her phone and shivered. She'd forgotten to take a jacket that day, and though she'd warmed up considerably at practice, the chill in the air had overcome the warmth of strenuous exercise.

She was alone in this forbidding place, and though she wasn't typically fearful of solitude, today it seemed different. She spun at the crackle of leaves or branches or whatever might make that sound. But nothing was there.

Steely determination had brought her here, the decision to take back the control she'd so readily given away. Since making that decision, she'd felt a return of her former strength, her fierceness, her confidence. She'd felt like herself again, though not completely. The events of the past few weeks had changed her, had opened her eyes to a dark world of depravity that she'd never intended to enter.

It had all been a fun adventure until then, something to answer the urgings toward independence from her over-protective parents.

But maybe they weren't over-protective. Maybe they were doing their job. An uneasiness and trickle of regret made its way into her chest.

Another crackle and her heart hitched into high gear. But she shook off the fear, and with it, the budding possibility that this somewhat remote meeting spot could be a very bad idea.

She'd practiced what she would say, and it had sounded good to her ears. Words of warning, her flashing eyes and superhero stance. And the message that she'd reveal him and what he'd done if necessary.

He'd back off after that message was delivered, for sure. He had far too much to lose to ignore her.

She'd almost given up when she heard the approach, the telltale crackle of leaves and small broken branches. She turned, a stern expression setting the stage, and her initial salvo seemed effective.

But she'd deluded herself, convinced herself that it would all turn out right. She discovered that she'd been terribly mistaken.

Later, she thought sadly about the familiar face of her friend, a close, best friend. And the terrifying things he'd done.

Continue scrolling for Chapter One from The Expert Witness

CHAPTER ONE

"But I'm not sure what it means," said Michael Fischer. Early thirties, single, and successful in his chosen profession, he was nevertheless somewhat clueless about women. His earnest expression and obvious intelligence belied the degree of his befuddlement.

He stared at the small screen he'd shown to her, shaking his head, touching it tenuously, as if he could bring back the affection of the woman he'd been yearning for, simply through the seeming magic of a tiny screen that offered so much promise of true love. If you only just swiped this direction or that.

As if the human heart worked that way.

This wasn't a difficult case for her, although it certainly must feel hard from his point of view. But this wasn't emotional resuscitation. He hadn't suffered a heartbreaking loss. Not one tear had fallen in the two sessions they'd had so far, and at no point had he expressed despair or even grief. Instead, he was deeply puzzled. That was understandable.

This was going to be education. With little emotional repair needed, the best course was a mini course on dating. Dr. Jill Rhodes provided such things regularly. She could almost do it in her sleep. Certainly, for others, for her clients.

Maybe for herself.

The frequency of these kinds of issues in her client base signaled once again that it was time to finish that book on dating, the one she'd been formulating late at night for months. She'd received a nice advance, and it had a deadline of sorts.

It would be great, at times like this, to simply lean forward, look into the current hapless single person's eyes, and hand over a book. *Her* book—filled with advice crafted to save the legions of tortured singles out there from shooting themselves in the foot so often.

The title, though, was a puzzler. *Swipe Right for Love* initially sounded good, but it turned out there were at least a dozen published dating books with the word "Swipe" in the title. Plus, it would be misleading for readers to think it was all about how to use a dating app effectively. Nope, not about that.

Instead, it was about all the stuff that happened so often *after* the swipe. Or without bothering to swipe. Or after the multiple vodka shots at the bar on a Saturday night.

Things she'd done herself, in the past, and other things that had happened to her. She touched the emptiness of her third finger, left hand. Emptiness that might never be filled but the filling of which remained a hope held dear.

Outside the window of her office, which was ground floor and looked onto an outdoor atrium, filled with live oaks, a squirrel dug frantically through the Asian jasmine, desperate to find what he'd hidden from himself weeks or months ago. Sunlight struggled to penetrate the leaves and branches of the trees, lending the area a soft, dappled, calming green atmosphere. Azaleas bloomed in their twice-yearly event, sparse blooms that sprang from the photosynthesis of the spare amount of sun that made it through the shade of her north Dallas office atrium.

"Dr. Rhodes?"

ABOUT ROXANNE

Her client had spoken, and she'd missed the last thing he'd said, meaning she'd broken the cardinal rule of psychotherapy: *listen*. Intently. At all times. She was a great listener, prided herself on her ability to hear what people said, and more importantly, what they *didn't* say.

"I'm sorry. My mind wandered for a moment." A terrible thing to admit, but how could you help people without being real with them? At his surprised look, she rushed to say, "Not because your story wasn't interesting, or that I didn't care. But I wonder—and I'm just feeling curious—why are you so focused on the meaning of Olivia's text?"

His forehead wrinkled in puzzlement. "Because I don't understand. She sent me this text message telling me she's *not ready for a relationship*, and that's after she went to a hell of a lot of trouble getting my name from a buddy so she could track me down, after seeing me on Instagram. We went out for three months, almost every night. We were inseparable. We were planning the whole summer together—trips, her friend's wedding—actually two weddings—everything. How do you go from that much... *intensity*, to a freaking breakup text?"

Time for a little education. "It does seem confusing. Let's try to untangle it, but first, I have just a couple more questions about Olivia. Actually, comments, guesses, if you will. When I get something right, hold up a thumb, like a thumbs-up. If I get something wrong, do a thumbs-down."

Sometimes you have to switch out of the usual therapist/client role and play a non-verbal game. To switch the brain off one track and onto another. "First, she goes out to bars with her girlfriends at least three nights a week."

He did a thumbs up.

"Second," she continued, "she has a job but not really a career. Maybe she's college educated, but she doesn't seem to be doing much with it."

Thumbs up.

"She talks about her siblings, or her friends, who are married and have at least one child already, maybe two. She talks about the kids a lot and takes care of them from time to time."

Thumbs up again, frowning. The train was getting ready to switch tracks.

"She wears really nice clothes, maybe too nice for her level of income. She's invited you over at least once while taking care of an adorable child—a niece, or a nephew, or a friend's little one."

Thumbs up, more slowly, frown increasing. The train was almost on the other track.

"She's sweet, but not especially deep. Your conversations usually revolve around other people in her life, gossip, if you will. A favorite topic is who's getting engaged and who's wedding is coming up."

Thumbs up and then, a "stop" gesture. "Okay, I get it. She's marriage and baby minded, and maybe that's her biggest goal in life, and yes, maybe she's husband shopping, but *what's wrong with that?* She's beautiful, she's sweet, and I want marriage and kids, too. *We were on the same page.*" The train was idling on the new track, still unsure.

"And you're right. There's nothing wrong with being on the same page about what you want. In fact, that's the whole point of dating—finding someone who wants what you want. But isn't there more that you want? What about a connection at a deeper level?"

"What do you mean?" He twisted a bit in the chair.

"Come on, Michael. You're a smart guy."

He shook his head and looked away. "I know what you're getting at." He sighed. "But I'm so tired of this cycle. Every time I meet someone new and think it's going somewhere, it just fizzles. Like this."

"Right. And that is the real issue. It fizzled because you weren't really on the same page. Yes, marriage and family. But no, you didn't really click in all the important ways. Yet you pushed for the relationship, wanting it more than she did. *Desperation*—and I don't mean because no one would want you, but because you've given

ABOUT ROXANNE

yourself some kind of arbitrary inner timetable—desperation of that kind attracts the wrong sort of connection. It's a pattern," she added.

Her words sat in the room, and slowly, he seemed to absorb them. "I know. But what do I do about that?"

"I'm not sure. It's hard to get yourself to *not* feel something you feel, to *not* do something you yearn to do. Sometimes, it's more about finding the substitute feeling, or action, something else that lights you up, something else to dive into. Focus on that, whatever it is, and learn to trust that the rest will follow. Be yourself, be real, and *let go of the outcomes*. No one can predict or control the right time to meet the right person." And as the words left her mouth, she knew they were as much for herself as they were for her client.

He swiped his hand over his head slowly. "I have no clue what you're saying to me, what you're suggesting I do. But I do see the pattern you're talking about."

She sat quietly. People need time to absorb new ideas, and he needed to understand the ones that swirled in their conversation. It was so simple, yet so complex, finding the right person, and finding your way to something that could bind you together for years, decades, of life.

She was the de facto expert on the subject. Heavy was the expectation that she be the knowledgeable, wise, guide to winning in life and love. She had a PhD, after all, and she specialized in relationships and family issues, or at least, that was what her marketing person put on her website and in social media. She was keenly aware of the expectations of her clients and anticipated that growing with the publication of her book.

It wasn't as if she didn't know what she was doing, it was that what she did wasn't measured in some sort of replication of her own life, like a template she could hand to her clients, one that she'd proven would work, the evidence her own carefully curated life.

There was no map to give them when they sat down with her for the first time, no way to point and say, *go down this road about eight-*

point-five miles, take a right on that road, slow down, take a left, and you are there at happily ever after with the soulmate of your dreams!

After a moment, she suggested they wrap up for today and asked if he wanted to set up another time. She was looking forward to a needed break after this session and before her afternoon clients. The antique clock sitting on her desk clicked softly with each passing second.

As Michael Fischer stood to go, he paused and turned back. "Dr. Rhodes. There's one more thing, and I'm afraid it's not about me. It's about someone who is in serious trouble."

OTHER TITLES BY NINA ATWOOD

Unlikely Return: A Novel, is available on Amazon.

Free Fall: A Psychological Thriller, is available on Amazon.

Nina's next full-length novel, book one of the electrifying Jill Rhodes mystery/thriller series, is scheduled for release in 2022. (See excerpt at the end of this book.)

Get Nina's FREE Novellas when you join her VIP Reader Club. Go to:

www.ninaatwoodauthor.com/freenovella

Reward Special note: If you introduce me to someone in the moviemaking industry [big screen, streaming content, etc.] that results in a signed contract and paid advance on <u>any of my books</u>, I will pay you a reward of $10,000!

– Nina Atwood

Contact: nina@ninaatwoodauthor.com

About the Author

Nina Atwood is a licensed psychotherapist and award-winning executive coach. A published self-help author for the past 24 years, Nina recently turned her pen to fiction. *Unlikely Return* is her first novel, *Free Fall* her second, with more on the way. She lives in Dallas, Texas, with her husband and their adorable fur babies.

Made in the USA
Las Vegas, NV
17 April 2024